NIGHTBONE

NIGHTBONE

A NOVEL BY
MICHAEL HARDWICK

Weidenfeld and Nicolson
London

**British Library Cataloguing in Publication
Data**
Hardwick, Michael
Nightbone.
1. Fiction in English, 1837–1900 – Texts
I. Title
823'.8

ISBN 0–297–79806–5

Photoset and printed in Great Britain by
Redwood Burn Limited, Trowbridge, Wiltshire

To Mollie, with love

CHAPTER 1

NIGHTBONE

PEASOUP time in The Smoke. All London spilling over with the stuff.

People and beasts groped, coughed, snorted exasperation and disgust. Unseen hooves dragged invisibly grinding wheels. Spectres of vaguely human form materialized, grew, menaced, then vanished.

Among all the fog-blind, one made his way unfalteringly. Heavy boots and strong legs moving in steady rhythm. Policeman's boots, confident from years of intimacy with every feature of these streets, bearing about his duty Number 773, age 28, height 6ft, weight 168lb, colour of eyes brown, colour of hair ditto, length of service 10 years: Nightbone, Sergeant, Metropolitan Police.

He made his rendezvous with two of his constables. Both were young and new. They were waiting for him under a futile gaslamp on a corner where the fog hung like sopping yellow rags.

'Nothing, Sarge.'

'Quiet as a wet Sunday.'

'Don't be too sure of yourselves. Peasoupers ought to worry you.'

'Too busy directing old folk. Oughtn't to be out.'

'Old lags, off to work. Half the villains in London, making the most of it. Keep your eyes double peeled and your ears extra sharp.'

'Yes, Sarge.'

He kept them waiting some moments while he stared about into the murk, as if expecting a mob of villains to materialize and prove his point.

'Carry on,' he ordered, and watched them resume their beat together. Officers patrolled in pairs round here. It had never been his preference. A man might miss something through chewing the rag with a mate. Solitariness concentrated vigilance. Nightbone paced on alone. The fact that he was pursuing an escaped criminal didn't make him hurry.

'Where is he, then?'

He filled the cellar threshold, legs planted, elbows wide, thumbs tucked into his black leather belt. The door he had thrust open stayed ajar behind him. The fog billowed temptingly beyond. A dash for it would not succeed.

'Why, arternoon, Mr Nightbone!' Bolting Harry Lumsden, spokesman for all present by virtue of greatest aggregate prison-time. 'Narsty go o' fog.'

They lounged on benches against dripping walls: Harry Lumsden, passer of false money; Manny Solomons, street vendor of stolen knick-nacks; Nag's Head Nat, public house beggar and nuisance; Fat Annie, washerwoman and drunkard; Bodger Blandy, used-up pugilist; Nell and Jenny Jacks, sisters of the street as well as of blood; Scotch Jimmy Andrew, occasional brewer's labourer and periodic tearaway, tending the plank table that was their bar. Petty crooks, idlers, tarts. The fog offered no special opportunities in their lines. They huddled from it in this dank hole under an empty house, to drink stolen liquor and conduct inane converse to the Palm Court strains of Blind Frank's squeeze-box.

The one Nightbone sought was, of course, not visible.

'Where?'

'Who was that, Mr Nightbone?'

'Not Tommy, by any chance? Tommy Cox?'

'Ooh, if it's young Tommy you needn't be chasing 'im. Took yesterday, wasn't you sayin', Annie?'

'Caledonian Road. Din' they think to tell you, Mr Nightbone?'

There was a time to browbeat and a time to humour, while his eyes checked what had been the kitchen stairs, a pair of long cupboards, the long-disused food hoist, the littered fireplace where fog hung in memory of cooking smoke.

'Tommy did a runner this morning,' he informed them unnecessarily. Such news travelled faster than policeman's boots.

'He never!'

'How, Mr Nightbone? Come over the rail, did he?'

8

'You know.'

Young Cox had vaulted clean out of the dock and dashed from the magistrate's court. Nightbone hadn't been there. Colleagues who had been would be lucky if they only got kicked off the force. The new Commissioner was proving unsparing of the inefficient and the corrupt alike.

'Three runners Tommy's done,' said Manny Solomons, the group's mathematician.

'Done a few meself.' Bolting Harry bore his nickname with pride.

'Not with me within reach of your collar.'

'True, Mr Nightbone. I give you that.'

'I'm waiting, then.'

'When in doubt, ask a policeman?'

The drawled sneer came from one half-seated on the edge of the bar table, an empty gin glass in his hand. Bailey Watts, formerly Edward Watts, Esquire, intended barrister-at-law, rebaptized after the Central Criminal Court. His voice had been heard in the Ancient Bailey only once. 'Not guilty.' The jury believed only the half of it.

Nightbone gave him the stare that was one of several portentous mannerisms more effective than speech. It took a bold man to defy that look, and Watts was anything but. He was a sneaking, degraded cheat; a confidence trickster and fraudsman, not yet thirty but as grubby and defiled as the suit he always wore. It had been made for him in Savile Row some years ago. A good suit and a cut-glass accent were desired assets in a man living off his wits. Ragged cuffs, a soiled collar and greasy tie-knot, together with many ineradicable patches of dark substances, detracted from the effect. Only the voice remained plausible.

Nightbone knew the story well. Wealthy widowed father. Pampered law student son. Sexual deviance. Disgrace. Imprisonment. Ostracism. All leading to hatred for the Law he could never practise and for all who served it. Nightbone had played a small role in Bailey's downfall. He knew he was high on the embittered degenerate's reprisal list.

He stepped a pace forward into the cellar. He backheeled the door and replanted his feet. He spoke civilly.

'You happen to know where Tommy Cox is, Bailey?'

'Mr Watts to you, Nightbone.'

Bailey put his glass down and slid off the table. He was trembling, and it was not only from drink. Pale, pink-rimmed eyes dilated and contracted. Nightbone heard one of the watchers sigh with anticipation.

'I asked you a question, Watts,' he said.

Bailey twisted his mouth contemptuously. He jerked his fists up in a feeble imitation of a fighter's stance. Gristly wrists protruded from frayed cuffs. Bunches of knucklebones quivered. He licked dry lips, exhaling the acid of fear.

Nightbone knew he had no need to watch his back. Bailey had no fighting cronies here. The sprawled onlookers would relish seeing him get spread about the walls, as he seemed to be inviting. It would serve him right and relieve their boredom a bit.

'Gow on, Bailey!' someone exhorted. 'Wotcher waiting for?'

'Chrissmas,' another supplied.

The ex-professional, Bodger Blandy, guffawed and beat his mug against the wall, simulating the bell.

Nightbone made the move. He stepped forward again, so abruptly that Watts couldn't draw back in time. The uniformed chest and the unsteady fist collided gently.

'Obstructing an officer,' Nightbone declared, to general guffaws. He seized the leading wrist in an iron grip. His other hand reached for the handcuffs in their pocket.

It never got them. As Watts proclaimed agony Nightbone flung him from him. Watts sprawled backward across the table. Nightbone spun round away from him, to wrench the door open. He almost dived out into the fog. They heard him clatter up the outside steps.

The slide of the old food hoist crashed back into place. Tommy Cox, wriggling frantically in the shaft, cursed the temptation that had made him peep out to watch Nightbone wipe the floor with Bailey Watts.

The upper rooms and passages and stairs were an obstacle course. Women and children screeched at the policeman in the escaper's wake. He tore down blanket partitions and lines of clothes. Two women struggled to shut a second-floor window sash. Nightbone shoved them aside and clambered out. He didn't stop to consider the drop down into the fog. Tommy had gone that way. So could he.

He was on the leads of a roof. Invisible scuffling in the fog indicated Tommy getting into the adjoining house. Nightbone rushed towards the sound, trusting like a plunging horse on unfamiliar ground that his legs would carry him surely.

A roof door in the slope of cracked tiles fell shut. He heaved it with both hands. A thick-soled boot crunched more tiles as he strained. The fugitive within gave up the frantic attempt to secure a latch, and ran on. Nightbone was in after him. 'I'll have you, Tommy!' he shouted. He hurtled down a shuddering staircase. 'Save us the chase.'

A disrespectful reply was flung back. A door slammed. A bolt snapped fast. Heavy shoulder work needed. Nightbone staggered into another full room. More beds to be hurdled, a boy's outthrust leg booted aside. Juvenile howls. Shrieks of filthy female abuse.

There was no open window. No other door, no cupboard, no exit to the roof. Only a fireplace piled with litter. Soot clouded about it.

As a young constable he had once gone up a chimney after a runner. He hadn't reckoned on the difference between an underfed slum kid and a well-nourished bobby. Sheer impetus had carried him until he stuck fast, cascaded with soot. Assistance from jeering females below had cost him his trousers.

Not this time. He dashed back out of the room. He leaped up another staircase and got out of a back window on to the roof. From the fog hiding the chimney stack he heard Tommy's wheezing gasp as he struggled out, to stagger coughing along the leads.

'Quit it,' Nightbone called. 'You'll break your neck.'

'Break yours!'

They clattered through two more buildings, alternating attic rooms and roofs. Then they were at the end of a block and having to descend. It was against a runner's instinct. Down in the streets the odds turned adverse. Other coppers, interfering civilians. But there was still the fog. Its ghosts were too surprised to intervene as Tommy ran through them headlong.

His thudding boots betrayed him. He wouldn't risk stopping to try anything clever. Nightbone grinned to hear him curse and skid to a halt. He stopped too, and listened to the tentative splash as Tommy lowered himself into the Regent's Canal.

Water wasn't his element. He was lost as soon as he went in, scared of tripping and drowning. His hands groped emptily. No spectral barge materialized to offer refuge. Nightbone found him standing helplessly up to his waist in dirty ooze. Tommy was black faced from the soot, panting hugely, near to crying from frustration.

'Having a wash, Tommy? Looks like you need one.'

He hauled in an unresisting wrist and snapped the handcuff.

'Why'd it have to be you, Mr Nightbone?' Tommy moaned. 'You wasn't even in court.'

'This is my manor.' They waded ashore together. 'Nowhere worth running to on my patch. You know that.'

'I can't seem to help myself. Sorry I told you to break your neck.'

'I didn't hear. It'll be a stretch this time, anyway.'

'Don't I know.'

'Getting nearer the big one, Tommy.'

'Yeh.'

'A big one can change a man. Never quite the same, after the Moor.'

They walked on towards a police station. Some coppers would have half-killed after being led such a chase. Twice before Nightbone had collared Tommy on the run and later spoken for him to tradespeople. He hadn't kept the jobs. Seemingly easier money had beckoned. Tommy never could resist it.

'Pity about Bailey,' he said.

'What about him?'

'I reckoned you was going to give him a doing.'

Nightbone said grimly, 'Keep away from Bailey Watts and his kind. That sort can land you in real trouble.'

He gave the arm he was holding a meaningful thrust, urging his prisoner faster through the fog towards the relative sanctuary of a cell.

CHAPTER 2

LUCILLA

W*HIZZ!* The leader's fiddle.
   Bang! The cellist's boot on the dais.
   Crash!!! Both bows and the lady pianist's hands
   hard down together. The last chord of a whipping
Viennese polka.

The trio bowed and filed from the platform. Applause was thin. Clatter of cutlery and plates superseded Strauss. Well-heeled Yorkshire ladies gossiped on. Viennese and Parisian melodies came with the fixed-price lunch. One didn't applaud the other courses.

Langenbach's Swiss Café had become a fashionable feature of Leeds city centre shopping. Until near the end of the 1870s Adolf Langenbach had been a senior chef at the Hôtel Beau Rivage, Geneva. Then, like a distant call from beyond the Alps, he had heard the *leitmotif* of Industrial Northern England: 'Where there's muck, there's money.' Strangely drawn, he had renounced humdrum security and clear air to create an oasis of Continental cuisine in the grimy, no-nonsense city.

It proved an attraction from the start. Expensive flowered hats bloomed in a setting that was all light paint and space and pastel napery, immaculate cutlery and glass; different but respectable; precluded from exaggerated foreignness by loud Yorkshire vowels. The food was rich but not too unfamiliar. Heeding advice urged on him when setting up, Langenbach gave generous portions at a modest price.

He ran the kitchen himself. His spotless long apron and chef's tall hat impressed the provincial ladies when he came out to bow among the tables. He was in his fifties, large, pink, bald and twinkling, an embellishment to the surroundings. His wife, Hilde, was not. She was small and sallow, darkly dressed, with greying hair in a tight little bun. From the cash desk next to the door she returned customers' greetings with dismissive winces and a grudging vocabulary of mispronounced phrases. She looked permanently displeased.

Lucilla Poole knew why.

Wherever she moved as she waited on the tables Lucilla felt the woman's eyes on her. Especially when she went towards the kitchen, where Adolf Langenbach was. His little nudges, sly pressures, accidental-on-purpose collisions, with his hand laid on her arm as he laughed and said he was sorry, were as unmistakable to her at seventeen as she could see they were to his wife, at fifty-odd.

Lucilla had worked there five weeks. He had started this after the first few days. She had tried to make him see she didn't want it, indicating by glances that his wife was watching. His response had been hopeless sighs. Now he'd taken to looking moony. She thought she saw customers nudging one another.

'I could go another of these, miss.'

The young man rang the bowl of his tall green hock glass with a fingernail. He was the only male lunching alone, next to one of the lime green iron pillars. Friendly dark eyes. Curly black hair and side whiskers. Slim and neat, in a quiet gingery check. Lucilla knew his accent was London.

'Unless you want rid of me.'

It was that time when lunch is over and tea not yet being served. The instrumentalists had trooped through to the kitchen for their meal. The room was emptying noisily. She put his empty wine glass on her tray.

'Don't you want pudding, sir?'

'I fancied an ice cream.'

'That's all right.'

As Lucilla crossed the floor she knew he was watching. Men did. Those with their wives peeped over the menu.

She knew she was worth it. The other waitresses were a waxy, blemished lot. Black dresses and white accessories did nothing for their lumpy, drooping figures. Lucilla, brought up among actresses and dancers, had learned how walking straightbacked made a skirt swing from the hips. She could toss her head proudly, chin up, speak with her hands and eyes. She only did these in private, to her mirror, but being aware of the effect gave her an aura of self-assurance. Men sensed it, as they admired the ripening curves, blue eyes, and generously coiled and braided buttermilk hair. They noticed her unusual way of speaking for those parts. The years among theatre people, on tour with her parents, had rid her of every flat trace of Yorkshire accent.

The touring and the theatre were in the past. She was a waitress, getting the eye from men and being pawed by her boss. She was sure his old woman was watching out for the excuse to send her packing. It wouldn't be fair, but it wouldn't break her heart. Especially on a day like this, when autumn sunshine had given summer clothes a last reprieve from tissue paper and camphor balls. There were better things for a pretty girl to be doing on such a day than carrying a tray.

Lucilla put down the fresh glass of hock. He picked it up and gave it a little bob towards her before sipping.

'Fresh as the day. Peasoup time in The Smoke.'

'Pea soup?'

'London Particular. Fog.'

'We got plenty of that here.'

'You're telling me. Niff of its own, Leeds fog.'

'It's the mills. Do you know these parts, sir?'

'I know Roundhay Park. Just the day for it.'

'That's right.'

'How about it, then?'

'Some chance.'

'Not your afternoon off?'

'We start teas at three.'

'After you finish?'

'No thanks.'

'Home like a good girl?' He didn't say it sarcastically. She gave him a rare little smile.

'That's it, sir.' She left him to his wine and ice cream. The other customers had gone. Mme Langenbach had quitted her desk, clutching the cashbox and spike of paid checks. She was at the head of the long kitchen table when Lucilla came in. Employers, waitresses, kitchen hands and musicians lunched together. The under chef dished up, but Adolf Langenbach arranged each portion on its plate. He served his employees food as good as the customers got. It saved paying more wages, but also he was a kind man. He had always chased his prettiest girls because he wanted to be kind to them. His wife didn't appreciate that fine feeling.

'Last one, madame,' Lucilla reported.

'Haff you the door locked?' Madame held out her hand for the check and money.

'The gentleman hasn't quite finished.'

'Sit down, child,' Langenbach told her. 'In one moment I go see to it.'

'*Nichts davon!*' His wife shook her head and got up quickly. She hastened to the service door. 'It makes never to leaf de kostomer allon, or they are taking avay de knifes und spunns.'

Veiled smiles around the table drew a secret wink from Langenbach. He bent close over Lucilla's shoulder to put her plate before her. She saw the other girls exchange smirks.

The door flew violently open again. Mme Langenbach stormed back in. She shouted at Lucilla.

'*Schwindler!*'

She was waving a piece of paper. Her other hand was clenched around something. She came to stand over Lucilla and dramatically revealed the last customer's check. A few copper coins quivered on her other palm.

'You giff back, or poleeze!'

Lucilla could see the coins made up only a fraction of the bill.

'That's only the tip.'

'Ja. You leef down de tip und de odder keep.'

She dragged Lucilla to her feet and went on shaking her, as if expecting the missing money to fall out of her clothes. Langenbach tried to intervene. His wife pushed him aside. Lucilla broke free. She stormed to the pegs for her coat and hat.

'No!' Mme Langenbach moved quickly to stop her. 'Adolf, *Polizei beruf*!'

Lucilla realized how it might look to a policeman. She pushed past. With Mme Langenbach in close pursuit and the others streaming after she hurried to the table beside the pillar. She scrabbled among the things on it, peered underneath, lifted the chair, though not expecting to find anything. The jealous woman was pretending, so she could sack her. That, or that sneaking Londoner had welshed on his bill. She turned to appeal to Langenbach. He looked sheepishly away. Someone started knocking at the street door which Mme Langenbach must have locked. A brown bowler hat bobbed on the other side of the glass. Arms were gesticulating.

'Sorry to disturb,' the young man gabbled when Langenbach let him in. 'Hadn't gone a block when I realized. Left the tip and forgot the check. Three and six? There we are. Sorry again. Here, anything up?' He stared round them all.

'It is nothing,' Mme Langenbach said frostily.

'Oh, isn't it?' Lucilla demanded. 'You accuse me. Start sending for the coppers. Call that nothing?'

'My dear young miss ...' Langenbach put a fleshy hand on her arm. She tossed it away.

'It's all you. Creeping and pawing!'

Langenbach began spluttering. His wife pushed him again in fresh rage.

'What is all this?' the young man asked.

No one heeded him. Without a backward glance Lucilla was off down the street, carrying her coat and hat. She heard him call after her, and then his running steps. She walked faster.

CHAPTER 3

BAILEY

'THOUGHT you was goin' to do 'im, Bailey,' Fat Annie mocked.

As the sounds of pursuit receded, Bailey Watts tested his limbs. For what it was worth he brushed himself down.

'Didn't give me an opening.' Their derision was beneath his notice. 'Anything left in that bottle?'

'Two and a tanner worth.'

Bailey stuck the exorbitant charge into Scotch Jimmy's hand and snatched the bottle. He put it into Bolting Harry's hand.

'Remember,' Bailey said.

Harry nodded, drinking.

The bottle went on to Manny Solomons and one of the others before Bailey reclaimed it. The excitement was over. General debate resumed. Blind Frank's concertina began to whine.

Bailey didn't drink from his bottle. He went to squeeze into the bench space beside Bodger Blandy. He held it out to the ex-fighter.

'Have a wet, Bodger.' Not pausing to wonder at being thus favoured, Bodger obeyed.

Michael Blandy was not yet thirty. He looked twenty years older. His appearance owed nothing much to age, but everything to rough usage. His jaw had been broken and had mended crooked. Both his cheekbones had caved in. His nose was spread like a bulldog's. His eyelids had been cut so often that they no longer closed completely, but left ghastly glimpses of irregular reddish white. Bodger asleep was a terrible sight.

Only one of the eyes was any use. The other had been pulped in a bare-knuckle mill with the Islington Monkey. It was said that Bodger had fought the last three of the twenty rounds with the eye popping out and his second running after him, thrusting it back.

He had long since done without teeth, though not before a roaring uppercut from the Finchley Growler had caused him to bite off part of his tongue. Half-intelligible mumbling was all he could manage. Fellow occupants of the cellar managed to distinguish whether he was amused or angry, or merely wanted a drink.

'Take another,' Bailey invited. He leaned close to a ravaged ear and spoke on. What he had to say succeeded in kindling a rare spark of understanding in the one intact eye.

Bodger had been a cheerful young giant of a porter in Covent Garden. The way he handled himself in a street scrap impressed his mates, who encouraged him to put himself up to stay three rounds with old pros for half-sovereigns. A promoter invested in having him properly trained and billed him to fight at London halls at £25 a side. Bodger – it was a corruption of 'bodier', in tribute to his fast smarting punching to the ribs and sides – had his run of wins.

Then his speed on his feet began to go. He started getting beaten. In an especially vicious bout he was knocked senseless while picking himself up already dazed. It blew away all that was left of his ring skill and most of his wits. There were a few more unlicensed fights in cellars and attics, with bare knuckles and no holds barred. A police raid mercifully brought that to an end. Bodger tried to go back to market portering. He was unable to hold a job. Sudden bitter rages made him a menace and he was warned off Covent Garden. His only subsequent work was occasionally carrying an advertising sandwich board. He lost his way in the streets, wandered into busy roads, held up traffic, cursed drivers and passersby. The police treated him patiently, but sometimes, dimly suspicious of persecution, he lashed out at them. Then they ran him in, and he would be terrible in court with his mumbled threats and his eye.

After one of his short prison terms he found his way into the Pentonville cellar. He passed most of his hours there now, in morose silence. When he began raving they calmed him with a drink. It was a rare thing, though, to have the bottle put into his hands. He tried his hardest in return to comprehend Bailey Watts's murmured confidences.

'Blasted copper' and adjectival variants were easily understood.
'*You* know what coppers are, Bodger. Picking on a man. Snapping
after him like dogs. Hounding him.'

Like the dog he himself resembled, Bodger stirred threateningly
and growled deep in his throat. Bailey watched him drink.

'That's right, Bodger. Mop up. Interfering bastards. But for them
you'd be in the ring still. Shame, for a champion like you. That
Nightbone, it was, you know. He got that fight stopped.'

A dim memory of the last interrupted bout fluttered in Bodger's
fog-filled mind. Police uniforms. A crowd struggling. Fists and trun-
cheons. Protests of 'Shame!' and 'Live and let live!'

'Nightbone,' Bailey repeated. 'Always said he'd get you turned off.
Put the word on you down at the market as well.'

He nudged Bodger's elbow, tilting the bottle towards the slack
mouth.

'Your turn's come now, Bodg. Listen. Can you follow what I say?'

The bulldog head nodded. Bailey went on speaking low.

From her corner of the cellar Nell Jacks watched them.

While Nightbone had been there her eyes had been on him alone. It
was a long time since she'd fancied any man. She knew Nightbone
wouldn't touch her with a bargepole, but she had no other fantasies
left. She knew how strong he would be. Strong. Firm. Clean.

There had been a freezing night when he'd shone his lantern into
the shop doorway that was her regular station.

'You'll catch your death, Nell.'

'Perishin', ain't it, Mr Nightbone?'

'Get on home and thaw out.'

'Can't. Jen's got an all-nighter. I got to stop out. He wouldn't
cough up in advance, so she couldn't give me the price of the dosser.'

Nightbone had walked her to the doss-house and given the tup-
pence bed money to the porter. He'd never come later, expecting
paying back in kind. Not like one bobby who'd not been seen around
any more lately. She wished he had.

Rum cove, Nelly Jacks reflected. All man, though. Nothing like
Bailey Watts, with his toff's voice going on about how clever he was.
He'd been on about it before Tommy Cox had run in all breathless.
Bolting Harry had bet them Nightbone would be round soon. She'd
noticed Bailey swallowing them faster after he heard that. Getting up

Dutch courage, she knew now. It had been almost a laugh, him squaring up to Nightbone. She'd have enjoyed seeing him flattened.

She looked across at him and Bodger. Bailey caught her eye. He was just getting up, giving Bodger a helping hand. The empty bottle rolled at their feet.

Bailey had to strain to help Bodger with one arm and open the door with the other. The fog billowed in like train smoke.

Nell got up when they had gone. She gave her emerald green skirt a shake and secured the pins in her hat.

'You coming, Jen?' she asked her elder sister.

Jenny roused herself. She glanced at the new drift of fog in the room, then into the tin mug in her hand. It still held enough to detain her. She pulled her shawl closer over her pink bodice and stayed where she was.

Fat Annie jeered as Nell passed her. 'Never caught me 'avin' to work a peasouper. Always kep' enough put by.'

'Put any cove off his stroke, meeting the likes o' you in a fog,' Nell retorted. She wrapped her muffler high and tight round her neck and slipped out into the choking gloom.

CHAPTER 4

JOE

'So she isn't my auntie really,' Lucilla explained.

'Just honorary,' he suggested.

'That's it. Honorary auntie.'

They were strolling the vastness of Roundhay Park, treading the gold and copper carpet-pile of leaves. Joe Pearson was pleased to see her laugh at last. It was an hour since he'd come calling after her as she stamped away from Langenbach's.

'Miss! *Miss!*'

People's heads had turned. She tried to ignore him and walk on. He dodged round in front of her.

'Let me past.' She was still half tears and half fury.

He held his brown bowler hat to his breast. 'All my fault. Came back quick as I could.'

She still tried to get on. He shifted to block her.

'Listen, I'll go back with you. Explain everything. Find a copper and take him, if you want.' He peered round exaggeratedly. 'Typical. Whenever you need one . . .'

'I don't,' she said. 'I'm not going back.'

'You'll get the push.'

'I have. Gave it myself.'

'You can't do that! Just over me.'

'Don't flatter yourself. It's nothing to do with you.'

'What, then?'

'Never you mind.'

'I do mind. Where are you going now?'

'None of your business.'

'Roundhay Park?'

'You and blinking Roundhay Park!'

'You've time now. Come on.'

'You've a cheek, haven't you?'

'Two. Not half as pretty as yours.'

A few minutes later they had climbed to the top of the Roundhay horse tram. Now they were wandering side by side under the limitless blue sky over the vast public park of lakes and ancient woodland where John o' Gaunt had ridden to the hunt five hundred years ago.

Lucilla had pinned her hat on for the tram ride. She carried it again now. She had shaken out her hair the way the actresses did. She let her hips swing freely. Joe Pearson noticed.

'Old trout, is she?' he prompted.

'When I was a little kid, stopping with her, she made me do all her washing-up.'

'She never!'

'Standing on a box to reach the sink.'

'Wonder you're not like those others in the caff – great horrible red hands.'

She was impressed that he'd noticed. She was vain of everything to do with her looks. The dancers and actresses had imparted awareness of what mattered most to a girl. She thought for a second that he might follow up his compliment by trying to take her hand. He didn't. He had sat clear of her on the tram seat and hadn't taken the excuse of holding her arm to help her off.

'What about her old man?' he asked.

'I help in his shop. Serving and wrapping.'

'What's he like?'

'Not as bad. Specially when she's out of the way.'

For years, on and off, Lucilla had been dumped on the stingy, bullying woman and her cowed husband, when her parents were out on tour. Her father was a scene-shifter, her mother sewed in wardrobe. Mr and Mrs Poole went together or separately where they were hired. Melodramas and pantomime, mostly. When they didn't take Lucilla they left her with Auntie Doris and Uncle Edgar. It was a general shop on a dismal South Leeds street corner. Lucilla had the narrow boxroom just under the roof, in return for doing the house-work and helping in the shop.

It was three years since her parents had left her there for good. She tried to believe they'd waited till she was old enough for them to split up and abandon her. She knew they hadn't. Not her mother, anyway.

She'd no desire to work hard learning lines to speak on stages. The theatre had been no magic world to her. Yawning hours in cheerless lodgings and backstage rooms, mostly. But its people had been kind. The women had seen she wanted mothering. They supplied it and she picked up what they showed her. She was sure it would come in handy some day.

'How about a slap-up tea?' he suggested.

'If I don't have to serve.'

This time he did take her arm. They walked more quickly along the tree'd avenue towards the Mansion House. Since no pleasure in Yorkshire could be complete without heavy eating, the old house on a hill between the two lakes was made over to catering. An outing to Roundhay implied tea at 't'Mansion'. They got a table beside one of the tall windows looking on to grey stone columns and the gold, green and blue vista of parkland and sky. Lucilla felt good. She was in a position to be sorry for the grey-haired waitress doing the same boring job all her days. Her companion read her thought.

'Not your cup of tea.'

'My auntie put me into it.'

'Better than skivvying for her.'

'I have to do that as well.'

'That's coming it strong. What d'you want?'

'Haven't the faintest. Get away from here, for a start.'

'By yourself?'

'I'm old enough. Nearly twenty.'

'Go on!'

'Well ...'

His expression turned serious. 'It's a dodgy place, the world out there. Take it from one who knows.'

He had given her his card when they had exchanged names:

JOSEPH PEARSON, Esquire
Maurice & Cie, Lingerie et Corsets
Great Titchfield Street, Londres W

'You don't work in my line and not get to know a bit.'

'What about?'

'Girls trying to make out on their own. What can happen.'

'I know about that.'

The disenchanted waitress was passing. Joe pointed to their teapot.

'Drop more hot water, ta, dear.'

'And our check,' Lucilla ordered.

'On me,' Joe said.

'I'm paying my half.'

'But for me you wouldn't have come. Anyway, have it on the company. "To entertaining client, two bob." Mustn't forget this time or I'll be taking that old girl out for tea . . . Cor . . . !'

He had struck his forehead with the heel of his hand. Lucilla thought he was fooling about, but he stared at her.

'That's it! The company. The company and *you*! Dearie me, what would old Ted say, Joe Pearson nearly passing up a natural!'

'Ted who?'

'My big brother. Ted and Joe Pearson. *Maurice et Cie, à votre service, madame.*'

His funny accent and the way he lifted his shoulders up to his ears made her laugh. Some people turned to look at them. Lucilla covered her mouth with the napkin.

'*Mademoiselle, pardon,*' he was correcting.

'Oh, do give up. They're looking.'

'Let 'em. Well they might.'

'I don't know what you're on about.'

'You and the firm. A model.'

Lucilla's stomach gave a great lurch. She understood as well as any girl in Leeds would what he was on about. The Leeds trade mostly supplied cloth for others to tailor, or men's ready-made. Just a few firms went in for ladies' high fashion. Like every other female who went down Bond Street, Lucilla always paused at a velvet-lined window where the stunning gowns on show were said to be from London and Paris originals. She had caught glimpses inside of elegant creatures showing them off to rich customers.

'You'll be fantastic!' Joe Pearson was telling her, impatient on his chair. 'Ted'll jump at you.'

'I don't think.'

'Listen, love, this is my job. I don't just sell. I've to keep my eye out for talent. Didn't suppose all London models are cockneys?'

'I never thought.'

'Not only down south do all the roses bloom. Who wrote that?'

'I don't know.'

'I did. Just now. It comes over me at times. Something bigger than me, that . . .'

'Mr Pearson . . .'

'Joe, love.'

'Do you really think Mr ... your brother ...'

'Ted. Joe and Ted. Design and showing is his side. One of the best. Uses models from all over. Never believe how tough it is to find ones with what it takes. Hard man to please, old Ted. Those who've got it don't stay long, either. Still, we see 'em all right if they buy the wedding outfit from us. Discount and a present.'

'And it's your job to keep finding new ones?'

'Plenty write in. You must have seen our adverts in the papers. Full details with photo if possible. Interview in town. All expenses paid.'

'Town? London?'

'Where else? Top end of the trade. Those that don't suit, half a sov' and no quibbles. Those that do, signed up on the spot. Experience not necessary. Full training given. Pay and prospects, better than most. Young ladies' hostel or approved lodgings. Just what you're looking for. Suit you down to the ground.'

'I haven't said I'm interested.'

'You don't need to.'

'Haven't had time to think.'

'Yes you have. It's all over your face. Eyes, mostly. Lovely blue eyes, blond hair, neck like a swan ...'

'Give over. They'll be looking again.'

'Figure like ...'

'Please!'

'It's how some write in about themselves. Lord knows what they can see in their mirrors. "Mirror, mirror, on the wall ..." You, love, Lucilla, take it from me, you've really got it. From where I'm sitting, all of it. Be up with the big earners before you can say:

> 'I wonder whatever I would have done
> If I hadn't met that hamiable Joe Pears*on*?'

There was the inevitable row when she got home and told them how she'd finished at Langenbach's. She stayed calm when Aunt Doris sneered that she'd turn out as bad as her mother. She reported nothing of miracles.

A few days at most, Joe had said. She would be sure to get a telegram from his brother early next week. When she came to London, she might as well bring all her things. Save having to come back for them. Certain as that.

To be shut of Leeds and what it represented. The sweetest prospect she had ever savoured.

CHAPTER 5

NELL

ALL very well for young Cox, drying nicely on a cell bunk with a can of coffee in him. Nightbone had partaken of coffee, too, but then it was straight back to work. His soaked trousers clung coldly to his legs, whose destination was again the cellar.

Bolting Harry Lumsden and company ought to know better than pretend Tommy hadn't been there. He had to be. He hadn't the imagination to run anywhere else. They needed reminding that if there was a bobby in North London not susceptible to being fooled like that, Nightbone was the name. There was also the more serious matter of Bailey Watts. That desperate goading had sprung from something more than drink and hysteria. He had nerved himself up to provoke a thumping. His witnesses there would take his money or drink and perhaps honour a bargain, whatever they thought of him. They respected Nightbone grudgingly. Not because he was a copper. Because he had made them. They might not be London's most creditable citizens, but their testimony would interest the new Commissioner of Metropolitan Police. On his orders, all complaints against officers, however trivial, were investigated. And there were the do-gooders, on the lookout for abuse of authority in everything a bobby did beyond blowing his nose. Some would question even that. Especially those who had it in for Nightbone. No one had it in for him more than Bailey Watts.

Hard times had fallen on the Metropolitan Police. Bad pay and conditions had done that which the old Commissioner had warned of for so long. Disobedience and strike threats were rife. Political troublemakers had moved in. Swell crooks with money were tempting

dispirited policemen who had none. Exhausted by apathetic politicians, obstructive civil servants, and ratepayers incapable of seeing
a connection between having a police force and paying for one, the old
Commissioner had resigned. A soldier had been hurried home from
India to take his place. The Met found misgiving turning to dismay.
In a few months his swingeing discipline had lost them several
hundred men out of the 15,000 who policed London's millions.

Bailey Watts was clever enough to see all this. Cunning as
monkeys, and far more dangerous. He had seen the chance he'd been
waiting for. This time he'd failed. Nightbone proposed to serve notice
on him not to try again. He would remind those others not to be
tempted to let Bailey use them for his dirty work. Use anyone, Bailey,
and without a qualm leave them to take the consequences.

Nightbone turned off the invisibly busy road into a narrow cobbled
alleyway. The fog's biting breath mingled with the fishy reek of
excrement, oozing between the stones. Even in fog you could almost
see the smell here. He was used to it.

As he turned into another alley, similarly perfumed, he heard
muffled voices calling. A woman's and some men's. One of the men
laughed and the girl called again. They sounded as if searching for
one another or someone else.

Nearer by, one of the men shouted again. This time it was a cry of
alarm or fear. The female started shrieking. The man called again,
urgently. Another answered. Nightbone ran towards the sounds.

Figures materialized in the hanging vapour. A woman in a bright
purple skirt and a big flowered hat sagged against a wall. Her face was
against the wet brickwork. Her arms were pressed about her ears. A
man seemed to be grappling with her. Another stooped over a form on
the ground.

Nightbone's grip fastened on the standing man's upper arm. He
cried out fearfully as he was spun round.

'Get away!' Then wide eyes recognized the uniform. 'It wasn't us.
Honest.'

Nightbone had seen that he was merely supporting the sobbing
girl. He knew her. She had sunk to her knees, clawing the wall. The
second man was tending the other woman, who lay still on the
cobbles. Nightbone knew her, too. Her skirt was emerald green. It
wasn't long since he had seen her last.

He loosed his grip. 'Which way?' he demanded. 'Quick!'

'Dunno. We didn't see no one. Only *her*.'

29

Not caring what he knelt in, Nightbone got down. The long woollen scarf she usually wore was absent. The acute angle of her neck between head and shoulders showed how savagely it had been broken. Her eyes bulged sightlessly and her tongue protruded bloodily.

'Shut up, can't you?' the standing man hissed at the moaning woman against the wall.

'Leave her,' Nightbone ordered.

He gave each of the men his searching stare. They were young porters or shopmen, genuinely shocked and scared. The kneeling one got up. He jerked his thumb.

'We was with her. She said we might find another round here.'

'That's right,' his companion agreed. 'We was calling out for her. When we found her we reckoned she'd keeled over.' He fluttered his fingers to his lips in a drinking gesture.

'Saw nobody else?'

'No.'

'Heard nothing?'

'Not a squeak. Did we, Tom?'

'You don't belong round here.'

'Market. Shut up early. We was taking a stroll.'

'In *this*?'

'We'd had a couple of jars. Bumped into her. Said she'd find a chum.'

The woman was quieter now.

'You all right, Mary?'

'Yeh, Mr Nightbone.'

'You see anybody? Hear anything?'

'It was like they say.'

'It was you that screamed?'

''S right. Is she . . .?'

'Just stay there quiet. No running off.'

Nightbone took down the men's names and addresses. He raked them again with his look.

'One of you – you – stop here with Mary. You, back that way to the road. Police sign fifty yards to the left. Say Sergeant Nightbone sent you to fetch them. Got it? Nightbone.'

'Can't you blow your whistle?'

A harder look was all the reply. The man went frightened into the fog, glancing uneasily about. Nightbone turned to his mate.

'When the bobbies come, tell them I said they're to take charge. Repeat what you've told me and anything else you can remember.'

'Where'll you be?'

'I've something else to do.'

'They'll run us in, won't they? How'll they know it wasn't us?'

'Mary will vouch for you. They know her.'

'Well – I say!'

'She was good enough for you ten minutes ago.'

Nightbone stopped again to retrieve the damp muffler that he had seen lying nearby. He spread it over the dead girl's distorted face and stood for a moment looking down at her. Then, resuming the direction he had been heading, he, too, went away into the fog.

He approached the cellar steps for the second time that afternoon. Some of them were droning a song to the concertina.

He thrust the door open again. There was no cocky greeting this time. The voices and then the old squeezebox died away as he surveyed them. They were in their customary places. All those he'd left there before, except Bailey and Bodger. And, of course, Nelly Jacks.

They waited for the tongue-lashing that didn't come. Instead, Nightbone went to where Jenny was slumped in a doze against the wall. Her tin mug hung empty from a crooked finger. He touched her shoulder.

'Jen.'

She raised heavy eyelids. Her expression was dragged down and lifeless-seeming. For a moment he saw a look of Nell. Not Nell as he'd just left her, though.

'Whassit?'

'Come on.'

She let him help her up without protest. He had nibbed her before without stopping to explain. If Nightbone came there was a reason. It was always a fair cop.

None of the others spoke. Jenny dragged her clothing about her to meet the cold outside. Nightbone followed close, ready to steady her on the slimy stairs. Someone kicked the door shut after them. The concertina whined again.

He had met Jen three years back. She had been new to the streets of North London. Twenty-three, she said. Blowsily pretty. Expecting to queen it over the local regulars, who hadn't had anything like her exotic career. She lost no time in telling them so. She told Nightbone, too. His sergeant's stripes had been new then, inviting a chaffing.

'What you get 'em for? Holding hands with the inspector? Want to see my stripes? Come up here and I'll show you 'em.'

She found it impossible to shock or provoke him. She abandoned ribaldry and told him about herself.

'Till they carry me out feet first I'll remember the day our ma sold me off. Said it was a friend I was to stop with for a bit. The landlord was putting us out and six kids was too many with a new one coming. I was twelve. I knew Harriet Minchin wasn't any friend of hers, but I had to go.'

'You were one of Mother Minchin's?'

'See! Something makes you sit up. Started in style, I did.'

Mrs Harriet Minchin, formerly of Southampton Street, Strand, had catered for all tastes. Virgins of either sex a speciality. The younger, the more expensive. It was said that young Viscount T—— had paid her 300 guineas for a ten-year-old girl. Prosecuting counsel at Mrs Minchin's later trial for baby farming had naïvely mentioned the alleged transaction. Mrs Minchin's counsel had been briefed thoroughly.

'My Lord, the defence objects to the introduction of hearsay evidence. I am instructed that my client was never acquainted with the nobleman named. She does, however, have the honour to number certain other members of the peerage among her friends. If it pleases your lordship, I have here a list of names for the gentlemen of the jury to peruse . . .'

'Thank you, thank you, but I regard the topic as irrelevant and inadmissible. May we get on?'

Mrs Minchin was acquitted. She retired to Brighton, where she worked admirably for fallen women.

'Where was your dad?' Nightbone had asked Jen.

'Where he always was – quod. Only ever came out long enough to put Ma up the spout. Then your lot hooked him back. Snuffed it on the Moor.'

'How did your mother know Ma Minchin?'

'The old bag had scouts everywhere. Do you know how many tarts it takes to keep one house going? They're always after new talent. Where we lived, twelve was a ripe old age to have never been . . . kissed. After Pa got sent to the Moor last time Ma knew he'd never come back. Must have been a sort of relief, but she couldn't keep us. Oh, cheer up! I don't look too bad on it, do I?'

She told him frank details of her initiation, and re-initiation, and yet further re-initiation. Then even the artful Mother Minchin couldn't go on passing her off as what she had ceased to be.

'I was coming up fourteen. They send the older girls to Brussels and those places. If they pass for twenty-one they can register and be legal. The best ones, the posh ones, they marry off to rich blokes in Hong Kong and South America. I'd been spoilt for that. She shipped me off to Turkey. I didn't mind really. Better than sewing shirts or pasting matchboxes.'

She professed a kind of veteran's pride in her service as a white slave, in establishments cruel and kind. Until they trusted her she was kept without money or clothes of her own. The penalties for making off with anything considered the property of the house were unspeakable.

'I'd nowhere to run off to, anyway. I sometimes thought of being back here. What could I do then? Same thing, I expect. Like I am now. Leastways out there, while you behaved yourself, you had a roof over your head and your belly full of food and drink. The blokes weren't all bad.'

'How did you get back?'

'Bloke fetched me. Old Greek ship's captain. Bought me out. Without a by-your-leave, mind you. Just told me he had, and I was to go with him. Said he had to catch the tide, so there was no time to fetch my things. I was furious. "What right have you, carting me about like I'm cargo? You can turn this old tub round and take me back. You get nix out of me!" But he wouldn't. And he got round me. Got what he wanted. Then the dirty rotter did a bunk on me after we docked at London. Nothing but what I had to stand up in. Bad cess to him! I thought of trying to get back to Stamboul, but I wasn't sure. He may have forgotten to pay for me, if he'd ever tried. And him a Greek. No guesses who they'd take it out on. Into the casbah with the has-beens. Besides, I'd found Nelly.'

'Nelly?'

'Kid sister. Two years younger. You'll see her round here soon.'

'On the game, too?'

'What else is there? She's had to keep herself and the boys since Ma snuffed it, and me away. Two of 'em in the navy now. One in the artillery. All right, Ernie's in quod, but you must admit she's not done bad. I don't like the look of the house she's in. Wapping. Too many sailors. I told her she'll be better round here with me. No more whorehouses. Furnished lodging. You lot can't touch us.'

'So long as you behave.'

'I know the rules. I'll look after Nell.'

She had done, but Nightbone had seen her own bloom and liveliness fading fast. She took to dyeing her fading black hair, with motley results. Her features thickened. She drank more and had got a reputation for mocking at men who walked past ignoring her. She taunted other girls, boasting of her superior experience. A fight cost her a month inside. When she got out she found she had lost her prime stand in a deep shop doorway at a junction of three roads. She had to share Nell's inferior beat among the alleys. From looking after Nelly, Jen had come to depend on her. Nell, who was quieter, and didn't drink much, and still had her unremarkable looks more or less intact, was the chief earner now.

Nightbone thought she hated the life but there was nothing else. He fetched Jenny from the cellar on that foggy, murderous afternoon, to tell her that her sister would at least never find out what it was like to be a used-up whore.

CHAPTER 6

UNCLE ED

THE weather at Leeds had deteriorated dramatically by evening. Thick cloud massed and the atmosphere turned muggy. At nine o'clock the rain came.

It poured all night. Too excited to sleep, Lucilla listened to it drumming on the slates, gurgling and slopping in the roof's iron guttering, inches from her head. It was still pouring when she got up in morning darkness. She dressed and went quietly down with her candle. She lit the back parlour gas jet and built up the fire in the range. Five o'clock was half an hour before her usual time, but she could stay in bed no longer.

Through the rain's wash she heard the clacking procession of clogs and heavy boots. For most men and women and many children it was the start of just another long working day in factory or mill. Lucilla had sworn to herself she would never be one of them. She'd sooner starve. Even this dismal house and shop was preferable. But that wouldn't be for much longer now. Her heart was unusually light as she went mechanically about her daily tasks.

Uncle Edgar could count on a good day when it rained like this. Women who might have gone into Leeds Market would shop locally rather than get soaked. When last evening's row had abated he had sent Lucilla to the home of the thin girl-child who helped him.

'She's no need to come in, with you at home.'

'They need her wage, Uncle.'

It was Aunt Doris who reminded her, 'You can tell them who they've to thank for not getting any.'

Lucilla went wretchedly to face the girl's family. She gave them sixpence of her own. She would soon have plenty of money. The girl was welcome to her job.

The shop stayed open till nine. This evening at six Aunt Doris emptied the till and took the locked cash box to put under the bed. Then she squeezed into her tightest corset and her sociable dress. In a rain bonnet and waterproof she went off under a vast umbrella to enjoy her weekly evening at the Ladies' Whist Club.

The downpour that had driven customers in during the day kept them away after dark. The doorbell tinkled scarcely a dozen times between six and eight. Lucilla saw her uncle check his watch yet again.

'Nowt much doing.'

Lucilla had been trying to see out, shading out window reflections with her cupped hand.

'There's nobody about. It's coming down buckets.'

'Happen we'll call it a day.'

He locked and bolted the door and pulled the blind. Lucilla put out the gas and followed him through into the welcome warmth of the parlour kitchen.

'Shut door,' he ordered. 'We'll not have anybody seeing light and knocking. Some folk reckon a shopkeeper's life's not his own.'

She had thought him unusually quiet in the shop. He tended to be quite chatty with her when his wife wasn't within earshot. Uncle Edgar Harrison was some inches smaller than Lucilla, who wasn't unusually tall. She could see down through his mousy hair to a balding pate. He was in his mid-forties, but a little downy beard and moustache made him seem older, and melancholy with it. She did feel sorry for him at times, married to such a wife and stuck here for ever. Otherwise, she despised him for not being man enough to stand up against the tyrant.

Aunt Doris's habits were rigid. She would be home almost precisely as the black marble mantelpiece clock chimed ten. Until then her husband could pretend he was master of his establishment, provided he kept the shop open till nine and didn't allow credit.

'Shall I make you a cup of cocoa?' Lucilla offered. She took off her apron and went to the big copper kettle.

'Aye. Take one yourself.'

The fire in the open range made the room snug. Her own room was at its most cheerless in wet weather. It was too early to go to bed. She had nothing else to do but spin fantasies about life in the London fashion trade. If Uncle was in the mood for chatting she might risk telling him her news. Perhaps he could make it easier to tell Aunt Doris. Perhaps they would be glad to get shut of her.

He surprised her by saying, 'On second thoughts, what we want is a drop of summat real.' He went to the dresser cupboard where one or two seldom-seen bottles were. 'What do you fancy, Luce? Glass of port wine?'

'Just a little, please, Uncle.'

It was the first time he'd ever called her Luce.

Her parents had given her sips of wine, and occasionally her own glass. She liked it in small amounts. It was a surprise to be offered any in this house.

He poured for them both, in tall fancy glasses, and brought them to where she was standing beside the chenille-covered dining table. She noticed his hands trembling. His mouth was tight from concentrating on not spilling.

Lucilla took a glass. He didn't look at her.

'Come and sit you down.'

He touched her arm and pointed to the narrow settee in front of the closed window curtains. She sat on it obediently and he joined her. There was just space close together between the end cushions.

Uncle Edgar took a drink. Still not looking at her he said, 'Nowt like a wet inside when it's wet out.' His voice was weak and husky.

Lucilla wondered suddenly if he was going to break something to her. Tell her Aunt Doris had decided she was to go into a mill. She took a sip of port and waited.

'Aye.' He had to clear his throat. 'Well, Luce, I reckon you and me have a bit of business.'

'What about, Uncle?'

'*You* and *me* sort.'

She knew at once what he really meant. She hadn't expected it, but she'd seen him sometimes looking at her in the way other men did.

She stood up and put down her glass.

'I think I'd better go up.'

'Aye. That's the ticket.'

He tossed back the rest of his drink and stood up. He came forward and pushed his face eagerly at hers. Taking her arm with one hand he reached behind him to put his empty glass on a small table. It toppled off the edge and fell to the linoleum floor, snapping in two at the stem.

The accident didn't distract him. He tried clumsily to kiss her and at the same time steer her towards the door leading to the stairs. She turned her face sharply away.

'Please, Uncle.'

'What's up?' He was craning after her lips. 'Come on, Luce.'

'No thanks. You're hurting.'

'I'd not hurt you, Luce. Not a bit.'

'I don't mean that. Let go.'

'Don't bother coming all over innocent wi' me. You know what's what.'

'Yes. And there's nothing doing.'

Her sudden spirit surprised him. He stared.

'Why not? Never mind *her*. She'll not be back. Listen, Luce, it'd be for your good. You don't like being here. I can't say I blame you. Having to put up with *her*. Same as me. Both in t'same boat. I reckoned, you and me . . . I'd see you right for brass. So much a week. You can tell her you've got a new job. Get one or not, as you fancy. Stop out all day, so's she can't be on at you to work for her . . .'

'Stop it. Stop saying such things.'

'What's wrong? An hour or two on her night out. Not much. Nowt wrong with me?'

He was reaching for her lips again. She struggled violently.

'What the hell do you think I am?'

'Language, Luce!'

'Stop calling me that. Oh, just you wait. Wait and see!'

'Hey! You'll not let on?'

'Frightened she'd give it you for wasting good brass?'

The taunt provoked him. He jerked her towards him and crushed her close. His puckered lips sought harder after hers. Saliva wetted her cheeks and chin. Though she wriggled hard her arms were trapped under his. She could only bend her body backward. She arched her neck away from him. He bent with her. Kisses slobbered on her throat. She felt herself going to fall. She gave a last desperate twist of all her body. They stumbled, locked together, on to the sofa.

Small as he was, he was strong. Lucilla began to panic. He managed to get both her arms pinioned in one of his, freeing a hand to fumble at her skirt. She threshed her booted feet.

It didn't occur to her to scream. Their combat was silent, except for gasps and breathy ejaculations. He forced her down further on the couch. She was on her back, weighted by his body. His hand groped and tugged. Exasperated by the amount of her linen, he dragged his other hand into play.

With a freed hand Lucilla made a snatch for where she thought the broken wineglass was on the floor. Her fingers found the base and stem. She got it into her palm and poised it like a dagger.

'Look!' she gasped.

He jerked his head round. The gleaming sliver was only inches from his eyes.

'For God's sake, Luce!'

'Get off! Get off me!'

She advanced the weapon to follow his retreating face. He almost fell off her, on to his feet. Keeping the glass stem raised in her fist at shoulder height, she got up. He tottered as he retreated. He stumbled backward on to the sofa again, panting and staring.

Lucilla stood over him. She didn't know how long she could hold him there. Her legs were trembling. The arm holding the glass dagger was shaking. She thought she might be going to faint.

It took only a hard push in her back to send her sprawling face forward beside him. The weapon flew from her hand and shattered against flowered wallpaper.

'Stay there, you little bitch!' Aunt Doris ordered.

She spent that night locked in her room. Her aunt had virtually dragged her there. Lucilla had put up no resistance. She was too shaken even to try to explain.

'Broke a glass and came at me!' her uncle had babbled. 'Went crazy. Worse'n her mother.'

His wife's contempt kept them both guessing how much she had heard before coming in the back door.

'Why was the shop shut up?'

'She must have done it.'

'Mrs Booth came and told me. Blind down and light out. Not gone half-past.'

'You're not making out that ...?'

'I've been watching you, Edgar Harrison. I know men. As for you, you trollop, we'll see to you tomorrow.'

From her locked room Lucilla heard them carrying on. Much later, the key outside her lock was turned quietly. She didn't believe he would try again, but it gave her another moment's near-panic.

The door didn't open, but she found it had been left unlocked. Just Aunt Doris's reminder that whatever had happened didn't let her off her early-morning duties.

CHAPTER 7

JEN

As they came up the steps into the denser fog at street level, Nightbone turned her in the direction of the lodging she and Nelly shared. Had shared.

He kept her arm to steady her. She leaned against his solid side. She was slightly unsteady from the drink. Her shivering was more alcoholic tremor.

'All right, Jen?'

'Ta.'

The cold air was clearing her head, but she still didn't ask what he had fetched her for. He didn't enlighten her. He wasn't going to break it out here in the fish-stinking, fog-filled street. She was entitled to her little bit of privacy. It was one room in a narrow house not far away.

'No more whorehouses for me,' she'd told him. 'I've earnt my freedom.'

He knew the score. Some girls worked in residential brothels, regimented not unlike nuns, except that their observances were somewhat different. They stayed from choice, or duress and unpayable debt to the proprietor. Some, independent and prosperous, had their own apartments. They gave themselves airs and received by appointment only. Many others slipped in from respectable suburbs to rooms rented by the hour, to make pin money their husbands wouldn't give them. Some lived with their pimps, ponces, fancy men, bearers-up, or plain bullies. The men took most of the earnings, robbed the clients, and gave a sort of protection and companionship.

Most – except the lowest and oldest and wretchedest, who performed anywhere they could get their back against a wall, and slept rough – had a rented lodging. It was somewhere to rest, lie sick, drag up a child. Neighbours in the trade gave some help and understanding. If the landlady wasn't the sort who charged extra high for pretending not to see or hear what her premises were being used for, there was an almost cheerful coming-and-going tenants' community round her kitchen fire.

When Nightbone had first known Jen and Nelly they had had a room apiece in a house that was clean enough and quiet enough for the police to ignore. Then their landlady had taken up with a sailor. He soon recognized an easier life ashore. He tripled the rent and tried to set himself up as the household pimp. The sisters moved on. They had kept moving since, with a downhill tendency.

'Hey! Where are we going?'

It had dawned at last that he wasn't taking her in.

'Your place, Jen.'

'What?'

She'd mockingly invited him often enough. He had been there, too, though only to inspect. Recently he hadn't liked what he'd found: the two sisters living and operating in the single cramped room with only one bed. They shared it when they were alone. When either brought a man the other made herself scarce.

'Nelly might be there.'

She was looking at him, curious to discern what he had in mind. She saw the grim set of his jaw as he faced into the fog ahead.

'Oh God!'

He held her arm tighter.

'Hold up. We're nearly there.'

'It's Nelly. Isn't it? Oh, God!'

He supported her the rest of the way. Her keening moans as they went up the lodginghouse stairs caused a couple of doors to open. Curiosity showed in wide eyes. At sight of the uniform the faces fled and the doors shut.

The room was very plain but tidy enough. The bed took up most of the space. There was a jar of yesterday's drooping flowers on the narrow little mantelpiece. Nightbone knew the flower woman who always gave Nelly the leftovers from her basket.

He sat Jen on the bed. Her hands drooped in her lap. Her damp hair straggled across her face. She stared sightlessly at the faded mat that was all the floor covering.

He unwound her muffler. 'Have you got a drop in, Jen?'

She didn't answer. He went to search the narrow cupboard and drawers that held their things. They didn't cook in the room. The Irish landlady provided food in her basement kitchen. Cash in advance for everything. She had been a tart herself and knew their tricks.

There was a corner cupboard, but no bottle in it. It was another of Ma Costigan's rules that drink was bought from her. He went to the basement. The Irishwoman was pouring gin from a stone bottle for one of three girls in loose wrappers who were smoking cigars beside the grate. He saw the girls nudge one another at sight of him. One of them wriggled her shoulders and made a performance out of modestly pulling her robe close.

'It's yourself, Mr Nightbone,' said Mrs Costigan. 'Anything the matter at all?'

'A glass of that will do.'

'Ooh!'

'For Jen Jacks.'

'That's nice. And will it be another for the Sergeant?'

'Make it two for Jen.'

He knew the girls were pushing each other and making faces. He turned his head and gave them his look. His bleak expression gave them something to stare at.

'What's she been doing this time, Mr Nightbone?' the landlady was asking.

'Nothing. Nell's dead.'

'Holy Mother! Nelly! How?'

'Strangled.'

He gave them the details briefly.

'Anything to tell me, Mrs Costigan?'

'What would I know?'

'Any of you?'

The girls shook their unpinned hair. They were suddenly very young and frightened.

'Anything at all. Bloke you've seen her with lately. Stranger, maybe. Might have taken against her.'

There was no response. He gestured impatiently for the gin.

'Jen would know,' Mrs Costigan said, pouring the second. 'Never two was closer than them.'

'I haven't asked her yet,' Nightbone said. 'This is to help.'

He left them, carrying the two glasses. The landlady hadn't mentioned payment. She had read his eyes.

He held the first drink to Jenny's lips. She sipped without expression. The bite of the liquor, and what he told her, made her shiver. She looked at him at last, beside her on her bed, holding the glass. Her fingers were at her throat.

'The garrotte?'

He nodded. From the way Nell had looked it hadn't been unexpected and unseen like that. Squeezing fingers. Face to face. Terror.

'Who, Jen? Any ideas?'

She shook her head.

'They always like Nelly, fellers. She's nice to 'em. Come back looking for her.'

'What about first-timers.'

'Not lately. She'd have told me. Told me everything. She was particular. I made her be. I told her what to watch out for. It's the eyes. The way they look at you while they bargain. You know which to tell to sling their hook.'

She took the glass from him. Her hand shook, but she drank without spilling. He ought to have been back at the station making his report, not sitting on a whore's bed feeding her gin.

'She wasn't done for her tin, that's sure,' she said.

Unless the man was inexperienced, he thought. Or he would have known they never kept money on them.

'Why else, then?'

'Dunno. She didn't have the glim. You can count that out.'

Not necessarily. If a bloke caught a dose he'd blame the last tart he'd been with, not one of his own class.

'Men!' Jen said violently. She might have thrown the glass at the wall. He took it from her. The other full one was out of her sight. He left it there.

She subsided again. 'Ta, Mr Nightbone.' It was almost a child's tone, and she put her hand on his. He put his other hand over it. It was cold as stone.

'Why not go down for a warm?' he suggested. 'I've told Ma.'

She shook her head. 'I'd sooner stop here. Will I have to ...?'

'I'll identify her. I'm sorry, Jen. Truly sorry.'

'She said once she fancied you. Will I tell you what she said?'

'If you want.'

'She said, "Just one time with him," she said, "and I might even chuck it." Know what she meant?'

'I can't see it. No.'

'Something to do with feeling clean again. Only she knew you'd never touch her. Said that made her feel dirtier still.'

'I'm a bobby, Jen.'

'That never stopped some of 'em.'

'They aren't bobbies now.'

'You're a queer one, Nightbone.'

'Not that, either.'

He gave her hand a squeeze and got up. 'I've got to get back. They'll be looking out for me. Anything else?'

Her brief spark had died. 'I'll manage. Funny, I meant to look after her. She finishes up looking after me. Now there's nobody left to start looking after no one.'

'None of that talk, Jenny Jacks,' he told her seriously.

'I used to blame our ma for selling me. Poor little Nelly got kep' home, and look how she ends up! Laughing, aren't I?'

Her voice shook. He reached quickly for the other glass of gin and left her with it.

'Keep an eye on her,' he told Mrs Costigan.

'Will I take her up another drop, Sergeant?'

'Presently.'

He began reaching into his trousers pocket for money.

'On the house,' she said.

'Good of you, Ma.'

'You're not so bad for a crusher. What'll they do with Nell?'

'Inquest. The parish will see to her.'

One of the girls broke in. She was the one who had put on the little act with her gown. Nightbone knew her slightly. She was a bit of a character, like Jen had been.

'Can we have her?'

'How do you mean, Sal?'

'Not a parish job. Could have been any of us.'

'It costs a bit.'

Sal glanced at the other girls. Their look might have been taken for bashfulness.

'Day's takings each. Think of Nelly while we're earning.'

When he had finished his report, which rounded off his day's duties, he tramped to his lodging behind the Caledonian Road. The fortress mass of Pentonville Gaol loomed almost invisibly in the autumn darkness and fog. It had grown colder. The gaslamp at the end of each street corner lit nothing beyond its own globe, a clinging pale blob.

Nightbone had never been a man to brood. The job was like any other, boring most of the time, sometimes busy, now and then more dangerous than some. Its solitary nature suited his lonely temperament. This evening, as he sat in his small room in his waistcoat and slippers, he thought of what Jen had said about Nell. What Nell had said to Jen. About him. He wondered if the brothers in the army, the navy, and the jail ever considered how their sister had brought them up. If they did, perhaps they would regard getting throttled in a back alley as an occupational hazard.

Such notions continued to crowd his mind after supper. His landlady served it to him in his room. Warming, satisfying Lancashire hotpot. He was always welcome to join Mr and Mrs Hilling in their parlour. He seldom did. It meant chatting and listening and offering opinions about things on which he hadn't any. He got out a bottle of the strong army beer that he usually reserved for Sundays, and sat alone drinking it. He smoked a pipe and stared into his coals.

A knock on his door eventually interrupted the reverie. The landlord peered in, grey beard and strong spectacles. He was a hardworking engraver from Lancashire, whose eyesight was going. He went to bed early to save it.

'Tub up, lad.'

'I'll be straight down, Jack.'

''Neet, lad.'

'Good night.'

In taking this room in an otherwise private house, Nightbone had made one odd stipulation. He must have a daily bath.

It had struck Mr and Mrs Hilling as so peculiar that they had almost turned him away. He offered to pay a little extra for it. It proved little enough trouble. All it involved was bringing in the long metal tub that hung outside the kitchen door, setting it before the kitchen range, and pouring in a few inches of hot water from the two big iron kettles always kept on the hobs. When Nightbone was on day turn he had his bath after the couple went to bed. Mr Hilling's last duty was to bring the tub in and fill it and give him a knock. Nightbone emptied it afterwards and hung it back in its place outside. When he was on night duty he bathed in the morning, before turning in. The notion of having a naked young man in her kitchen, and her husband gone off to work, wasn't one to unsettle Mrs Hilling.

His bath's purpose wasn't solely hygienic. He called it his patent refresher. It soothed away fatigue and gave him sound sleep. An added ingredient helped work the magic. Before stepping into the tub he reached from the kitchen mantelpiece a big stone jar. Lifting its lid released a sweet country garden aroma of herbs and flowers that pervaded the room when he sprinkled a fistful of the contents on to the water.

He had once helped a couple of gipsy pedlars, being threatened by a mob of women. They were accusing them of a theft Nightbone knew they hadn't done. He sent the mothers off with advice to keep a closer eye on what their kids got up to. The pedlar tried to give him a half-sovereign. He refused it.

'Ever take a tub?' the didicoi wife surprised him.

'When I can.'

'You look a clean 'un. Have this.' She picked a small bag off their barrow. 'Perk you up when you've bin on your pins.'

She loosed the bag and held it up to his nose. He smelt summer sunshine on flowers and leaves.

'Juniper. Peppermint. Chamomile, Orris Root. Handful in the tub afore you gets in.'

He had found the refresher so good that he looked out for them coming round again. A copper chasing after them with cash tickled them hugely. They promised to keep him supplied.

This night, for once, the bathing ritual failed. The infusion that soothed his muscles didn't ease his mind. Images of Jen Jacks's overwhelmed features alternated with Nelly's, alive and dead. For a rarity, Nightbone was a long time going off. And then he slept uneasily.

CHAPTER 8

THE COMMISSIONER

S TANDING before the Commissioner's big desk, Chief Superintendent Charles McNorris eased his knees under his considerable weight. He had learnt the bobby's bend from the
old constable who'd taken him out on his first beat. That had
been back in the 1860s, about the time when they exchanged frock-
coats, white duck trousers, and the tall top hats that kept blowing off
for the more army-style uniform of blue serge and a helmet with
wind-defeating chinstrap.

Nowadays Charlie McNorris came to work in a civilian suit and
bowler hat. He was Assistant Commissioner, Metropolitan Police, at
New Scotland Yard.

The only uniform he kept now, worn on ceremonial occasions, was
rather a splendid get-up. His wife cherished it in tissue paper in their
bedroom wardrobe. He looked quite grand in it and less portly.
Lately, he had got it out surreptitiously a couple of times, to look at it
for reassurance. In his fifties, and ranking second in the metropolitan
force, Charlie McNorris was feeling almost as insecure as any other
bobby. There was no predicting this rigid little soldier-chief, with the
probing grey eyes, hair like an iron skullcap, moustache of spiked
wire, and skin yellowed by Eastern suns. Being paraded before him
wasn't McNorris's notion of his office or rank. He had been used to
being consulted, to voicing opinions to be valued. In the old chief's
presence he would have spoken his mind from the visitor's chair.
Now, he only answered questions. Like all others, he stood. There was
no chair.

Colonel Arthur Naish Saltby, stiff backed on his plain chair's edge,
looked up again from his papers.

'What *sort* of man?' he repeated with more emphasis. His wiry frame, tightly buttoned up in a black suit, looked too slight to produce the deeply resonant voice.

'Excellent officer, sir.'

'Sort of *man*?'

'Prefers to go his own way.'

'How well do you know him yourself?'

'Since he joined. Little over nine years.'

'How *well*?'

'He's served most of his time out in O Division. We cross paths now and again.'

The Commissioner sighed.

'Is it conceivable. Chief Superintendent, that my questions and your answers might cross paths rather more often?'

Policemen and soldiers mostly wore uniforms, and served their Queen and country without thanks or adequate reward. Apart from that, they were as chalk and cheese, oil and water to old hands of Charlie McNorris's vintage. His acquaintance with the army was chiefly from years of picking it up drunk off London streets. When it came to knowing bobbies he deferred to no one. He had been Chief Instructor at Wellington Barracks, where every Met recruit spent his first week. It had been McNorris's boast that he could pinpoint a man's quality in a seventh of that time. His snap assessment of Col. Saltby had been of a stiff-arsed so-called Leader of Men, spoilt by almightiness and the fawnings of junior officers, servants, and females. Used to having all about him jump at his least utterance. A sort to make any old copper groan.

Nothing in subsequent weeks had changed that opinion. McNorris had kept his patience. He had been waiting to see the miracle of a police force transformed by the flourish of a military baton. He was still waiting. Now there was a situation for which patience and caution were not enough.

He raised a thick finger, aiming it like a pistol barrel at the documents on the desk.

'Anyone who'd believe that would believe anything.'

The Commissioner didn't cry mutiny. He cried nothing. He let the outburst spend itself.

'That Watts. Scum. Dregs ...'

'Dregs *and* scum?'

'Rotten. To his diseased marrow.'

'I'd gathered that was your opinion, Chief Super. You've thoughtfully recorded your comments on his record.'

'I reckoned you might want them, sir.'

'You reckoned I should *need* them, where my better-informed predecessor would not.'

'Standard procedure, sir.'

The Commissioner didn't comment. He brought forward some of the papers to study for a few moments.

'Tell me, why has Nightbone never made Inspector?'

'It's up to the officer himself to apply.'

'I'm aware of that. *Why*?'

'There is no requirement to state reasons for not so doing.'

'Has anyone *asked* him?'

'Not procedure, sir.'

'Not procedure to hold friendly conversations, in which such a subject might conceivably come up? Anything prejudical known? On or off his record.'

'Definitely nothing.'

'Family problems?'

'Unmarried. Both parents deceased. No close family. No, er, entanglements.'

'Lodges privately, I see. Accommodating landlady?'

'Nothing of that sort, sir. Very respectable old couple.'

The Commissioner referred back to another document. 'Plenty of hard arrests.'

'He can handle himself, sir, Nightbone.'

Col. Saltby put down the document as if dismissing it from parade. He left his chair abruptly, to march briskly round the desk. He stood inches shorter than his deputy. He had the air of a whippet, tensed for a race.

'It's his handling of others that I am concerned with, Mr McNorris. Specifically, this complainant, Watts.'

'Like I said, sir, if you'll believe that . . .'

'*I* say, Chief Superintendent, kindly do not condescend to me.'

'Not intentional, sir.'

Col. Saltby knew better. He saw before him an uncouth hulk of chest and paunch, thick red neck, fat cheeks as pink as ham, soggy eyes too close together. He heard the tones of East London and the corporals' mess.

It was as he had expected to find when he had accepted this

appointment. He had come to it believing that policemen were cast from a base metal unrefined since the days of the Bow Street Runners. In the army, an officer promoted from the ranks was a rarity. The opposite applied in the police. Col. Saltby knew that bringing in civilians of "good education and social standing' to senior ranks had always failed. It didn't surprise him. Looking at McNorris told him why.

This uncomfortable interview sprang from a communication received at the Yard some hours ago. It was from a lawyer acting on behalf of one Edward Watts, Esquire, complainant against a Sergeant Nightbone, O Division, Metropolitan Police. It alleged unprovoked assault by said Sgt. Nightbone against said Edward Watts, Esq, resulting in actual grievous injury and distress. It was accompanied by the report of a Paddington doctor who had examined complainant yesterday evening. He had found evidence of severe blows to the region of stomach and abdomen. Complainant had named said Sgt. Nightbone as his molester.

The Commissioner had sent for his deputy.

'What action on this, Chief Super?'

'Usual procedure, sir. Sent to the district superintendent for copy of officer's report on any incident of yesterday's date, involving himself and complainant. Requested statements from witnesses named.'

'Has the officer been questioned?'

'Not procedure at this stage, sir.'

'A plain yes or no would suffice.'

'No, sir.'

'You haven't spoken to him yourself, informally?'

'Certainly not, sir. And if I may say so, sir, I know them both. Nightbone and Watts. It's a put-up.'

'The lawyer – know him well?'

'By reputation.'

'Fully qualified to practise?'

'Yes.'

'The doctor?'

'Not personally known to me. There's some will sign anything.'

'Any reason to suppose he's one?'

'No evidence, sir. I'm having him looked into.'

'Not in any way, I hope, that might be interpreted as warning off or intimidation?'

'Not my habit, sir.'

'I merely mention it. The complainant? Have our own doctors seen him?'

'Not found him so far, sir.'

'Not *found* him?'

'His own doctor says he put him into a cab to take himself off to hospital. Hasn't heard from him since.'

'What about the hospital?'

'No record of him being admitted anywhere. No outpatient treatment. Can't have been that bad,' McNorris couldn't resist putting in.

'Isn't his lodging known?'

'Landlord hasn't seen him. Doesn't know anything. You ask me . . .'

'Yes?'

'He's gone to ground. Played this trick on Nightbone and holed up with some other rats, till it's safe to crawl out.'

'Afraid for what Nightbone will do to him?'

'I don't say that, sir.'

'Very well, Chief Super. Let me know what you find out, Meanwhile, no further approaches to anyone. Doctor, lawyer. Nothing that the Home Secretary, the police committees, the public, might question.'

'The officer, sir?'

'Nothing at present. When his report of the incident arrives you will please have it brought straight to me. Unread by anyone else.'

'Very good, sir.'

'And Chief Superintendent . . . No words with him meanwhile.'

The old policeman's hands tightened at his sides. Although he was not in uniform he came to laborious attention. If the chair behind the desk had been empty he would have given it an ironic salute. But the chair was occupied, and it was the Commissioner in it.

Since then the Commissioner had examined Nightbone's report in the station logbook. He had read Nightbone's personal documents again. He had allowed his back to rest against his chair while he thought. He had got up from his desk, marched about a bit, looked out of the window, and sat down to think further. Then he had sent for the Assistant Commissioner again.

The interview that was proving so distressing to Charlie McNorris was nearing an end.

'Have him fetched in,' the Commissioner ordered. 'No explanations.'

He opened a drawer and took out an envelope. He handed it to the Assistant Commissioner.

'This is to go by cab to his duty inspector. It's a letter authorizing him to go to the man's lodging and collect his mufti. Then bring it straight here.'

He saw McNorris's expression. 'Kindly don't tell me it will be a shock to his landlady's sensitive soul. If I'm not satisfied with what he has to say for himself he doesn't leave here in uniform. Yes, Chief Superintendent?'

'I was going to say, sir . . . suggest . . .'

'That . . . ?'

'It wouldn't go down well. In the force.'

'It would not be intended to. It seems I have been mistaken. I believed I had made enough examples. Clearly not, so the worse this one "goes down", as you put it, perhaps the better.'

'Watts is a con man. Any bobby would see through his game.'

'And I'm not a bobby?'

'It's what will be said.'

'Because I'm not, such people as Watts are outside my experience? Is that it? You've heard of self-inflicted wounds, I take it?'

'Exactly what I'm suggesting, sir.'

'I can smell them, Chief Superintendent. One of the commonest army crimes. It used to fetch a flogging. There are those who say it should still. The recourse of the shirker and the coward. Minimum pain and no lasting disability. Show me a man who has "accidentally" shot off a toe or sliced his little finger end with his bayonet. I will show you a malingerer, and punish him.'

'Watts, to a T.'

The Commissioner picked up the medical report and read from it aloud.

'"... Injuries apparently administered with considerable violence ... Severe enough to give rise to fear of damage to internal organs ..."' He tossed the paper back on to the desk. 'Self-inflicted?'

'I don't believe in any injuries, sir.'

'But you could believe in professional men conspiring against a police officer?'

'There has to be something of the sort. Nightbone, sir. I'd back him anytime.'

'And most loyal that you should. Tell me, when Watts is found, what then? Do you expect he'll confess? Admit this has been one of his confidence tricks?'

'If he's not injured, he'll have to.'

'Then our next move would have to be to bring serious charges against the doctor and lawyer? Aiding and abetting?'

'Naturally.'

'So they must be realizing the danger they're in. Do you suggest Watts is lying low to conceal the fact that the doctor's report is a fake? That the entire affair is a conspiracy? Chief Superintendent, I beg that you will not be so indiscreet as to let any such opinion gain currency. They would only have to produce Watts, complete with injuries, and my head and yours would be on the block, side by side. Unless, of course, you hold that such a joint sacrifice would benefit mankind in general and the Metropolitan Police in particular.'

McNorris wasn't deceived that the Commissioner was joking for once. His thick cheeks flamed with the frustration that burnt within him. As though aware of it, and deciding it needed damping down before his deputy dissolved in flames, Col. Saltby suddenly assumed a quieter manner. His keen eyes never wavered, but he became almost confidential.

'Tell me frankly, McNorris. Is it pure justice you're chasing? Or the interest of a fellow policeman?'

'Both, sir. They go together.'

'Well, here is something to accompany them. *Lay off*. Abandon this enquiry, both professionally and personally. Consider what situation it puts us in. The force is at rock-bottom strength. I am in the middle of urging that upon the Home Secretary. I'm reminding him how watchful and critical the press and public continue to be. Everything we do, every penny we spend, is scrutinized and commented on. Don't you conceive it hard to justify devoting time and resources trying to counter an allegation against an officer who the bulk of evidence suggests paid off a score against an old antagonist, and thought he could get away with it?'

'Why should he report it, sir, if he didn't do it? That's not getting away with anything.'

'That suggestion implies grave accusations. Against the conduct and probity of members of the medical and legal professions. On what grounds? What evidence? No, no, Chief Superintendent. I prefer not. Kindly concentrate your invaluable experience and our slender re-sources on more important and less dangerous matters. When Watts does show up again he'll be spotted soon enough. Let us wait to see what shape he's really in. The longer he lies low, the more his wounds, if any, heal. So, the weaker his allegation gets. But even then, any examination or interrogation, on or off police premises, must be rigorously correct and witnessed. No possibility of alleged pressure or inducement.'

In spite of the Commissioner's parade-ground tone, Charlie McNorris thought that, for the first time, he was seeing him worried. Not so cocksure of himself. A shade vulnerable until he knew how this was going to work out. Could it be the chink in the armour that he'd begun to fear was never going to show? Could Saltby be seeing at last that dealing with shysters, backstreet quacks, and the likes of Bailey Watts was real policeman's work? Saltby's way of running the Met was to keep the Home Office and police committees sweet at any cost. Those people had been glad to see the old Commissioner go. He'd pestered them endlessly. They wanted somebody who would cut costs and reel out the red tape. They had got one in Saltby, but Charlie felt suddenly more optimistic than he had for weeks.

'Very well, sir,' he accepted obediently. 'Where does this leave Nightbone, though?'

The response unsettled him again.

'Very precariously placed,' the Commissioner said. 'If Watts has those injuries, and we discover no other cause for them, then the case represents a serious condemnation of police methods. It will be seized on by our critics, to the severe detriment of the entire Metropolitan force.'

Charlie McNorris saw that his time had come to protest no more. He had done his duty. Warned his chief as a faithful deputy ought. Spoken up for Nightbone as a colleague and friend. Enough said. He would obey his superior's orders. He would go straight across to his own office and summarize them in writing. He would date-stamp the document and bury it in the files. Somewhere it wouldn't be found by accident, but could be retrieved from later.

Let Saltby sack Nightbone. Let him fall on his arse. Each man for himself. Nightbone included. *And* Charles McNorris. Next time they let him sit in that chair he'd make sure he stuck. He'd had one brief chance, but botched it. He knew how to do it now.

He saw the Commissioner's impatience to get back to his Home Office memorandum. His desk was strewn with notes. Col. Saltby picked up his pen, but paused.

'By the way, Chief Super ...'

'Sir?'

'One further thought for you. Have you considered Nightbone's position if Watts should *not* show up again? Ever?'

'Sir?'

'Suppose his disappearance means he's played his last trick, but overdone it? You might feel that that sad eventuality could be prejudicial to your friend's interest. Fatally prejudicial, perhaps.'

The Commissioner dipped his pen-nib dismissively and resumed his writing.

CHAPTER 9

STRANGER IN THE SMOKE

No immediate sentence having been passed on her, Lucilla decided to cheat her aunt of the postponed pleasure.

When she went downstairs next morning it was earlier than usual. She stepped very quietly, carrying the carpet-bag and hatbox she had packed, and unpacked, and repacked, until late in the night. She took a workers' tram to the railway station. After buying a third-class one-way ticket she went to the telegraph office. A clerk fancied the look of her enough to help her address a wire to Maurice et Cie, Great Titchfield Street, London W.

'ARRIVING KING'S CROSS STATION 10.47.'

She was unsure how to sign herself. She settled on 'L. POOLE'. Afterwards she thought she ought to have put 'MISS'. Not being personally acquainted with Mr Edward Pearson, she addressed it to his brother Joseph.

Further afterthought that perhaps he wouldn't be back in London yet, or might be away from his office that morning, came too late. By the time these and other doubts began nagging her she was on her way to The Smoke.

Mrs Costigan unlocked Jen's door, and she wasn't in the room.

'How am I to know?' she answered Nightbone's demand. 'I'm not her keeper. Mine is not that sort of house.'

The bed was made. He couldn't judge whether it had been used. The few possessions he had noticed last night were still there. The flowers hung dead over the jar's rim. The landlady picked up the three empty glasses. One was a tumbler. She saw him notice it.

'Didn't you tell me to fetch her another? I gave her a big one.'

'Then it wasn't last night she went out.'

'Jen can hold it.'

'Have you ever known her go out of a morning?'

'Maybe taken herself to a boozer. Drown her sorrows.'

He hoped they were all she'd gone to drown.

The fog had cleared overnight. The noisy chaos of street life was visible again. Nightbone looked in at a few more places where they knew Jen.

A newsagent's was placarded with 'MURDER!' They hadn't seen her this morning.

'Keep 'em off the streets a bit, this,' said the newsagent. Nightbone didn't return his matey wink.

He looked into five pubs. She hadn't been in any of them since yesterday morning, when she had been in them all. They hadn't seen Nell for some days.

'Pore little duck,' a barmaid said. 'Didn't drink much. Never have known her for a judy if she didn't dress up. How's Jen took it?'

'It's what I want to know.' Following his night thoughts he had woken up wondering if he had done enough for her. What else? He wasn't a detective. He couldn't go trying to find Nell's murderer. Not officially, anyway. It was unlikely anyone else would. Too busy. Short-handed. Just another tart, asking for it like all the rest. Wonder there weren't more.

At least, he wanted to know that Jen was all right, and to tell her he'd do what he could. He left messages for her at the places he visited. She was to go the police station and wait for him. He kept looking in there, but the Station Sergeant continued to have no news. When he returned yet again at 9.45 Nightbone thought they were eyeing him curiously.

'I'm going down to the Thames Police,' he told the sergeant. 'Maybe the railway. Cover for me, will you?'

'Why not use the telegraph?'

Nightbone went out without answering.

For a wonder, there had been no overnight river incidents. Most mornings produced their haul of corpses. Mainly female. With all those skirts to float them they were easiest spotted.

Nightbone took a bus from the river police wharf to King's Cross. The railway station was second choice for girls with misery too much to bear. They'd sooner spoil their looks under the wheels than risk getting rescued alive from the river.

The great terminus from the north was busy with morning arrivals and departures. Lines of carriages were disgorging and loading. Oily steam clouds billowed towards him as an express locomotive with a long line of coaches braked and slithered beside a vacant platform. A porter was shouting around the concourse that it was the 10.47 from Leeds. Nightbone knew him.

'Morning, Harry.'

'How do, Sergeant. Bloody fog's gone, then.'

'That's right. Anything doing?'

'Plenty in my line. Nowt in yours that I've heard.'

'Quiet night?'

'So they say. Hey up!'

He hurried off with his barrow in response to a waved umbrella. Passengers were streaming from the Leeds train. The concourse was a teeming stage of separate dramas. Tears, laughter, kissings, embracings, handclasps. Hands and handkerchiefs were being waved. Anxious expressions lightened with recognition. Hats were swept off. Children dashed. Mothers screamed. Porters bustled laden trollies to the cab ranks, enjoying the anxiety of dispossessed owners left panting far behind.

Nightbone shared something of the arrived travellers' relief. He thought it was unlikely that Jen had gone into the river or under a train. It had to suffice. He ought to be on his rounds. At least he'd tried. He looked at the station clock and thought he had better get a cab back. As he turned to go to the rank he noticed a woman. A young woman. One female out of the many there, but distinctive enough to catch his eye. She had on a short dark coat over a deep blue dress. Her wide hat, tilted to one side, had a band of the same blue, and imitation white roses. Her hair was combed up above her neck and ears. To Nightbone the hair was whitish-yellow. A woman might have called it buttermilk.

She caught his attention with her striking poise. She seemed to float across the concourse, as if there were no crowd. The carpet-bag and hatbox in her hands might have been filled with feathers. Her back was ruler-straight and her shoulders squared. Her head was held high. She moved in the way Nightbone had seen grand ladies pass by as he'd stood on duty at public functions.

59

As she stepped through the ticket barrier Lucilla was feeling anything but the confidence she had resolved to show. The crowd she faced looked gigantic and unwelcoming. Her empty stomach was churning, her heart beating fast.

She had been mad to do this. All the way to London she had sat in the chilly grip of fear. She noticed neither scenery nor fellow passengers. She could only think of getting there, finding the ticket office, and asking for the next train back. But she had to pass through the barrier, and as she did she thought of Joe Pearson, somewhere in that crowd, looking out for her. Perhaps his eminent brother was with him. They may have spotted her already. It wasn't Lucilla Poole's way to let strangers see how she felt. The actresses had impressed on her to reveal only what one wanted people to see.

So she put her head up and wafted through into the crowd. She kept going. Obstacles proved no problem. People stepped back. She was indifferent to the crush and the noise it was making. Only her eyes hesitated. They flickered left and right, seeking a curly brown bowler and a familiar grin.

They found brown bowlers, but not that one. Nobody touched her arm significantly or called her name. She was at the far end of the concourse, where the exits and entrances were. She stopped, and turned to face the milling crowd. She put down her two pieces of luggage beside her feet. Chin still up, back still straight, she stared imperiously round. What now?

Plenty of people were still coming in past her. Some were obvious latecomers, looking anxiously for people they were to meet off her train. She watched for Joe among them. He would have a joke about it ready.

He didn't appear. The crowd was thinning. Then it was starting to grow again, mustering for other trains. Lucilla knew finally that she was on her own.

She had spotted the ticket office. There were plenty of trains, she knew. Time to risk a bite in the buffet to calm her famished stomach. She would be home before dark. Home? Aunt Doris and Uncle Edgar. The shop. The mill.

Putting on the show of aplomb, though, had done something for her courage. It came to her that to slink back defeated was beneath her. It would take away from something big she'd achieved on her own for once. She'd escaped. Got to London undetected. No one was here to take her back. She was independent for as long as she chose. It was something she'd never been. Nothing had gone wrong, except that she'd arrived too soon. There simply hadn't been time for the Pearsons to act on her message. It was all her fault. Maurice et Cie sounded decent people. What had she to lose by going through with what she'd begun?

She had a few guineas, if it meant taking a cab. It was early enough in the day to go there and hope to be seen. If Mr Pearson wouldn't see her today there were those lodgings Joe had mentioned. They would introduce her at one of them. Joe had said his brother would jump at her. It was only a matter of how soon.

Suddenly she felt quite adventurous. Where were the cabs? But she must go to the waiting room first. And she was so hungry. A wash and a cup of coffee and something to eat. A few noisy folk and some unaccustomed surroundings weren't going to defeat her. Not for Lucilla Poole the role of Frightened Provincial Girl.

A bobby was coming her way. A sergeant. So much for Joe saying they were never there when you wanted them. One was just what Lucilla did want. She didn't know whether Maurice et Cie's was halfway across London or just round the corner. Bobbies knew everything about streets and places. Even in vast London, she supposed. She didn't have to approach him. He was coming to her. Youngish. Solid, but no giant. The way he moved reminded her of a heavy horse. He saluted.

'Good morning, madam.'

The deference pleased her.

'I'd be careful leaving your luggage down like that, madam.'

'Oh?'

'There are people with a nasty habit of snatching and bolting. Safer to hold on to it or have a porter.'

Lucilla picked up her things.

'Thank you, officer. Sergeant.'

Close to, she was younger than Nightbone had thought. Not a woman. A girl. Eighteen? Seventeen? Attractive. Confident sounding. Well spoken. He gave her a reassuring smile.

'All alone?'

'I was expecting to be met.'

'Far to go?'

'Titchfield Street.'

He frowned. 'Titchfield Street's pulled down. For new building.' He noted the flicker of alarm in her look.

61

'Great Titchfield Street, I mean. Is it different?'

'Miles apart. You don't know London, then?'

'Actually, I haven't visited it before. If you wouldn't mind directing me, Sergeant.'

'You'll need a cab.'

'Of course.'

'Just through there. About fifteen minutes, depending on the traffic.'

Lucilla followed his eyes to the cab rank sign. She noticed another policeman who had just come in by that way. He was looking all round. He saw her talking to the sergeant and came towards them briskly.

'I'll take your bag out for you, madam,' the sergeant offered. 'I'm going that way.'

The other officer had borne down before she could answer. He was very tall and wore a trim grey beard. His tunic front was impressive with dark braid. In place of a helmet he wore a stiff round hat with a shiny peak. He looked very official and stern.

'Sergeant Nightbone?' He ignored Lucilla. Her friend turned and saluted.

'Good morning, sir.'

The bearded officer acknowledged the salute. He looked at Lucilla. She knew she was being sent on her way.

'Thank you for your help, Sergeant,' she said. He at least had been polite. She made off with her bags towards the ladies' waiting room.

'Any trouble there?' Inspector Gillen of Scotland Yard asked Nightbone.

'Just directions, sir.'

'Off your manor, Sergeant.'

'Furtherance of an inquiry, sir.'

'And?'

'Nothing, sir. I was about to get a cab back.'

'I have one outside. To fetch you to Scotland Yard. The Commissioner.'

'Very good, sir. Has my station been notified, sir?'

'They told me where I might find you. One of your colleagues has taken over the rounds you should be making.'

The inspector turned and stalked towards the cab rank. Nightbone didn't know him. Probably one of the Commissioner's new brooms, transferred from a provincial force.

Inspector Gillen said nothing further throughout the journey to Westminster. Nightbone sat looking straight before him, deferentially not looking out of the window. He had no idea why the Commissioner should have sent for him. Not over Nelly Jacks, surely? He'd soon find out.

He thought briefly of the girl at King's Cross. In a cab by now, safely on her way. She'd seemed capable enough. The other sort stuck out obviously. Pale thin faces. Frightened eyes. Colourless clothes, and clutching their things to them. It made them such easy marks for those people who frequented the railway termini, looking out for such as them. Offering them help that led into nightmares. Not enough bobbies to keep moving them on. Time cut out with dippers and lost kids. Leave the girls to the do-gooders who competed with one another to save them.

At the Yard the inspector led the way up many stairs to an ante-room. Left to wait, his helmet under his arm, Nightbone saw that the office the inspector had entered bore the label Assistant Commissioner. The other door off the ante room was the Com-missioner's.

Nightbone recognized the timbre of old Charlie McNorris's voice in his room. The inspector soon came out again and left without so much as a nod. Nightbone expected the Chief Super to come out to greet him, but his door stayed shut. When he did appear his custom-ary smile was missing.

'Commissioner's ready for you. Helmet on.' He led the way into the other office.

'Sergeant Nightbone, O Division, sir.' The Assistant Com-missioner withdrew and shut the door.

Nightbone marched to the desk where the slight, grey man in black mufti sat bolt upright, watching him approach. He had seen the Commissioner before. He had been seated stiffbacked on a horse, reviewing a parade at Wellington Barracks soon after taking up office. He had made a speech in a surprisingly deep loud voice. What he'd said had obviously been meant to unsettle them all. Full of dire warnings. Serving notice that old easygoing ways and irregularities that were generally winked at were now things of the past. All changed. From now on, his way of having things done would be the only way. Heaven help the man, no matter what his rank or length of service, who didn't remember that.

Nightbone halted and saluted. The Commissioner made no acknowledgement. He plucked a paper off the top of the pile before him and pushed it across the desk.

'Edward Watts.'

It was all he said. Before even reading, Nightbone knew that Bailey had done him.

CHAPTER 10

BELLE AND FLOSS

Two middle-aged ladies together were looking for places in the busy buffet. They hesitated beside the table where Lucilla sat alone.

'These aren't taken,' she told them.

'Thank you, dear,' one said, smiling gratefully.

'If you're sure you won't mind?' said the other.

It proved to be an extraordinary encounter. Inside five minutes' drinking coffee together the three of them had found places, events, and even people in common. Lucilla felt her energy and courage growing with every sip and each mouthful of paste sandwich. They were Theatricals. To her that accounted for everything in the familiarity line. No people easier to talk with – listen to, rather – and she was well attuned. They were retired now, but she knew that the flow of chatter didn't wane with detachment from the talking profession.

'All that rushing about the country. Half one's life standing on Crewe station.'

'We kept meeting on tours, and sometimes shared digs.'

'Both hankered to settle down, didn't we, Belle? Before any sweet-talking gentlemen might get round us and nobble all we'd saved together.'

'Plenty ready to try, weren't there? But we kept them out.'

'Nothing against gentlemen *as such*.'

'Except, in the profession, half aren't gentle and the rest aren't men.'

Lucilla laughed with them at the old joke. She'd always thought actresses and dancers oddly disparaging of men, considering how much of their spare time they gave to them.

They smiled a lot, and were not abashed to laugh out loud. There was much 'Well, fancy that!' and 'You don't say!' and '*Isn't* it a small world?' Some of the performers Lucilla had met with her parents were their 'very dear friends'. They couldn't place her parents themselves, but they knew some of those very same North of England backstages. They had reminiscences about pantomime acts she'd watched from the wings, where her mother had stood holding the costumes for the quick change, while her shirtsleeved father prepared to lower Asia Minor on a rope and erect the Grand Vizier's palace wall in five seconds.

She thought they looked well off, much more stylishly dressed than Langenbach's customers. One was rather tall and dark haired, with heavy shoulders and a big bosom. The other had more a dancer's bones, slim and feminine, though she would be about fifty. Her hair was dyed a light shade between brown and fair. Lucilla saw that she noticed her natural colouring. She thought she detected envy.

A mention of Leeds jerked her back to reality and King's Cross Terminus, London. They had been gossiping for over half an hour. The smaller woman, addressed by her companion as Floss, saw Lucille look at the buffet clock.

'What time is your train, dear?'

'Oh, I'm not *going*. I've only just come.'

Lucilla explained what she was doing there. Her friends were much amused.

'The Pearsons?'

'That's right. Maurice and See.'

'Ted and Joe to us. Aren't they, Belle?'

'They use us all the time. Going on three years. Four next month. Their young ladies.' She was getting a card out of her handbag. She gave it to Lucilla. 'This is us. Flobell Select Lodgings for Ladies. Newman Street.'

'Our nest since we retired,' Floss said. 'Almost on their doorstep.'

'It's amazing,' Lucilla said. 'I might have come knocking at your door myself.'

'It's mostly only the long-term ones they ask us to take.' Belle informed her. 'They know how particular we are. One can furnish more nicely if there's no fear of moonlight flits.'

'I'm sure it's very nice,' Lucilla said, feeling a little put in her place. 'Are you meeting somebody now?'

Both heads shook. Their expressions saddened.

'Just been seeing one off.'

'Back to Wakefield.'

'I told you she wouldn't do, Belle. Didn't I?'

'Not in the long run. No. One of their rare mistakes.'

'We can usually tell at a glance. Ought to by now, Heaven knows.'

Belle explained to Lucilla. 'They're very particular. Proper behaviour. Doing as you're told. It stands to sense, being responsible for girls under their charge. Ted sees himself as a sort of uncle.'

'Oh, uncle, yes. Kindness itself, but no nonsense. Least sign of – what's the word, Belle?'

'Waywardness. Disobedience. Back to where you came from. No second chances.'

'Can't afford to risk their reputation, you see.'

'We did warn her. She wouldn't listen. Just had to go. And so must we, Floss. Sitting here gossiping. We only came in for a cup of coffee.'

'But it's been so nice talking to you, dear,' Floss said. 'We do hope they take you. Don't let what we've been saying put you off. I feel sure they'll give you a chance. Don't you, Belle?'

'Mustn't raise hopes, Floss, but I'd say ...'

'Please,' Lucilla said hastily. 'If you're going back to your house, could I come and share your cab? Since you're so near there. I'd be glad to pay.'

Belle smiled. 'Good heavens, why didn't we think, Floss?'

'Of course, dear. No need to think of paying. In fact ... Belle, do you think we might, just for once ...?'

'Why, of course, Floss!' Belle exclaimed. 'How clever.' She turned to Lucilla. 'Not one of our best rooms, I'm afraid. But if you *should* need to stop over, just for this one night ...'

'Oh yes, please!' Lucilla cried.

Floss was all smiles. 'You could have a nice tidy up before you go to see them. Leave your things with us ...'

'A little lunch. Then pop across this afternoon.'

'So near.'

'And if they take you – I'm sure they will ...'

'So am I, Belle.'

'It's marvellous,' said Lucilla, springing up. 'I'm so glad I met you.'

'We're glad, too. Aren't we, Belle?'

'Any friend of Ted and Joe's . . .'

'The fact remains, Nightbone. Your report makes no reference to Watts whatever.'

'He was trying me on, sir. They all were. They knew where Cox was hiding. There was no point singling out names.'

'Have you arrested any of the others for aiding an escaping prisoner?'

'If we went in for that, sir, half London would be behind bars.'

'Perhaps half of London *ought* to be behind bars, Sergeant. At the very least you could have been expected to name a man you insist set out to defy you. His purpose was clearly to distract your attention from the escaped man.'

'No, sir. He'd been screwing himself up to it for some time. He knew I'd be coming there for Cox, and took his chance.'

'His complaint states that you provoked him deliberately.'

'It comes down to whose word you take, sir.'

'But I have only *his* word, Sergeant. Here is his statement. Witnesses. A doctor. What have I from you? A report which doesn't even mention the incident.'

'There didn't seem need, sir. He wouldn't have tried it on again. Not after I'd had a word with him.'

'Did you have that word?'

'Not yet, sir.'

'Actions speak louder, perhaps?'

'I hardly touched him.'

'Easily overlooked, you thought. If questioned, you could say he impeded your inquiries.'

'No, sir.'

'Annoyed you without reason.'

'He *had* a reason.'

'I have yet to hear one good enough to convince me, let alone the Home Office.'

Col. Saltby's voice had boomed ever louder. A volume capable of covering vast outdoor spaces must have broadcast his anger all over the building. His tone, if not his actual words, reached plainly enough to the Assistant Commissioner's office. A head came round McNorris's door. He saw the sergeant he had deputed to take the Commissioner's letter to Nightbone's district inspector. While they were talking, the loud harangue in the nearby office subsided. McNorris took the bundle of Nightbone's clothes and put them on his table. He ushered the sergeant silently away. He was tempted to linger at his open door, to try to hear what the Commissioner's low rumbling voice was going on to say. He didn't dare. It was too distant, and the Commissioner's door might open suddenly.

Charlie shut his door quietly. Looking at the clothes on the table, he realized at last why they had been sent for.

You couldn't send a bobby to jail in his uniform.

'It's lovely!' Lucilla exclaimed, staring round the room. It was much bigger than hers at Auntie and Uncle's. Her two pieces of luggage, carried up before them by a little maid, looked shabby and forlorn lying there on the light carpet.

'Quite nice,' Belle agreed. 'But you should see the ones we have for the permanents.'

'If you'd like just a peep into one?' Floss invited.

'No, please,' Lucilla said quickly. 'If they don't take me on, I couldn't bear to know what I may have missed.'

The room was twice the size of what she was used to, and with no sharp slope of ceiling to slice a wedge out of its space. The white metal bed was inviting. It had a pretty pink quilted coverlet. There was a wardrobe, a chest of drawers, a marble-topped washstand with a swing mirror and toilet things, and a towel rail. All the furniture was painted in light tones.

'Quite right, my dear,' Belle approved. 'One step at a time. Miriam, see to some towels for Miss Poole. You'll stay tonight, whatever happens. We insist.'

'Oh, certainly,' Floss agreed. She put her head on one side and gave Lucilla a persuasive little smile.

'There's running water, you see,' Belle pointed out. 'Have a nice wash and come down to the room marked Private. That's our parlour. We have our little snack at half past twelve, and you must join us.'

'Wouldn't it be putting on you?' Lucilla objected. 'And I ought to be going to Maurice and See.'

'Company, dear,' Floss said. '*Cie* is French. *Companie*. For company.'

'I don't know any French.'

'You'll pick up all you need,' said Belle.

The kind ladies left her alone. She almost tore her hat off. Her hair fell half down. She shook the rest out impatiently.

Then she shrugged off her coat and shoes. She bounced full length on to the bed, her loose hair tossing around her. She had never felt so free.

'Chief Superintendent, this man is discharged from the force. Immediate effect. You have his things?'

'Yes.' Charlie McNorris found it hard to speak. His mouth had gone too dry for courtesy.

'See to it personally, please. He leaves the building speaking to no one else.'

The Commissioner turned from his window. Nightbone was rigid at attention.

'Count yourself lucky, Nightbone. Your record saves you from worse. But don't depend on that. If the man's injuries take a more serious turn you will be called to account. That's all.'

Nightbone saluted. He swivelled on one heel, brought his boots together, and marched out, stiff armed.

The Assistant Commissioner shut his office door. He indicated Nightbone's civilian clothes on the table.

'Sorry, son,' he said.

Nightbone had his helmet off already. He used his tunic sleeve to massage his forehead where the rim had left its red weal. It had been a very long interview.

'I did what I could,' Charlie McNorris said.

Nightbone didn't respond. Like a prisoner being booked he emptied his pockets on to the table. He didn't swear, or fling his uniform across the room as he took it off, or boot his helmet across the office, as McNorris had seen some others do. Nightbone folded his tunic and trousers as neatly as if he expected to be putting them back on soon. He put on his own suit.

McNorris realized he had never seen him out of uniform. Civvies seemed instantly to shrink and diminish him. Without the helmet and thick-soled boots he was a foot shorter. That was not all. He looked somehow compressed. His shoulders were less square. His chest lacked the profundity of thrusting silver buttons. The texture of the man, as well as his clothes, was softened. The change from heavy blue serge to grey worsted was like shedding armour for velvet. McNorris thought he would have to look twice to recognize him across a street.

'There wasn't any shifting him,' he tried again.

'You're welcome to him,' Nightbone said. The customary 'sir' had been dropped already.

'What'll you do?'

A shrug was all the response. Nightbone laced light brown boots on the rim of the wooden wastepaper bin.

'Just one warning, son.'

'Yes?'

'Don't go after Bailey Watts.'

'Why?'

'Anything happens to him, you'll be up to here in it.'

'I might not be home when you come looking.'

'You're known. Just remember, for your own sake.'

'Bailey's, don't you mean?'

Nightbone straightened up. He took his coat over his arm and gave the nap of his grey beaver hat a rub against his sleeve. He put out his right hand. McNorris took it.

'No hard feelings? Nothing personal.'

'What do you think?'

Nightbone left without another word. He spoke to no one he passed in the corridors or on the stairs. None gave him a glance. Like an invisible man he melted out of Scotland Yard, to merge unnoticed with the millions.

CHAPTER 11

TED

As he walked from the Yard he felt like a disembodied spirit. His sensations weren't his own. Everything that he had taken for granted was gone.

He crossed the Embankment and walked several hundred yards eastwards towards Blackfriars. He didn't stop until he was well out of the ambit of policemen who might know him. He leaned on a stone parapet, ignoring the river's stink to stare over the busy Thames.

He remained there for half an hour. Then he took a cab to his lodging. Mrs Hilling stared at the civilian letting himself into her hall.

'Only me, Mrs H.'

'My heart fairly turned, Mr Nightbone.'

'You've had visitors, I gather.'

'I didn't know what to say. They showed me a paper and made me take them into your room. I thought you must have got hurt or something.'

'One way of putting it.'

'You don't look yourself. What is it?'

'Order of the sack.'

'The ... You? Not ever!'

'Seems I hit a man harder than I ought.'

'I expect he deserved it.'

'More than I knew.'

'But if it was in your duty ...'

'Not so easy to define, nowadays. They keep changing the rules.' He laughed sharply, unusually for him.

'Whatever shall you do?'

'Clear out. They might have a change of heart, and not in my favour. I'll just go up and pack the rest of my things.'

'Oh, you're not going like that, Mr Nightbone? Jack would be that upset.'

'I don't want you and Jack bothered. No more strangers with bits of paper. Anyway, the neighbours will start gossiping.'

'Who cares? Come through and have some tea.'

'If you don't mind, Mrs H., I don't want to talk.'

He went up to his room. It took him only a quarter of an hour to put the rest of his belongings into his small brown tin trunk, painted with imitation iron bands. He carried it down, dangling it by one handle. The landlady heard him and came from the kitchen. He had some coins ready.

'Here's for a week's notice. Say so long to Jack for me.'

She ignored the money. 'You'll come back if you can, lad. We shall not be letting again.' She held up what she was carrying. It was his herb jar. 'Don't forget these.'

His street-pounding days were finished. His implacable tread would patrol North London ways no more. There would be soothing enough needed, all the same. Nightbone took the jar. He leaned down. For the first time he gave his landlady a kiss. Then he left her house.

'Just once more, walk across the room from me. Now turn – slowly – now towards me, and ready to turn again. Slow – that's it! And for the last time, across, turn – and back. Capital!'

'Wasn't I right?' Joe Pearson grinned at his brother. Ted was putting Lucilla through her test.

'Take a little breather, Miss Poole.'

Prettily flushed from her exertions, Lucilla sat on the plush covered chair that Ted indicated with his cigar. She remembered to perch only on its edge and keep her back straight and her hands folded, palms upward, in her lap.

The test had lasted ten minutes. From behind a littered desk Ted Pearson, shirt sleeved, waistcoated, bowler hatted, had directed her. He had made her walk a great deal to and fro. It gave her plenty of chances to swing her hips the way she thought so professional. He had asked her to mount and remount several times a set of four dummy stairs. She knew that only her legs should move. She held the rest of her body proudly steady and erect, head high, hands turned out at her sides. She had picked things up for him, carried them, put them down. Reached up to a high shelf. Bent down. Lain on a sofa. Twirled rapidly on a spot. Skipped and pranced. Even, briefly, danced with Joe for partner, to a time beaten by Ted with his round black desk ruler.

'You've *never* been on stage?' he said again, with a note of incredulity. She had told him her theatrical background.

'Not actually on.'

'Hard to credit.'

'I told you.' Joe was hiding none of his pride of discovery. He had greeted her delightedly when she had presented herself at the showroom at two o'clock.

'Cor, the relief! Didn't see your wire till after your train was due. Dashed across in a cab. Not a sign. Thought you'd gone straight back.'

'I'm sorry I put you to the bother.'

'Don't mensh. You got here safe. This is a wicked city.'

'Won't your brother be too busy to see me?'

'After my spiel? He can hardly wait. Come on up.'

Maurice et Cie was on the first two floors of a modern corner building. Its windows displayed winter outfits in bold styles and strong colours. Lucilla thought them much more cheerful than anything they would wear in the North. The spacious ground floor was a forest of garments on wheeled racks. Sewing machinists were at work. She heard the massed whirring of more machines in a room beyond. Women were doing the sewing, carrying bolts and pieces of material, racking garments. Men were silently cutting and hand-sewing. The women were mostly young and attractive, dressed in an almost uniform way. Lucilla noticed that each one's dress colour matched the shade of her neatly done hair. They looked happy and interested in their work.

Ted Pearson's desk was in the middle of a big room upstairs. It was unlike Lucilla's idea of an office. Easels stood about displaying designs. Young men were making cotton models from them on dummies. They were cutting, pinning, trimming, experimenting, standing back to compare with the sketches. Ted Pearson was calling to one of them to try some other way with the collar. Maurice et Cie was a bustling concern.

Lucilla approached apprehensively. She thought Ted and Joe not very alike for brothers. Ted looked older. His black hair was grizzled about his ears. It and a large black moustache gave him a foreign look. But when he greeted her he sounded as London as Joe. He was less forthcoming, but she felt he approved of her so far.

After some questions he put her through her paces. So many other men in the room daunted her a bit to start with. She soon saw they were too busy with their own concerns to stare at her. Their lack of interest made her show off harder, trying to force them to take notice. She enjoyed it. All the things she had done in front of her private mirror were called for, and others. It was the first time she'd been asked to perform, but she was well rehearsed.

'There's just one last thing,' Ted Pearson said, to end her rest. She was disappointed as she stood up. She'd thought his decision was coming. 'I want you to go with our Mrs Goldman for measuring.'

A stout Jewish-looking woman had joined them. She was darkly dressed, with a tape measure about her neck. She nodded reassuringly to Lucilla. Ted placed his cigar in an ashtray and stood up. He seemed faintly embarrassed.

'Not to be indelicate, Miss Poole, modelling for our house doesn't stop at putting on pretty frocks. We do the complete range. Outerwear and underwear. Because a young lady's suited to showing off this or that, she may not be right for the other. That's Mrs Goldman's department.'

Lucilla was afraid for a moment that it meant she wasn't suited to proper modelling. He was trying to let her down lightly. But Joe was still smiling behind the chair. He winked. She felt the woman's touch on her arm. She was led out to another room.

'I shan't keep you ten minutes, dear,' Mrs Goldman said. 'If you'll just take all your things off, please.'

'All of them?'

'Put them on this chair. I've locked the door. No one will come walking in.'

Lucilla obeyed. It was less embarrassing than she'd feared. She could see that a firm like this had to be choosy. Ted Pearson had written down her answers to all his questions on a big pad. He'd wanted her exact age, particulars of her parents and any other close family. She hadn't any. She explained about Aunt Doris and Uncle Edgar. He wanted to know why she'd hurried to London without waiting to be sent for. She told the truth. She included the experiences with Langenbach and her uncle. She noticed Joe's concerned look when he heard about the latter. His brother wrote dispassionately, only looking at her to ask his questions.

'There, my dear,' said Mrs Goldman, who had worked briskly with her measure all over her. She, too, had made many notes. 'That's all. Just put your things on. I'll come back for you. Take your time. Lock the door again after me, and I'll knock.'

Secure behind the lock, Lucilla looked at herself for some minutes in the oval cheval glass. She placed her hands on her hips and turned her body slowly from side to side. She held her head high, as Ted Pearson had directed her. It was some years since she'd seen herself like this, full-length naked. She had changed in that time, both in development and in awareness of herself. The girl in the glass, with the haughty stare of narrowed eyes and pursed lips, wasn't herself as she was used to feeling. Except for having nothing on, the Lucilla Poole she was face to face with for the first time must be the one others saw. She was intrigued. And impressed.

A bit excited, too. She saw herself blush. She turned her back on the stranger in the mirror and got dressed.

Ted Pearson stood up again behind his desk.

'Miss Poole – Lucilla – congratulations.' He gave her a little smile.

'Measured up perfectly,' said Joe.

Mrs Goldman lifted her nose at him and left. She gave Lucilla a passing nod and smile.

Ted ignored his brother's remark. 'Sit down, Lucilla,' he said, serious again. 'As a company that employs many of its young ladies away from their families, we take our responsibilities more heavily than some. I'm going to offer you a place with us. Before you accept it, though, you must listen carefully to the terms and conditions. Stop me and ask any questions you want. All right?'

Lucilla wanted to give one answer to only one question, but she nodded and listened.

'These are standard terms,. All our young ladies begin the same. To begin, £35 a year. After one month's probation, subject to satisfaction on both sides, £40 per annum.'

It was more than twice her pay at Langenbach's.

'Help in the showroom as required. Gives you a feeling for the range. Do you know what walking out means?'

'I don't think so.'

'Going into society with an escort – professional, that is. Show our clothes off. Get them noticed. Extra allowance and expenses for that. Commission on any sales directly due to you. All right?'

'Perfectly, Mr Pearson.'

'He's Mr Ted,' her sponsor put in. He gave her his wink again. 'I'm Mr Joe.'

Ted ignored him and went on. 'As to everyday wear, there's nothing to stop you providing your own, if Mrs Goldman approves it. Bought from the house it will stand you only four guineas. Eight to ten anywhere else. Fitting and alterations gratis. Shoes, underwear and corset as Mrs Goldman directs. Ten or eleven guineas all told.'

The amount startled her. It was more than she had. He reassured her with a smile. 'You don't have to find the money. It can be set against wages.'

'Will I have to get anything else?'

'A gown. One of our gentlemen will run it up specially for you.'

'Nice blue for those eyes,' said Joe.

Lucilla was growing too alarmed to be flattered.

'There's my lodgings . . .'

Joe answered before his brother. 'Belle and Floss's. Since you've moved in already.'

'Oh! Would they take me?'

'If we say the word.'

'If I could afford it . . .'

'You can. Take a year minimum and the company goes half. Eh, Ted?'

'A year!' Lucilla exclaimed, not waiting for Ted's confirmation.

'Two, if you want,' Joe breezed. 'See how confident we are.

'Famed throughout the fashion trade is
Maurice et Cie and their spiffy ladies.'

Lucilla looked at Ted. He didn't seem amused. He had heard it too often, no doubt. 'Haven't you anything to do?' he asked Joe, quite irritably, she thought. Joe sounded unconcerned.

'Expect so. Don't forget, though, it was me found her. If it hadn't been for a mess-up over a lunch bill . . .'

'I'm really grateful, *Mr* Joe,' Lucilla said.

He gave her a wave and went away.

'Can I really afford to stay there?' she asked Ted Pearson.

'There are cheaper places. Hostels, too.'

'Oh, that doesn't matter. I'd love to be there. They're so nice.'

'It's your decision, Lucilla. Anything else?'

There was something. She was almost afraid to ask it.

'If ... for any reason ... I want to leave ...'

He nodded. 'Usual notice. On either side. If it's you, you return any monies advanced. Do you understand why? We're prepared to invest heavily in you. Time and money. A girl trained by Maurice and Company is assured respect everywhere. Some have even found husbands through us.'

'Mr Joe mentioned it.'

'Forget that side of it for now. Think of it as the best chance you'll ever get to make something exceptional out of what you've got already. Take it from me, Lucilla, you have all the qualities. It will be hard work, but do your best for us, and we'll do ours for you.'

'Thank you, sir.'

'But ...' He seemed to hesitate. 'But if you do ever come to the point where you want to leave ... feel you must ... then you must come to me and say so. No one else. Only to me.'

'I'm sure I shan't.'

'I hope not. But remember.'

'Still on the address of welcome?' Joe said. He had come drifting back unobtrusively. 'Your escort back to Flobell's, ready when you are, ma'am.'

Ted put down his cigar again. He pushed a sheet of paper across to Lucilla.

'Read it first,' he said. He got out a fountain pen and uncapped it while she scanned hastily, trying to concentrate on the statement of terms. She couldn't.

'Just sign it,' Joe advised. 'Before you find it's a mirage.'

She took Ted's pen and signed. He stood up and shook her hand.

'Well done,' he said. Joe made her a little mock bow.

'As stranger to the premises, you're
Entitled to a guided tour.'

Again Ted didn't share Lucilla's smile. Another too familiar sample of Joe's personal wide range, she was sure.

She left the room with him. She didn't even notice whether the other men raised their heads. She no longer cared.

CHAPTER 12

OLD MAZURKA

NIGHTBONE knew that his undoing would not go uncelebrated. Villains would toast it in wines or spirits, befitting their status. Certain parlours and vestries would be festive with milk and rusks.

He had done his job as he saw it needed doing. Not by the book alone. It was the chief reason he had never looked for higher rank. It would have cramped his style. That style had included taking justice into his own hands at times. There were men who smarted at the memory of Nightbone's unofficial punishment in lieu of arrest. His kindnesses were not entirely blessed. Good deeds had their own curators. They were jealous of one another, but united in disapproval of a policeman who was known to help prostitutes and crooks, saw fit merely to box the ears of children who ought to be arrested and workhoused, and could never be found by a landlord wanting help with an eviction. Now he himself had been evicted.

His immediate concern was to clear out of that neighbourhood before word of his sacking was widespread. He didn't want to be there to face jeers, questions, commiserations, or anything else in the gloating or sympathy lines. He hailed a cab and directed it westward. The address that he gave offhandedly might have been an everyday destination. In fact, he had been there only once before.

The ride took him across Islington, Camden Town and Euston to a district behind Oxford Street. It was cleaner, less labyrinthine than the one he had quit. Its buildings were survivors from the Regency jerry-building boom, decaying behind pretty pastel stucco that peeled like old nursery wallpaper. Delicate fanlights were opaque with grime. Fine balconies of wrought iron sagged on unsafe mock verandahs.

The narrow houses were no longer family homes. Those that were not compressed into lodgings and studios were depressed into offices, workrooms and poky storeplaces. A few, slightly better maintained, kept their blinds and drapes always drawn. After dark, when the human meat market got busy, they glowed pink and red.

Nightbone's cab halted before the solitary shop in one of these squares. Its nature of business didn't need describing on the fascia. Its window revealed all: groceries, Continental sausages, sacks of coffee, biscuit jars, candles, vegetables, smocks, overalls, hats and caps, artists' palettes and brushes, tubes of paint, sketching pads, pencils, envelopes and notepaper, books, and a few editions of sheet music. Like Nightbone, its proprietor was one for disdaining any but his surname. It was painted above the window: MAZUR.

Nightbone paid off the cabby and went in. Several housewifely women were waiting to be served. The proprietor was alone behind the counter. Tall, round shouldered, bony, skull pated, with wispy grey hair and whiskers, all untrimmed. He served unhurriedly. All the while he commented to the shop at large. Nightbone put down his tin box with the herb jar on top of it. Beyond a glance as he entered the old man paid him no attention.

'You don't hear me complain. You never heard me grumble. What?'

'Not ever, Mr Mazurka.'

'What? You could expect a tradesman should grumble. Can't turn his back without a half dozen rashers goes. What?'

A murmur of unanimous sympathy.

'Not fair, Mr Mazurka.'

'The very idea!'

'Liberty!'

'Some people want locking up!'

'What? When I am closing down you know who you thank. It won't be for me a pleasure, calling in the credit. And the loans. No pleasure to me. But what can a man do when he is ruined?'

Like his accent, his national origins were indefinable: Middle European, Slavic, Levantine, Palestinian, overlaid with London. His often-reiterated 'What?' was a bitter laugh. It had as little to do with humour as the crooked leer that never left his mouth. They gave his litany of complaint the bathos of a music-hall monologue. His lot in life was ingratitude, bad debts and thieving. For as long as he could remember he had endured them all. Ruin was waiting its turn to be served. Stark disaster would be delivering shortly. Yet he struggled on, he told his audience ceaselessly, because they needed him.

The claim wasn't wholly exaggeration. Mazur was both a neighbourhood institution and an economic force. This was to some extent an artistic quarter. The everyday things he sold financed his arts and crafts side. Eatables commanded cash. Oil colours, cartridge paper, brushes and pencils were available on credit. So was money itself. Half his customers depended on his loans. They didn't dare shop elsewhere, for fear he take offence and foreclose. Even facing ruin he remained ready to oblige further. His interest charges were such that once in debt to him it was almost impossible to get out of it.

As a shopkeeper he had unique style. Instead of throwing away anything that was past its freshness he kept it on a side. Day by day he knocked a penny or two off its price. Some housewife eventually couldn't hold out against the cut-price offer that made stale food palatable.

'You got a bargain, madam. Fresh as the day it was sliced, almost. I knock it down too quick.'

'So sorry, my dear. Didn't I tell your mamma yesterday she should buy? What about this here instead? Again today reduced. What?'

It was inevitable that someone should have known Mazur to be German for mazurka. He had become Old Mazurka by reference and Mr Mazurka to his face. He never corrected anyone. They bought his goods and paid his interest. He should care how they called him. What?

It was Nightbone's turn for attention. He had been the last to come into the shop and they were alone. The old man's carping halted, though the false leer remained. Yellow eyes were watchful over the counter.

'Do you remember me, Mr Mazur?'

'Sure I remember, Sergeant.'

A bony yellow hand came across to shake his.

'Step through, before any more comes in.'

Nightbone picked up his belongings and followed into the back parlour. The smell of coffee was on the stuffy air. Moving a pan on the stove, Jenny Jacks raised her face in amazement.

'Well, well!' Nightbone said.

'Nightbone! How . . .?'

She turned questioningly on the shopkeeper. His shrug disclaimed responsibility. They heard the shop bell tinkle. He raised his hands then let them flop.

'Never no peace. Be comfortable, Sergeant. Give him coffee, my dear. Cocoa, if he wants. Anything. All right! All right!' He went out, muttering about persecution by trade.

Nightbone nodded towards the coffee pan. Jen got an extra cup from a row of hooks under the mantelpiece.

She was wearing the things she had had on the night before, flamboyant against the mundane background of untidily piled shelves of stock of all kinds. She looked washed out, but she was sober. She handed Nightbone his coffee and took one of the fireside chairs.

'Are you all right, Jen?'

'Be better if he had a drop handy. I didn't like to ask. Yeh, I'm all right. Bit touch and go first thing, with my head and remembering. Why've you come? What are those things?'

'When did you leave Ma Costigan's?'

'Bit after dawn. She would have kept on about Nelly. I couldn't stick it. What's it to you, anyway? What are you doing here?'

'I looked for you. Left messages.'

'What about? Oh, I get it. No, ta. Bosphorus, Thames, they both stink. Anyway, who'd have been left to care about Nelly?' She looked at him eagerly. 'That why you've come?'

He shook his head. The eager look died. She eyed the little trunk again.

'How'd you know where I was? He send for you?'

Nightbone shook his head again. 'He'd nothing to do with it. I just came. Why did you?'

'I dunno. Just did.'

It was a question neither had tried yet to answer for themselves. For both, it had been largely instinctive.

Their acquaintance with Old Mazurka went back to one of those street-corner chats that made the do-gooders sniff. Jen was apt to boast of her adventures in the white-slave trade. She reminded Nightbone of some of his father's fellow soldiers, bragging of experiences that must have had them scared stiff at the time. For a change, she was being serious.

'There was this kid. Rebecca. Yid, I reckoned. Plenty were, from Russia and places. She was from London, but she spoke a bit mixed.'

'Another of Mrs Minchin's?'

'No. Snatched.'

Everyone knew the stories of abductors with turned-up collars and hats over their eyes, swooping on girls in London streets with hypodermic needle or ether pad. Of drugged hatpins and paralyzing rings. Of the lurking hansom, waiting to whisk the victim to the docks. Of the sinister black ship, said to creep endlessly from port to port, collecting new girls and dumping their worn-out predecessors overboard. Nightbone had never heard of a verified case of any of them.

'Don't be taken in by all that stuff about drugs and suchlike,' Jen confirmed. 'When I'd been out there a bit I got chatty with some of the blokes who ran us. They told me, "There's plenty ready and willing, without need of that." Most girls I ever met wouldn't have needed drugging. Couldn't wait. Better than pasting matchboxes, any day.'

'What about this Rebecca?'

'The old trick. Flash cove gets round her with sweet talk. Big mouth. Says he can give her a swell job in Paris.'

'You said she was snatched.'

'I'm coming to it. When she tells him her folks won't let her go he gets her in a room, strips every last stitch off her, and leaves her shut up. Some others come at night and smuggle her to the docks.'

'Not the black ship!'

'It's not funny. It was the end of her. Poor little cow's under the Bosphorus.'

'What happened?'

'They fetched her to where I was. Big house in Constantinople. Middling high class. She wouldn't have it, though – what they'd brought her for. Cried and struggled. Some of us tried to talk her round. Well, it was for *her* sake. "Just do it," we told her. "You don't care after a while. Get used to it. Anything to stay out of harm." But she wouldn't. It suited them fine. There are blokes will pay over the odds for one who'll fight. I've played that game myself in my time. Wasn't all pretend, neither. Nails, teeth, boots. They loved it. I warned her. Men!'

'So?'

'One did his nut. Went berserk with her. I saw her when they'd hauled him off. Ugh!'

'Dead?'

'Not half.'

'What became of him?'

'What do you think? Don't reckon they pop out for a bobby? "Hi say, horfficer, hactually we seem to 'ave a spot of bother with one of our clients." Turks? Bottom of the harbour. Both of 'em. In a sack. Something heavy to keep 'em down. Thousands under there. Hundreds of years of 'em. I'll be down there with 'em if they get me back. If anybody asks after me, I *don't* think.'

Her concluding sarcasm had stayed in Nightbone's mind. It had paced with him throughout an uneventful night beat. It made him ask another question when they met again.

She shook her head. 'Didn't go in. I could see him serving. I knew it must be him. Well, don't look at me like that. What d'you expect? "I'll take a haporth of licorice, and if you're wondering where your little girl's got to, she's in a sack under the Bosphorus"?'

'I'm serious, Jen. You saying if anyone bothers to ask after you. Don't you think they wonder about her?'

'Fat good it'd do 'em to find out.'

'Anything's better than not knowing.'

'Knowing *that*?'

'That she's dead. Not having to keep asking the questions. Where is she? What are they doing with her? Will she ever come back? It's the worst of it. You could spare them that.'

'Why me?'

'You were there.'

'I wish I'd never bloody told you."

'You did.'

'I made it up. I was having you on.'

'Why did you go to the shop? You didn't make it up.'

'Crushers! Poking their bloody noses in!'

Nightbone held her arm to stop her stalking away.

'You went to tell them, and couldn't face it. You walked away.'

'You'll get a name, holding my arm.'

'Of course they wouldn't want to know it as it was. But they'd be glad to know she's out of it.'

'They'll have guessed. Anyway, why believe me?'

'You've no reason to come pretending.'

'They'll think I'm after a handout.'

'Tell them you aren't. Tell them . . . Say you were on the same ship with her. You tried to look after her. She fell overboard and got drowned.'

'That'll please 'em!'

84

'Something of the sort. I'll work it out for you. You can lay it on heavy, what she missed.'

Jen had gone on resisting, demanding to know who he thought he was, lecturing her, making her go where he said, say what he told her to. At last he'd hit on the argument that swayed her.

'Suppose it was your Nelly. Didn't come home one day. How long could you stand wondering?'

After a minute's stubborn silence she'd said quietly, 'If you come with me . . . Like you are now. In your uniform. Tell 'em you made me come.'

'If you want. Why?'

'They'd believe it. With you there.'

'Good girl. Where's the place?'

It was how they had met Old Mazurka together. He was a widower by then. Rebecca's mother had died without even a concocted yarn to console her. In this parlour, already deteriorating for lack of a woman's hand, Mazur had listened to Jen, while Nightbone sat silently looking on.

That unnatural leer of Mazur's, his camouflage for true feeling, had appalled him. *Risus sardonicus*. The frozen grin of the strangled. A living corpse. 'Spooky,' Jen had said afterwards. It had scared her more than having to go through with the act. The unnatural grin and yellow eyes that pierced like knife points. Neither was sure the tale had been believed. But after it, and a few questions which Jenny answered well, the old man – as catastrophe had made him seem to be – thanked them. He offered to pay Jen for her trouble. She refused. He invited them to come back sometime. If he could ever do something to pay them back for their consideration, either of them, they'd only to come.

Now Jen had lost Nelly, and Nightbone had lost himself. And each had returned to Old Mazurka.

CHAPTER 13

FLOBELL SELECT LODGINGS

JOE had taken Lucilla on her tour of Maurice et Cie's premises. She was impressed again by the prosperous bustle. She saw models showing winter dresses and coats to wealthy-looking customers in small salons. There was a bigger room, like a ballroom, with rows of cane-seated chairs painted gilt and black. Joe told her it was where the big seasonal showings for the trade took place. He sent her to stand on the platform, facing the rows of chairs. She easily imagined them all filled. She could picture rich men and women leaning towards one another, remarking on Maurice's stunning new girl . . .

Joe escorted her back to Flobell Select Lodgings for Ladies. He started to look for a cab, but she asked to walk the short way. She wanted to parade her triumph among the less favoured. He gave her his arm. She took it readily and even squeezed it.

'I'm really grateful, Joe.' She was wholly comfortable by now with both him and his name.

'Don't mensh. All in a day's work.'

'What if you hadn't gone there that day? You'd never have seen me.'

'Fate, love.' He tapped his nose, as though it were Fate's own organ. 'It would have led me to you if you'd been in a nunnery. Lunch mightn't have been so good, though. Here, heard the one about the Mother Superior and the case of burgundy? Bit too ripe for those dainty shell-likes, maybe.'

'You should hear some actors' stories.'

'You going to tell me them? One evening? Tet-ah-tet. Somewhere we can have a good chortle.'

86

'I'd like that.'

It was his turn to squeeze her arm. She pressed his into her side. Their eyes met as he smiled down. She reminded him, 'You're my boss now. One of them.'

He leaned down confidentially. 'Old Ted can be a bit touchy. Mustn't make the other girls jealous, either. Still, isn't a pretty new girl entitled to looking after in this wicked city?

'If you need to study life, Miss Poole,
Joe Pearson's is the top-notch school.

'How did you find the old boy, by the way?'

'Mr Ted? Quite sweet, I thought.'

'He'll be tickled to hear it.'

'You wouldn't.'

'It'd make him blush. Rather what they call a prude, considering the trade he's in.'

'I think he's a bit shy. Is he a married man?' She meant, is either of you?

'Who, Ted? Not on your life. Not like yours truly.'

'Oh!'

'The type. Not that I'm irrevocably spoken for yet. Postponing the fatal decision. Still surveying the field.'

'Are there many in the running?'

'Oh, very good, love. Wit as well as beauty. Yes, you could say there's a fair line-up. Keeps growing. Like only the other day, in a caff in a place where they talk like this.'

His mimicry of the Yorkshire accent made her laugh. Most of his droll asides did. She was tempted to ask what he'd thought when he'd watched her at Langenbach's that day, but it would sound too much like fishing for compliments.

'Ted give you all the spiel?' he asked.

'I only half took it in. I was too excited.'

'Happy with what you did catch?'

'I'll say.'

'Good pay. Didn't I tell you?'

'Marvellous.'

'Adult rate, did he explain?'

'Beg pardon?'

'Like him not to. Bit of a swizz. Old Ted wouldn't admit anything like that.'

Joe had lowered his voice melodramatically, glancing about, pretending furtiveness. With his free hand he lifted a lapel across his lower face.

'Factory Inspectors. Heard of the Factories Acts? Rules about working hours? Kids doing grown-up jobs?'

Lucilla had heard grumblings in Leeds about busybodies telling folk how to run their businesses. Stopping lads and lasses earning good brass their families needed. More rules getting brought in every year. Wouldn't be allowed to live your own life before long.

Joe told her, 'They've had one or two goes at the rag trade. Quite right, where the sweatshops are concerned. Make a woollen mill seem like Roundhay Park. But you've seen our place. All clean and decent?'

'Wonderful.'

'But what goes for some has to go for all. And, being high class, they pick on us. Dead jealous.'

'How?'

'Take walking out. Smart feller and flash bird parading the new designs. Best places. Races. Restaurants. The Park. Best advertising going. So, what do those factory-wallahs do? Lay down it's not suitable work for unattached females.' He spoke down his nose this time, in a prissy, clerkly tone. '"Without parental consent in writing."'

Lucilla's heart thumped. 'That's barmy!'

'"And on no account below the age of twenty-one."'

'Oh no!'

Agitation had made her halt. They stood in the middle of a busy pavement. People had to side-step to pass them. She didn't notice. She didn't care about anything, except what Joe had just said. And that she was only seventeen. She felt her glittering prospects falling from her, as if someone had cut all the tapes at once.

'All that sort of thing's old Ted's department,' Joe said. 'Don't wonder he's the worrying kind. You've seen how particular he is.'

Lucilla didn't care about old Ted's worries. She cared only that a daft, unnecessary law delayed her being a real woman for over three more years. She could kick herself for having owned up to her true age. She'd told Joe she was seventeen, that first day when she'd never dreamed she'd be seeing him again. He'd made one of his rhymes about it. Why hadn't he remembered, and warned her not to let on to his brother? Ted hadn't asked for proof. She was certain she didn't *look* only seventeen. This was what you got for giving honest answers to people. She could have lied. She *should* have. Given a second chance, she would.

Joe was looking at her seriously. He was no longer acting a part. She didn't dare ask why he hadn't thought to warn her. He was one of her bosses. Being told off might make him very shirty. The only risk she was considering was asking him a favour. To have a word with his brother. Explain. Persuade. Suggest altering the register. Nobody but them would know. It wouldn't be doing harm. She was as good as twenty-one in all the ways that mattered.

She thought she could risk asking Joe that. He wasn't the strict sort his brother sounded. He was responsible for her being here. He'd picked her and given her all that praise. She hurried the words, trying to convince him that it would be for the company's benefit. Their customers weren't going to find out and take their business away because Maurice et Cie's new girl was under-age. But pleading made her feel childish.

'If you could only make Mr Ted see,' she ended. Despair had made her babble stupidly. Yearning up into his eyes, she was relieved to see his smile creep back. Then his grin.

'Already have.'

'Spoken to him? What did he say?'

'Nothing. But you're on the books as twenty-one years and eight months. You've gained exactly four years, and not one wrinkle.'

She could have kissed him. He took her arm and walked her on. She might have skipped.

'When? While I was getting measured?'

'Ages before that. Well, last night.'

'Last night!'

'When I was telling him all about you. That you were one he was definitely not going to want to miss. Of course, being old Ted, he was straight on to the age thing. Thought it might be best for you to do a couple of years in the workrooms.'

'I couldn't. It would be like the mills.'

'Well, hardly. Anyway, I told him somebody from one of the other houses would be certain to see you in the streets. Spot you like I did. They're not all so particular about the rules. "Anyway," I said, "now or in two years she'll still be under-age. What's it matter? Can't waste talent like that because of figures on a bit of paper. Figures inside dresses are what matters."'

'You didn't! Joe, you *are* good. Can I say Joe still?'

'Out of hours, all the time. If you'd noticed, old Ted didn't say anything when you told him your age. I saw what he wrote, from behind his chair. It wasn't seventeen. He'd never admit it, but he's done it. Now he'll make sure he forgets it. Promise me you'll never never let on you know he's broken a law for you.'

'I won't tell anybody.'

'Belle and Floss know your age?'

'They haven't asked. Nobody has.'

'You're clear, then. But remember, tongues wag. There's no trade like this for jealousy. Even inside the firm. You'll meet plenty of proud beauties who'd do you down. Beautiful woman's prerogative. If anyone's ever ill-mannered enough to ask your age, spit in their eye. *Pardon mon Français.*'

Lucilla laughed. 'What happens when I am twenty-one?'

'Enjoy a second go round. How many get the chance? Now, Miss Poole, m'deah, kindly state your age.'

'I don't spit.'

'Just answer, then.'

'I'm twenty-one, eight months, and, I think, four days, kind sir.'

'By gad! Don't look a day over seventeen.'

'I wonder what I'll really be like then,' she mused.

'A changed girl. Woman. Know it all. Ma Goldman doesn't quite go for me, but she's a regular brick at her job. As for old Ted, don't worry about him. Work hard, be a good girl, and he won't trouble you. You won't see much of him day-to-day, anyway.'

'Will I see you much?'

'I comes and I goes. Got to keep up supplies, you know.'

'More runners for your field?'

'I somehow doubt it. Bear in mind the immortal lines of the Bard:

'When you've found the one who seems the best,
You can forget about the rest.'

'Do have another cup, dear,' Floss urged her.

The expensive furnishings and decoration of her landladies' sitting-room made a cheerful setting for their congratulations.

'We told you, dear. Didn't we, Belle?'

'Yes, Floss. We've seen enough of Joe's discoveries to know who'll suit.'

Bright rugs and cushions, china and glass ornaments, deeply polished wood. She could have basked on there, but she also wanted to be alone. The flattery she most wanted awaited in her mirror. She put her cup and saucer on the beaten brass tray beside her chair and got up.

'If you don't mind, I'd like to go up and unpack.'

'That's right,' Joe said, disposing of his tea things. 'Time I was toddling, or old Ted'll be after me. Ta ta, dears all.'

'Always the life and soul,' Belle said when he had gone. 'You really don't know how lucky you are to be with them. Does she, Floss?'

Floss nodded and smiled. They had pressed her to call them by their first names.

'As a matter of fact,' Belle said, 'we've a little surprise for you. Just the time for it. Come along, dear.'

She led the way to the door. The procession went up the springy crimson carpet, secured by gleaming brass rods. On the first landing Lucilla would have turned towards the narrower stairs up to her floor. Belle led instead into a deeper part of the house. There were some doors off the passage and one at the very end.

Belle turned to smile at Lucilla. Then she opened the end door. Lucilla moved forward. And gasped.

She had never seen a boudoir. Only in a picture. She stepped into it spellbound. Then she turned back to her friends. Their smiles confirmed the unbelievable.

'Oh!' was all she could manage.

'We hope you like it, dear.'

'Anything you need, Lucilla, just press the electric bell next to the mantelpiece,' Belle instructed. 'Miriam or one of the other girls will come and see to you.'

'That's right, dear. Remember you're a full paying lodger now. You may give them any orders you wish.'

'And we'll see you down in the parlour later. Say at six? There's the clock. We'll all have a little glass of something to celebrate. Come on, Floss. Let her get on with her unpacking.'

Minutes passed behind the closed door before she was able to take in the details that made the room so elegant. It was much bigger than her temporary one upstairs. Bigger, and higher-ceilinged. All its woodwork was ivory white. The wallpaper had a pink bloom, with strings of pinker roses from ceiling to carpet. A big window had beige velveteen curtains over a froth of ruched white lace ones. A dressing table was angled near it to catch its best light. Lucilla thrilled to see that the mirror had adjustable wings. She hurried to sit on the white fur-topped stool. She craned forward into her triple reflection. Her flushed face and provincial travelling outfit marred the effect, but there was enough to promise exciting hours seated there.

The dressing table was picked out with gilded lines and scrolls on the white. It had a shaped glass surface. A crocheted runner all along it set off an immaculate arrangement in cut glass, silver plate and tortoiseshell. There seemed to be a complete vanity set. She examined an oval hand mirror, hairbrushes, clothes brushes, cylindrical hair tidy, nail scissors and buffs, ebony glove stretchers, a miniature corkscrew for opening bottles of scent and toilet water. There was a porcelain pin tray, a branched tree for rings, a tray of hair combs in several sizes and shades of tortoiseshell. And a collection of dainty little bottles, boxes, bags and miniature wicker containers.

An electric table lamp with a broad orange shade stood to one side. Lucilla found how to switch it on. The effect in the mirrors startled her. She moved their wings, to catch her profiles in turn. She saw the reflection from behind her of a marble-topped washstand. A blue and white ewer in a matching basin dominated a collection of other things. Intriguing wafts drew her there to investigate another assortment of bottles, jars and packets. She found porcelain candlesticks, a porcelain sponge tray, soapdish, toothbrush holder, all freshly equipped. When she unscrewed some of the jars her eyes widened. She had just enough restraint not to daub and spray herself willy-nilly.

The white metal mantelpiece above a copper canopy and a quietly glowing fire had on it a little white porcelain clock. Wreathed pink cherubs cavorted on it and smirked knowingly. There were candlesticks and vases of the same design. A garden aroma proved to be from a broad bowl of pot-pourri. It was on a circular table in the centre of the room. She was surprised to find beside the bowl the pewter-framed photograph of her parents. It had been posed in happier days, the only intensely personal thing she owned. There were some books on the table. A glazed chintz armchair, patterned with birds and foliage, invited her to lounge and browse, when she could spare a little time from the looking glass.

The biggest piece in the room, so prominent that she had scarcely glanced at it, was the broad bed. Its head and foot were brass rails, tall as park railings, she thought, but with scrolled knobs and enamelled plaques populated by yet more cherubs. Cupid presided, dart at the ready. Lucilla saw that the mattress was so high up that she would have to climb a miniature flight of wooden steps.

On the lace-fringed counterpane was draped a filmy pink garment. She picked it up. It was like a handful of feathers. She could see her fingers through. Wherever her own cotton nightdress was, she wouldn't be using it. She opened drawers in the chest and dressing table, and gazed on slips, step-ins, corsets, camisoles. Their styling whispered secrets of the France she didn't know. There were silk stockings, short and long gloves, dainty handkerchiefs. In a mirrored press hung dresses, mantles, shawls and hats. On its floor lay a rack of shoes for day and evening. Three fringed parasols of different shades stood in its corners.

There was no sign of her carpet bag and hatbox. Hardly any of her own things were on view. She wasn't bothered if they didn't reappear. Perhaps she would find that the life they had belonged to had been discarded with them. Lucilla had seen Cinderella transformed often enough. Watching from backstage, as a child, she had known that the ball gown was just another costume off the wardrobe rail. It was as worn and fake as the ragged dress it replaced. She had watched her mother carefully making the tattered effect. She had seen through the illusions that made audiences believe fantasies.

She saw how these present effects were meant to spellbind her. She guessed how it had been worked. While Ted Pearson was giving her what Joe termed 'the spiel', someone had been sent hurrying here with word that she would be staying. Definitely star material, the landladies would have been told. Lay it all on! While they'd kept her lingering over tea the maids had been busy here.

She knew that when she came to try on those shoes and corsets and things they would fit perfectly. Mrs Goldman's measuring and expert eye, and Maurice et Cie's complete range, would make it certain. Gowns specially designed for her would come later. Everything had been done to show her what value they were putting on her, in a world she would never want to quit.

Yorkshire waitress into princess. 'Why not?' she thought. 'I'm worth it.'

She was standing beside the round table. She picked up the framed photograph that was the only material relic of her past. Her mother's stare was as cold as Lucilla had always felt it. Her father's heavy round features were waiting to relax. He was the one she'd loved. She'd trusted him. She wanted to believe still that he'd given her up only under protest. Where was he now? In a pub behind some northern theatre, yarning over his favourite mild and bitter until curtain time. Did he ever wonder about her? He would get a shock to see her now. Poor Dad. All his drops and flats and gauzes couldn't build a scene to compare with the one in which his little Cinders was about to change into Princess.

Never mind what other people would be at the ball. She and the girl in the mirror would upstage them. Lucilla went back to the glass to share her new friend's reassuring smile. The girl's arms were behind her back. She felt her own fingers tugging at hooks and buttons, impatient to get on with the Transformation Scene.

CHAPTER 14

REBECCA'S ROOM

'Y ou're kidding,' Jenny accused. 'Having me on. Aren't you?' But the way he looked told her he wasn't. 'Who the Hell's he think he is?'

'Commissioner of Police.'

'And he doesn't know a bashing from a shove?'

'A doctor would.'

'Doctors! I could tell you things. Make you never go near one.'

'Witnesses.'

'Harry, Manny. *That* lot?'

He had given her a brief explanation of the circumstantial case against him. He told her the difference, as he perceived it, between constabulary and military ways of looking at things. She wasn't taking it in.

'He was looking for a backhander.'

His laugh made her boil.

'Green as grass, you are, Nightbone. I know things. Those Turk coppers didn't only expect free bed.'

'I don't see Saltby after that, either.'

'What do you know? Higher up they are, more they can get. All right. Go on. Find excuses for him. Anybody would think you're bloody glad.'

He was glad she was all right. It sealed off his conscience about her. His old manor, and Jen with it, was someone else's concern now. He was exiled from it. He wanted to put it out of his mind. He wished she hadn't shown up here. But he was relieved.

He didn't want her being indignant on his behalf. Her or anyone else. Her challenges were too soon for him. He wasn't ready to explain and argue. He hadn't worked things out for himself yet.

Jen persisted. They faced one another from the hearthside chairs in Old Mazurka's back parlour. The shop sounds were a faint background.

'Anyway, witnesses. What about me?'

'What about you?'

'I was there, wasn't I? I saw it. You only shoved Bailey away, so as to go after Tommy.'

'Your word against the others.'

Jenny's exasperation made her jump up. 'What's that supposed to mean? I'm a whore? Whores can't see what's plain in front of them?'

'All right, Jen.'

'It's not all right. Who are Harry and that lot, anyway? What are they worth?'

'Just leave it. It's not your concern. And stop shouting. There are people out there.'

'I'll shout if I want. Any other time you'd have gone back and torn the little squirt apart.'

'And get stretched for it?'

'What's come over you, Nightbone? You don't want to know.'

'No.'

She had moved closer, staring down at him there like a heap a horse had just dropped.

'Here!' she said. 'What are you into? Why'd they really give you the boot? It wasn't Bailey, was it? There's something else.' She jerked her thumb towards the shop. 'You and the old cove. You're on the run, aren't you? Didn't think I'd be here. Come here to hole up.'

Her eyes widened. She had started to shake. Her tone was rising.

'Nelly. Is that it? You was out there in the fog. She was soft on you. You always was a queer one. You only say you found her. What did you do . . . ?'

Nightbone had risen swiftly. He snatched the wrist of the clenched hand she was making towards him. His palm and fingers enveloped it like a strangler's two hands about a neck. She knew what pain it would bring to try to wrench away. She stayed quite still, hissing with suspicion and dread.

'Just hear this, Jenny,' he said, speaking very low. 'All I knew about Nell is what you do. Nothing. I didn't find her. I found the blokes who did. Mary was with them. Ask her.'

She risked the pain.

'She was dead when they found her.'

'Who told you?'

'You did. Last night.'

'Why would I tell you that if I'd done it?'

He thrust his face towards her. The unaccustomed flare of his cheeks and the intenseness of the usually calm eyes frightened her. She made one last reckless defiance.

'If you're chucked out, Nightbone, you're on the street with the rest of us. Bloody see how you manage. Only don't come bossing me no more. You got no more right, and you're not worth hearing. Ahhh!'

His tightened grip had hurt her desperately. He had had to shut her up. Her voice had risen to a shriek, enough to draw Mazur to the other side of the slide in the connecting door through which he kept watch for sneak thieves. He saw them locked in that attitude, only inches apart. Jen's face was suffused with pain, Nightbone's from earnestness to silence her. He was maintaining the cruel grip, crushing her defiance with its warning.

The customer Mazur was serving rapped her coin on the counter. He turned back to her. She didn't appear to have heard the noise.

When he went through, a few minutes later, he found Nightbone alone. He was standing staring into the fireplace, leaning on one arm that was outstretched against the wall. He turned when he heard the old man and nodded towards the stairs.

'She needs a drink.'

'I don't keep none. You want to fetch some in? What?'

'It'll keep. Did you hear?'

'Not much. She's in trouble?'

'Didn't she tell you? About her sister?'

'She told me. You come about that, Sergeant?'

'No. And it isn't Sergeant.'

'What? They make you Captain already?'

'They make me mister. Finish.'

A call on the shopkeeper's professional attention interrupted them. Nightbone went back to staring into the fire.

Upstairs, Jenny rubbed her hurting wrist with her other hand. Her eyes burned with tears of pain and frustration. She stared round the little room that had been Rebecca's. Things of hers were still hanging and lying where she had left them. It was spooky. Jen saw the small window. She stood on the narrow bed to reach the catch. It wouldn't turn. She saw that it had been secured with wire. The window frame was nailed all round against burglars. Jen sank on to the bed. She seized the pillow and beat it against a wall. It burst. Feathers cascaded and flew. She threw herself full length on the bed and shook the headrail, like prison bars, with her two hands. She felt crazed for a drink.

Old Mazurka came back to rejoin Nightbone. He lifted his eyes to the noises through the ceiling.

'It was Becky's room. Her things are there. We waited for her to come back to it. So, you don't come about Becky this time?'

'She told you the truth last time. Becky won't come back.'

The shop bell summoned again. Nightbone heard him chiding, and the customer's peevish objection. Then a door banged and a bolt clashed. Old Mazurka came back. His grin seemed briefly to fulfil the proper function of grins.

'They got all day. They want a shopkeeper must be like a clock, never stopping. What?' He took one of the fireside chairs and motioned Nightbone into the other. 'Now you please tell me why it is not Sergeant no more, and why you come back to Old Mazurka. What?'

It was easier this time, without interruption or bursts of outrage, but Nightbone wondered again to what extent the story was believed. Although the grin was so patently an artificial effect that had become permanent the yellow eyes were alert. Alive, where so much of the rest appeared moribund. Nightbone had the impression of being studied intently by eyes that were on watch for something. Something they would recognize on instant sight.

'I had to get out quickly,' he concluded. 'Away from that patch. Somewhere I could lie low for a bit and think. Sort myself out. You'd said to come any time.'

Mazur nodded. He had lived in London for thirty of his forty-seven years. His certainty of the nuances of English language and character was not total, but he believed he could pick a liar in any tongue. He was looking for bitterness and self-pity in Nightbone's tone. He wasn't hearing them. His London years hadn't rid him of inbred mistrust of officials paying innocuous-seeming calls.

'What you plan to do?' he asked carefully.

'Find a job.'

'Nothing much round here. Shops. Offices. Rag trade. Not policeman's work.'

'What is?'

'Maybe you're a bit short?' It was risky to ask, if the two of them had come back with some idea of putting the word on him for his cash. He was relieved that Nightbone shook his head.

'You know where to come if you are,' he risked further. His principal business was common knowledge round there. Nightbone's mere nod dispelled his fear completely.

'I don't have no more rooms,' he said. 'I tell Jen she can stop a while.'

They heard her say, 'Don't bother.'

They turned to the stairs. Jen had crept down again. She couldn't stay up there alone in that room. The old man had told her to use anything she wanted. She couldn't bear to think of it. After her spasm of rage at Nightbone had subsided she had begun wondering about him again. She couldn't work it out, that story of his. He'd been quick enough to make up a story for her to tell that first time. What was he up to now? She heard the rumble of his voice, telling the old man something at length. She had to know what it was. She had sneaked out of the room on to the stairs, but a board creaked loudly under her. There was nothing for it but to come openly down.

She didn't like the way they stopped whatever they'd been saying and stared at her. She put on her perky tone.

'Tell you what. I feel ever so better. A nice rest. And the coffee. I'll be hooking it off now. Back to Ma Costigan's. Mr Nightbone can have your room.'

'What? You come back, and I let you go so soon?'

'I can look out for myself.'

'Stay here, Jen,' Nightbone told her. 'I'll find a place.'

The shop doorbell had attained unceasing clangour by now. Mazur got up, wringing his hands.

'You stay, Jenny. I find him a place. Make him to eat first. You, too. There's things in the cupboards. Plenty in the shop. Me, I don't bother.'

Jenny moistened her lower lip. 'I don't suppose you happen to have . . . ?'

'What?'

'Never mind.'

'Blooming all right for you,' she grumbled to Nightbone when they were alone. 'I'm used to having one or two.'

'Do you good to lay off.'

'Ho! In what capacity, may I ask, are you preaching?'

He was relieved at the way she said it this time. He gave her a grin and she stuck out her tongue. Together, they scraped up a meal. Jenny was incompetent, Nightbone not much better.

'You could be a fireman,' she startled him.

They were sharing sweet tea biscuits from a tin decorated with an oval portrait of a handsome young hussar and his sweetheart, all Regency roses and ribbons. It was the first time in her long experience of getting men to talk about themselves that Jen had had recourse to the Fire Brigade.

'Me? What for?'

'You'd have a uniform again.'

'Is that what I want?'

'You don't look yourself without.'

She'd been thinking so as she watched him eat and drink. She had never seen him out of uniform before. He looked quite different. Not himself a bit. Not Nightbone. He didn't look his same size, especially sitting down at the table. His face seemed changed, like he was acting being somebody else. That, and being so mild about what that bloody commissioner had done to him. Not to mention Bailey Watts. Not the Nightbone she knew. Definitely not.

'Bet you was born with a helmet,' she challenged.

He surprised her. 'Just about. My pa was in the Army.'

'Sergeant.'

'How do you know?'

'I can tell things. What made you go for a bobby?'

'Tell me, if you're so clever.'

'Nobody else would have you.'

'Could be right.'

His tone changed suddenly. 'Jen, I'm sorry about Nell.'

'You said so before.'

'I mean that I can't do anything.'

'Suit yourself.'

'It's not like that.'

She shrugged. 'You can't help me. You don't want me helping you. Wait till I meet Bailey next, though!'

He was down on her instantly.

'No, Jen. You leave Bailey alone.'

'Who's giving orders?'

'All right. I'm asking, then.'

'Just say why. Got something on you, has he? You wouldn't be the
first.'

'Think anything you like. I'm in it deep enough over him. I don't
want it stirring.'

She decided not to tempt fate, sitting as close to him as she was. She
got up and went towards the stairs. She mounted half-way then
turned.

'Don't expect the Fire Brigade would have you.'

'Why?'

'Lost your guts. Gave 'em back with your uniform. Went with the
job, didn't they? Don't bother. I'll yell the roof off if you come near.'

She ran up the stairs, and into Rebecca's room, and locked the
door.

Maybe she was right, she left him thinking. The uniform had meant
more to him than he'd known. More than a suit of clothes with badges
and silver buttons. It had been what set him apart from others. Made
it possible for him to follow the lonely way that he preferred. He faced
being even more alone now. It was as if he had stepped out of the fog
into a different world. He was a stranger in territory he didn't know.
No longer in a position to order and enforce. The uniform and what it
signified had been that much part of him.

He realized Mazur had come back into the room, glancing at the
stairs.

'You fight again? What?'

'She's in a bad patch. She'll survive.'

'About her sister you fight?'

Nightbone told him his incidental part in Nell's killing.

'She wants somebody to blame. I can't help her any more so she's
taking it out on me.'

'I should give her to drink?'

'Tomorrow. She's not that far gone.'

'You want she stays?'

'Till she calms down. I don't want her going telling all and sundry
where I am.'

'If they come asking?'

'I won't be here. You haven't seen me. Don't know me. You said
you know a place.'

He was surprised by the change the question brought to the twisted
features. Though the grin remained its nature seemed to alter. The
yellow eyes, too. Nightbone saw the look that he'd recognized in many

suspects he'd questioned. The crafty ones. The sly ones. Ones he knew were hiding something. They might tell him it, but only in their own time, when they'd ascertained how he would respond. How far he'd go with a bargain.

'There is a place,' Mazur said. 'High class. Cost a bit. What?'

'I can manage a few days. Sort myself out. Find a job.'

'I know a job.'

'Round here?'

'Sure.'

Nightbone said nothing. He had been at this point often before. The point at which an offer would be made or withheld. A moment of confidence or mistrust. An ill-judged word could spoil that readiness to come clean. It might never be won back.

'I make you a proposition. For Becky I make it.'

'I don't know any more than Jen told.'

The old man made the gesture of muffling his ears with his palms. 'I don't want more. It doesn't bring her back.' He uncovered his ears again. 'You want to hear?'

'Without obligation.'

'You know what she says about you? Jen?'

'What?'

'You're lost without your uniform.'

'I can always be a fireman.'

'What?'

'It doesn't matter.'

Beyond, the shop sounded as though it were under siege. Mazur shook his head impatiently.

'Never no peace! Listen quick. That time before, you bring her here. You make her come. You make her tell lies to help a foreign man whose heart is broken. I don't believe, but I think I trust you. Now you come back, and I know I trust you, because I pray that you come.'

'What do you want, Mr Mazur?'

'Him. Who takes Becky. The coppers don't help. I pray a long time for some way, and now you come. In my country I don't pray. I pay a gang. A copper, maybe. We shake hands and I pay. Here, where the laws is crazy, if I try to buy a policeman I will be in jail. If I will pay a gang I am in jail also. Crazy. All in Europe know English laws is crazy.'

'It's why they come here.'

'Crazy. Every man must be free. What? It don't matter he is a monster. You don't have the jackboot and the knout, but a man may take away a maiden and nothing is done. Because he must be free! What? He is a monster and he must feed. He knows where he may feed and be safe. In crazy England, where no coppers hunt him. So he comes back.'

The old man's passion had been rising with every sentence. Nightbone recognized a plea that must have been rehearsed over and over. He had been saving and compounding it against the time when it might be spent. It was his life savings. His most treasured thing. The only one worth holding on to.

'Becky is gone. Her mamma goes, too. Only Old Mazurka is left. I make one prayer, many times. I ask there shall come the means to catch this monster that crazy English laws don't touch. I pray, and nothing comes. Almost I quit to pray. And then comes Nightbone back. And I know that it is meant.'

'I'm not sure I can help.'

'I tell you. I got one thing left. Tin. Gelt. Money. Them out there, they owe me. I call in the bills and half the neighbourhood is ruined. So what? I call it in. I ruin them. I give it all to you, Nightbone, to find this monster who thinks he is safe.'

He was leaning far forward. His clasped hands were stretched out like a beggar's. He might have fallen to his knees.

Nightbone asked, 'Where do I go looking?'

'I send you there. To lodge.'

'He's at that place?'

The tousled head shook impatiently. Someone was pounding the shop door so hard that it was near to collapsing.

'I ruin you all!' Mazur yelled in that direction. He turned urgently back to Nightbone.

'I cannot go there myself. You can go. The landlord comes in soon. I send you with him. I pay everything for you, only you don't say. You come here. I give you tin. All you need. All you want. Only you find him. What?'

'There's still the question of proof.'

'What is proof, if the law is crazy? Only find him.'

'Then what?'

'I give you all I have for him. I buy him off you.'

CHAPTER 15

PEINE FORTE ET DUR

*Let there be laid upon his Body, Iron and Stone
as much as he can bear, or more; and the next Day
he shall have three morsels of Barley Bread,
without Drink, and the second Day, he shall
have Drink three times, without any Bread:
And this shall be his Diet till he Die.*

BAILEY couldn't swallow even the water the doctor put to his lips. His stomach hurt so much that the bedsheets pressed on it as if weighted with stone and iron. Its framework of bones must imminently give way. Then his intestines would be pulped. Dying would be agony.

He knew all about *peine forte et dur*. The history of punishment had been a part of his law studies that he'd attended to keenly. It was an old torture meant to change the minds of prisoners refusing to plead guilty, or even not guilty. Without a plea there could be no trial. Without a trial no sentence could be passed. Without a sentence there could be no seizure of estates and possessions. For their families' sakes, there had been those prepared to endure the hideous crushing to death.

Eddy Watts had done little for his family except disgrace its name. The blow had fallen one night four years ago. Returning to his father's big Hampstead house from one of the narrow pink-shaded ones in Fitzroy Square, he had been triumphantly informed by his enemy the butler that the master wished to see him.

'In his study as soon as you came in, sir.'

Eddy, who for the past hours had been inhabiting his alternative persona, Mademoiselle Blanche, was half-drunk from unladylike amounts of champagne, brandy and sweet liqueurs. He was exhausted from pleasure.

'Tell him I had prior engagement with pillow. Good night, What's-your-name.'

'The master's order was most particular, sir.'

'I tell you particular thing do with it, 'f you don't get *out my way*!'

His raised voice had brought the opening of the door at the side of the hallway. His father's silhouette was against the yellow lamplight.

'Eddy, please come in here.'

'Off to bed,' he called back. He turned to the stairs, to find the butler unmistakably blocking his way.

'You will come *here*!' he was surprised from his father.

'Get out of it!' he snarled at the butler. Joynson was elderly, but he needed only one white-gloved hand to grip the young master's arm just above the elbow and march him into the study. A heavily built man in a grey suit was standing there. There was a gleam of uniform buttons in the shadows beyond the lamp's sphere. When Joynson had gone, Eddy's father, full bearded and unnaturally haggard and speaking as if his tongue were numbed, introduced the standing visitor as a Superintendent Williams, of Scotland Yard.

Without a handshake or an introduction to his uniformed companion the officer proceeded to tell Eddy things about himself that he could not have believed were known outside the intimate circle in which he had passed the evening. What went on at Fitzroy Square was only part of the narrative. There was the weekend he had spent at the country house of a baronet and Member of Parliament. That other one at Deauville, with his father's male secretary and a pair of boys from one of the country's most highly regarded schools. They were detailed without recourse to notes. His father, motionless at his desk, had his face in his hands.

'Stop, for Heaven's sake!' the old gentleman cried out at last. 'Is there nothing you are going to deny?'

Eddy shook his head. He knew no common blackmailer had done this. There was only one man with all the knowledge. That was the secretary, recently dismissed for dishonesty to do with the family shipping firm's accounts. There had been massive embezzlement, yet no arrest. Now Eddy knew why. The one man who had seemed to love him had promised not to make public the details of their relationship. In return he would not be prosecuted for fraud.

'For your sake, your father misguidedly tried to keep it quiet,' he heard the superintendent say. 'It's always a mistake to expect people of that sort to keep their word.'

'Where it involved *me*, I would,' Eddy burst out. He was close to tears. 'Whatever else, I'd expect that.'

Great sobs overcame him. They had let him cry for some minutes. When his shoulders ceased to heave his father had asked him tensely, 'Tell me one thing, boy. Tell it truly. Had you any part in this crime against the company?'

'No. *No!* That's what really matters to you. Isn't it? The money.'

'As it happens, *sir*,' the officer answered for his shocked father, 'you're not entirely wrong. There are more ways of wrecking people's lives than killing them. The fraud will be a tragedy for scores of innocent folk. If you were involved in that you could count on Dartmoor.'

An anguished cry from Mr Watts interrupted him.

'I'm sorry, sir. A word of what to expect, though. Your son is a first offender, and the law isn't too concerned with some of the matters. But cases involving young boys are always taken seriously.'

'For God's sake!' Eddy had shouted. 'I'm a law student. Another year and I'll be called. Pay the man, Father. Pay him whatever he wants and send him away.'

The superintendent had left without another word to him. The young uniformed sergeant, who had been sitting so silent and un-stirring in the shadows, escorted Eddy in a cab to a police station. At the charge desk Eddy heard the sergeant addressed by name. Even without the circumstances, it was a name not to forget. Night-bone.

Bailey, as he had been rechristened after his appearance in the Central Criminal Court, left jail two years later. Like a voyager from distant parts, he found everything different. His father was dead. The big house at Hampstead and its contents had been sold off by cred-itors. He had no honest friends. It was beneath his surviving conceit of himself to expose himself to snubs from relatives. His legal career was over before it was begun. All he had was the bespoke suit he had been jailed in. His suit, a few shillings, and a paranoiac hatred of the Law and all who served it. Especially those who knew all about him. Since his trial he had never come across Superintendent Williams again. But his speedy descent into the North London depths had rein-troduced him to that sergeant of memorable name.

Eddy's past name was not entirely wiped out. There were some who still spoke of 'dear Eddy', and a few with tender memories of Mademoiselle Blanche. One was a doctor, whose name alternated between Charles and Carlotta, depending on the company he was in. Eddy and he and some other men had been co-tenants of the house in Fitzroy Square. With its staff of young male servants, who came there part-time and mingled equally with the members on the special evenings when everyone wore their nicest hair and new gown, and the atmosphere was heavy with scent and powder, it had been a cherished retreat for supping, drinking, chattering and fondling. And further things that kept the upstairs rooms aired.

The police knew about it, but kept a closed eye. Until an unsophisticated boy, who somehow had got taken on for Friday nights, was terrified by the maid's dress he had to wear and what he was expected to do. Fleeing home in a state of shock, he had met a clergyman he knew. He told him all. The police had no choice but to make a raid.

It had been Eddy's quick thinking that had rescued himself, Charles, and their special friends, Simon (Stella) and Angelo (Angelina), from ignominy. He had spirited them off the premises by a back way just in time. Getting home still in their dresses and heels and paint was thrilling in retrospect, but had been full of danger. Their escape spared them being paraded with their associates at Bow Street, in full drag before a packed house. It saved them from the jeers that greeted the recital of *nommes des femmes* and other intimate particulars.

After a diplomatic interval the sisterhood had reconvened at fresh premises. Mademoiselle Blanche was not seen there. Eddy's own big trouble had overtaken him. Some brutal encounters in jail turned him off his old tastes. After his release he had gone to the pack, physically and criminally. It made him dangerous to his former friends. His mind was known to be affected. There was no guessing what he might give away in one of his hysterical outbursts. Charles and Simon were especially concerned about it. They had cause to feel indebted to him, but he knew more about them than anyone. They had been discussing the danger of this not many days before Eddy turned up in a cab at the doctor's home at Paddington. He was in a state of near collapse and had to be helped indoors.

'Pissed,' diagnosed the cabby. But Charles's examination revealed severe bruising to the stomach area and lower. Eddy's painfully gasped story was of unprovoked assault by a vindictive police sergeant. He was able to name him, and witnesses, before collapsing.

Charles acted decisively. He maintained a second house, in the mews behind his home. Its half-dozen rooms were all equipped as plain bedrooms. They were for the accommodation of patients, chiefly female, needing to lie up briefly after illegal operations performed by Charles in what had been the basement kitchen. That, or injured during activities about which unwanted questions would be asked in a public hospital.

He took Eddy round there under cover of the fog and put him to bed in a room at the top. No other patients were in residence. He revived him and took down his statement in writing, and got him to sign it. Then he left him a carafe of water, patted his hand for old times' sake, and locked him in. He took a cab straight to the Maida Vale home of Simon, the lawyer.

'The witnesses make it awkward,' Simon said, after studying the statement and hearing what Charles proposed. 'If they don't hear anything more they may ask why they haven't. Depending what sort they are, of course.'

'They won't. They got the drink he promised them. That's the end of it.'

'Presumably the peeler will have made some sort of report. Not necessarily true, of course. The police are certain to cover up for him.'

'That's what I thought. So, do you agree it's safe for me to do as Eddy wants? Send his complaint direct to Scotland Yard?'

'Without delay. Together with your report. If they're forced to follow it up you'll be seen to have acted properly.'

'Presumably they'd want to question Eddy.'

'I fear so. *Could* it be fatal?'

'Internal injury's always tricky. The poor dear's certainly taken a bad bashing.' Charles hesitated. 'Might take a turn for the worse.'

'You think it will?'

'I rather do.'

'How long?'

'Matter of days, say.'

They communed in silence for some minutes.

'Poor dear,' Charles mused. 'I've always been grateful over that evening.'

'So have I. Such a waste. Not much of a life for her since that other beastly trouble.'

'Nothing to live for, really. Will you redraft the statement into proper form?'

'All right. I see you've left ample space above the signature. What shall you say, if they come asking?'

'That after examining him I advised him to go to hospital at once. He said he could manage in a cab. I gave him money and saw him into one. I simply haven't heard from him since.'

'I doubt they'll take it further than that. Close ranks behind their own kind.'

'Brutes of policemen, taking it out on defenceless little things.'

'Poor dear. Give her my love.'

At the top of the mews house in Paddington Bailey Watts cried out his fear. No sound came. His stomach was hurting increasingly. He wanted his friend to come back and attend to him. He could hear nothing in the house.

He would have tried harder to scream if he had known quite how alone he was.

CHAPTER 16

CONCERNING NIGHTBONE

'WOULD ye believe such a thing?' Ma Costigan demanded again. 'Jenny Jacks running off with a crusher!'

The girls sniggered. They were dressed for their occupation. Just taking a stimulant and a last warm. Their qualms about going back to work so soon after Nell's killing hadn't lasted. Their bullies had intimated graver perils if they didn't carry on earning.

'She always had a shine for Nightbone,' Sal observed. 'Leastways, Nell did.'

'Wouldn't mind him meself,' said Joan.

'Comin' sniffin' after her soon as Nell gets croaked,' objected Maggie. 'Disgusting.'

'Yeh, Ma. Suppin' your slosh together. Wot you give for nix. On account of your good 'eart.'

'That's right!' cried the Irishwoman, in the agony of the bilked. 'The crafty divvles!'

'It's not *sure* they're off together,' offered Patsy. She was new to the game and relatively innocent.

Mrs Costigan disposed of such reasonableness. 'Wasn't he leaving word after her in every boozer? Why else would the both of 'em go off sudden, and him once a proud sergeant?'

'I might give you a bob for her clobber,' offered Joan. 'Pay you back for their slosh – and a tot now.'

'Ye will not. She's paid up and her things won't be touched. Anyway, the day youse try keeping a bob back Alfie will kick your head off.'

The girls sighed, and sloped off to enrich the drab streets with their lustre.

'Charlie – whatever do you keep looking for? Moth?'

For the second successive evening, Mrs Assistant Commissioner had sniffed camphor and tracked her husband to the open bedroom wardrobe. She took his best uniform from him and returned it to its folds. She rewrapped the tissue paper and laid the bundle on the shelf among the mothballs.

'You got into it easily enough last time. I haven't noticed that you've swollen since. Except perhaps in the head.'

'What's that mean?' Charlie demanded.

'That spell as Acting Commissioner. You've not been quite yourself since.'

'Three months? Keeping the chair warm for Saltby's arse.'

'Chas! You know I won't have language, with the girls in the house.'

The two Misses McNorris were enjoying genteel tuition at a day college for young ladies. In the academic line, their father could read, write, and count. Not a great deal more. He had ascended in thirty-five years from beat constable to Assistant Commissioner of Metropolitan Police without educational advantage. His life's accumulation of knowledge was vast, though. It was crammed in a minute cavity inside a cranium that had served also as battering ram and punch bag. It comprised tens of thousands of names, faces, records, regulations, judges' rulings, gazetteer of evil whereabouts, *modi operandi* of bludgers, buzzers, dragsmen, dippers, cracksmen, kidsmen, fine wirers, palmers, shofulmen, fences, screevers, smashers, and myriad other practitioners of crime, alive and dead.

Custodianship of such an archive, in Charlie McNorris's view, as good as entitled him to the Commissioner's job. His brief experience of it had been between the abrupt departure of its former holder and Saltby's arrival from India. It had made Charlie less sure of himself. He hadn't known where to start, so had put off starting at all. Saltby, marching briskly in, had appreciated the situation at a glance. He had taken over as energetically and dogmatically as he meant to go on. Charlie resented such qualities.

Anybody could be an Army officer. It only wanted good connections, money, and that plummy way of talking that people took for brains. To make a senior bobby needed experience from the boots up. Plenty of hard kicks taken and given on the way. Watching Saltby going about things in his pig-headed fashion, disciplining and dismissing, and imbuing those who survived with the fear of God, had revealed to McNorris how the job didn't want doing. In this knowledge, he was ready for another crack at it.

Saltby was appearing too confident for his assistant's liking. If he saw out his three-year secondment it would be too late for Charlie. His best hope could be that the Commissioner's smugness would send him arse over tip in a great fall. What he had done to Nightbone might turn out to be just the thing.

'Another good young chap turned off today,' the Chief Superintendent told his wife as they made their way downstairs. 'No force left soon, this rate.'

She paused and turned to beam affectionately on her life's partner. 'There'll still be you, dear. Who else do they need?'

Colonel Saltby sat late in his office. His blinds were down. The electric lamp on the big desk was the only light. He read with narrowed eyes, but had never considered eyeglasses.

His door was locked. No clerk or messenger waited in the anteroom. The Assistant Commissioner had gone home long since. The Commissioner wished to reflect in solitariness.

He could have done so in his study in Kensington, in the fine house he and his wife had leased furnished for three years. She wouldn't interrupt him. The Indian orderly he had brought back as his man would enter only when rung for. But the thoughts occupying the Commissioner's mind were wholly to do with his work. He preferred the austere surroundings of Scotland Yard for meditation and contemplation.

The piles of documents on his desk were minutes from police and civilian committees, the draft of a Home Office commission's report, advice and criticism from politicians, judges, lawyers, magistrates, clergymen, private citizens, charity workers, and two ex-criminals turned reformists. Every page bore annotations in Col. Saltby's disciplined hand. That handwriting, without crossings-out or inserted afterthoughts, also covered sheets of notes of his own about manpower figures, cost estimates, drafts for new regulations and emendations to old ones.

He rubbed his eyes with his forefingers. The thick files were closed now. Only one other lay open.

Commanding the regiment had involved nothing like such concentration on detail. Most things could be deputed to lesser officers. Their minds so matched his that they could be certain to arrive at conclusions he would endorse. Here, he knew, he could rely on no such help. Only bloody-mindedness and hostility.

He had expected it. He had never known a military unit that had actually welcomed gingering-up. He had gingered many, though, and left them healthier, more competent. Even grudgingly appreciative. What his three-year spell of command would do for the Metropolitan Police would not be recognized until he had moved on. It could scarcely be in a worse state than he had found it. It had to improve. It didn't wish to, but it was going to. In his style. If his style wasn't what they wanted, they should have appointed someone else. He was giving up three years' Army seniority to it. He wasn't going to waste them. His skin was thick. If determination led him into a few mistakes he would blame himself. If others made them he would call them to account. If they repeated them, they were out.

Sitting late at the big desk, with the limited pool of yellow light on the one file open before him, he had a single misgiving. It flawed the smooth surface of his self-confidence like a mud-splash on a polished boot.

It bore a name. The one on the label of the file that Col. Saltby closed at last, to go home.

Nightbone.

Deaf to the scratching and squeaking of the Thames rats crawling near, and occasionally over, his legs, Bodger Blandy snored on one of the straw-leaking mattresses in the depot corner. Though his pulped eye drooped open it saw nothing. The other men grouped nearby, talking before lying down, took care not to look at him. He was too horrible even for them, who were far from being beauties.

He had worked here before, and they had been glad when he had gone. He had come back this time indicating that he wouldn't carry a sandwich board. He would pack or heave or paste, or anything of that sort, but not go out on the streets. It was understood that he wanted to keep out of police notice.

Strangulated noises from his misaligned mouth betokened a tormented dream. In parts it resembled the fantasy tormenting Bailey Watts's mind just then. Except that Bailey figured in Bodger's nightmare, and Bodger in Bailey's. The other people in both were identical: the cellar occupants, Nelly Jacks, and Nightbone.

Another of Bodger's phantasms merged with it. This recurrent one was peopled with men in tights. Stripped to the waist, sweating torrents. Crop-headed, savage-eyed men, bloodied behind great broken fists. And others, crimson faced, sleek and paunched. In straining yellow waistcoats, frock coats, high toppers. Chewing cigars, shouting resentment against constables pushing through them to enforce the end of Bodger's career.

He had to finish off his opponent before those crushers reached him. Had to finish it, or he wouldn't get paid. He smashed and smashed at the face. It was Nightbone's. The blows had no effect. That staring look of his never winced. Bodger's knuckles and wrists ached beyond bearing. His knees were going. He smashed on. Nightbone kept coming forward. He never raised his fists. The hard-set stare was all he used.

The tumult and shouting spiralled into an echo. Fog blanketed the scene. Nightbone's face was still in it, though. Still with that look. Still coming on. Bodger felt the iron grip enfolding his powerless wrists. The steel-cold snaps. He glimpsed the cell bars, the grim warders, the hangman displaying the rope.

Bodger made one last despairing effort. Switching his attack from Nightbone's face, he lunged lower with all his remaining strength. He felt it go home. A smash. The best bodier he'd ever landed.

The crowd knew it. Their cheers broke through again. The invading bobbies stopped to cheer with them.

But it wasn't Nightbone's face that fell back and away, mouthing agony. It was Bailey's.

Bodger threshed on the straw. The unearthly groan rattled his throat. It made one of the others, a young newcomer, turn curiously to look. What he saw of Bodger Blandy's eye gave him ghastly dreams of his own that night.

CHAPTER 17

ANGELO'S

'WHAT it is to have had artistic parents, Mr Hilling. Not so profane as to run the names together, though. There was a trend towards Michael for a time, but nowadays Angelo is the established preference. And yourself?'

Nightbone, who admitted to a Christian name only when officially pressed, gave the first to come into his head.

'Bob.'

'Well, Bob, it's all first-name terms in my humble abode. Quite Bohemian. But I believe you'll find it agreeable. Won't he, Mr Mazur?'

'Can't help but appreciate your style, Signor Martini. While you're in, is there anything you want? Nice bit of gorgonzola? What? Fresh yesterday.'

Nightbone already had his little trunk out in the shop. He waited beside it while his new landlord made the inescapable purchase, which he stuffed into his coat pocket. Then they walked together to the house, not far off in another of the squares.

It was the second time that he'd had to improvise hurriedly. When Old Mazurka had introduced him to the customer with a room to let it had been as Mr Hilling. It had been Nightbone's last-minute idea. Haste would allow no more inspiration than his former landlord's name. At least it was unremarkable. Not like Michael Angelo Martini.

He was late middle aged, white haired, smooth cheeked, puffy, pink. Very exactly mannered. He tiptoed rather than walked, as if wanting minimum contact with anything so gross as paving stone.

His arms hung forward from the elbows, neat hands and fingers dangling. They fluttered from the wrists as he talked. His accent was East London, with just enough odd pronunciation to justify Signor.

'Know Mr Mazur well, Bob?'

'Only just met him.'

'Really? I quite thought, from his recommending us to one another . . .'

'Called in there on the off chance. Shopkeepers know everybody.'

'Oh, yes. Especially that one. A local character.'

'Told him I wanted somewhere to stop a few days. While I look about for a job.'

'Any particular line of business?'

'If you can call it that. Ten years' army. Infantry. No, no particular line.'

From his eye corner Nightbone noticed the glance.

'I think you'll find my place suits you, Bob. Let's hope so, at least.'

The house was one of the Regency survivors. It was narrow and not too tall. The pink stucco had been cared for. Decorative wrought iron had been repainted glossy black. The fanlight panes were scrupulously clean. Reliefs of a pair of white plaster urns, trailing white plaster laurel strands, were on the threshold walls. The porch stone was black and white checked marble. The decorations and furnishings inside were just as smart. Looking for a place to stop, Nightbone wouldn't have gone for anything half so done up. It would cost a bit, Mazur had said, but in the circumstances it didn't matter. And if Nightbone was a bit short of the necessary he wouldn't mind paying an advance. Nightbone declined.

Signor Martini's tariff proved surprisingly reasonable. Nightbone guessed he had decided on it as they'd walked there. He said he could fancy stopping for a bit, while his cash held out. He said it was a pretty house.

His room was airy and high ceilinged. He thought his bit of luggage looked pathetic in the middle of the floor.

'Linen and towels changed weekly,' Martini told him. 'If you're short of anything else you've only to say. Fully equipped bathroom down the end there. Constant hot water. Bathe as often as you please. All part of the service. Glad to help in any way.'

He had bathed straight away, filling the house with the aroma of the potion he hadn't thought he'd be using again for some time. The first time he'd dared sprinkle it in the Hillings' bath he'd apologized.

They'd all had a good laugh about it. From what Mazur had told him, apologies wouldn't be necessary here. No jokes would be made. He didn't know – but it wouldn't have surprised him – that his new landlord, attracted by the scent, had come to the bathroom door, and hovered, wondering whether he dared open it and forgetfully walk in. He'd decided not to risk it. A strapping young infantryman who perfumed his bathwater was too precious a catch to lose through impatience.

'That's a very nice perfume you use in your bath, Bob. Like flowers. Very sweet indeed.'

The two other men at the supper table added their compliments on the odour still lingering about their lodgings. One was grey haired and distinguished looking, with a high nose, like the old Duke of Wellington on pub signboards. The younger was plump and sleek, with greased black hair and a blue chin. Michael Angelo Martini had on a quilted, bottle green velveteen jacket and an embroidered round cap. With his white hairs curling out under it he looked to Nightbone like somebody's grandmother.

Nightbone was conscious that the suit he was wearing was his only one. The meal was quite fancy by his standards, far removed from Mrs Hilling's Lancashire hotpot. A glass of wine was served. He didn't try to pretend that he knew the order of cutlery to use. He saw Martini watching him follow the others' lead. He returned his encouraging smile. The talk was chiefly gossip, with a good many names bandied about. Nightbone didn't know them. When anyone thought he was at risk of being indiscreet before the newcomer he resorted to 'You Know Who' and an apologetic glance. Nightbone smiled back.

The distinguished-looking man ate hardly anything. At length he rolled his napkin into its silver plate ring and got up.

'Duty calls.' His tone was pained. He gave a disdainful sniff. The dark man smirked.

'Evening off for once, thank God. I'm stepping across presently. See you there?' he asked their landlord.

Martini glanced at Nightbone before replying.

'Not this evening. I'll stay and make our new friend feel at home.'

'Take a glass of port, Bob?' he asked when they were alone.

'Very kind, Signor Martini, I'm sure.'

'Oh, *Angelo*, please, dear boy.'

'Angelo. Nice name. Angel, does it mean?'

'There are those who've suggested . . . ' He came back to the table with a decanter and glasses. The little maid who had served the meal seemed to have retired. 'Bob,' he said. 'Bob.' He tried it like a wine. 'I'm not sure . . . Bobby, perhaps?'

Nightbone realized where lack of foresight might have landed him. It would take an already suspicious mind to make the connection, though. Angelo gave no sign of one. He tried another variant.

'Robby. Yes, I think Robby. Do you permit it?'

Nightbone was glad to.

'To Robby, then.'

After the toast they chatted circuitously about life in London. In particular, its limitations for men disinclined to mixed society. Nightbone knew he was being manoeuvred. He was expected to volunteer something more than that he'd come originally from Kent and that his father had been a lifelong soldier.

'The Buffs. Me, too. Mother didn't want me to go, but I had to. Broke her heart, God rest her. She was right. Best ten years of my life wasted. I don't want to talk about it.'

Angelo blew his nose delicately.

'It can help, you know. My gentlemen tend to tell me their troubles. I believe I must have a sympathetic face.'

With a show of reluctance, overlain with peevish grievance, Nightbone spoke of the monotony and petty tyrannies of soldiering in a peacetime army. He had heard it all often enough from his father and his mates. Things that bored a man. Tempted him into mischief.

'Order of the boot,' he said bitterly. 'Thanks for nothing.'

Angelo murmured sympathetically.

'Is one allowed to know why? Or might one guess?'

Nightbone lowered his eyelids and remained silent.

'They don't make things easy,' Angelo prompted. 'For *us*.' Still getting no response he gave a long sigh. 'Anyway, you could have fetched up worse in life, Robby. Comfortable enough here, I hope?'

Nightbone answered peevishly, 'How long d'you reckon I can pay for a place like this? No more port, thanks. Can't start getting expensive tastes.'

'You might find you could.' Angelo poured again for them both. 'Youth on your side. Good looks.'

Nightbone made an angry fist on the table. 'Don't start coming that. I only just missed jug already.'

'Really, Robby! Angelo would be most sad if he thought you were misunderstanding.'

Nightbone gave him a suspicious stare, but slowly unbunched the fist. He left the hand lying on the table. Martini glanced at it. He smiled.

'On the contrary. How are you with the *other* sex?'

'Birds? I don't know any.'

'Oh, come. A soldier?'

'It was on account of one I had to get away into the Service. What a price. Mother's heart, and ten wasted years.'

'How sordid! Still, we can all profit from mistakes. I think you might find, Robby, that you've fallen on your feet at last. Just the job for you.'

'I don't get your drift. What's this about judies?'

'Get on with them at a pinch, could you? Walk out of an evening? Bit of dancing? Supper?'

Nightbone made a face. 'Old widow women? That lark?'

'Not at all, my dear. *Au contraire.* Young. Very young. Birds, one might say, of rare plumage. Exceptionally succulent to those of that taste. Clothes and get-up that might make you envious.'

'Whores?'

'Dear me, Robby, how impulsive we are!' Angelo slid a mottled pink hand across the tablecloth. Nightbone pretended not to notice it. He picked up his glass. 'Model girls, dear boy. Showing off new fashions in public. Personable male escort, who'll keep them out of trouble and not get 'em *into* any. Strictly hands off. I'm not wrong in thinking you could fill that bill, Robby?'

'For pay? Depends what the catch is.'

'None. I promise you. Our friends at supper looked well enough on it, didn't they? It's how they live. Very well, too.'

'You don't tell me!'

Angelo smirked. 'You noticed Frank scarcely eating? Saving his appetite for later on. Big charity supper. A dozen courses at least. You know those charity people. Well, you soon will. An exceedingly busy time of year for modelling. The winter fashions, you know. Then the spring ones. Arthur happens to have an evening free, but it's quite an exception just now. Good money. Eat and drink as much as you care. Mostly evening work. All day to follow your own fancies.'

'And you're saying I'd suit?'

'Take my word, my dear. Angelo knows. All the best houses come to Angelo.'

'Houses?'

'Fashion. Someone has to find them suitable walking gentlemen. That's what they're called.'

'Nobody ever called me a gent.'

'Shame! Natural bearing. Grace. Looks. Nothing a few of Angelo's tips and an evening suit won't transform.'

'And there's nothing the law can touch?'

'Absolutely not. A legitimate commercial practice. Widely recognized in the fashion and theatrical worlds.'

'I dunno . . . '

'Made for you, Robby. And you for it. A fresh face is always welcome. Here, too.'

'You've certainly made me welcome Angelo. When would I start?'

'As soon as possible. As I say, this is a busy time. Not too many eligible men around. Not your type. *Masculine*.'

'Well . . . Mind, the wet canteen's my usual level.'

'We must learn not to underestimate ourselves. Something tells me you've been wasted.'

'These birds . . . '

'Nothing to worry about there. They're professionals. It's as much as their job's worth to start playing games. Remember, it's what they wear that matters. Mere clothes-horses.'

'Mares, don't you mean?'

'Oh, very good, Robby. Very droll.'

He reached for Nightbone's hand again. Nightbone lifted it and gave the table a slap.

'I'll give it a go.'

Angelo sprang up and almost ran to the sideboard. He came back with his hands full of cutlery. He deftly set it out.

'Now, the simple rule. Work from the outside inward . . . '

With each separate instruction he made a point of touching Nightbone's hands, lifting them lightly to the appropriate items. Nightbone didn't flinch.

'Certainly beats soldiering,' he said after a time.

Angelo smiled down at him and patted the back of one hand.

'It does, Robby. In every way.'

CHAPTER 18

A MASKED BALL

TED Pearson had said she would find there was more to it than just looking her pretty self and parading in nice things. She soon did. They put her immediately to hard labour, but of the pleasantest kind.

She was to massage her hands and arms day and night with Rose Cream, and sleep in long gloves over a coating of it. Lip salve was to be applied at intervals, and body creams and jellies after an evening bath in warm water fragrant with lotions.

'No powder or cosmetics of any kind,' ruled Mrs Goldman, her duenna. 'The complexion must first be fully ready to receive them. Yours is not. It must be thoroughly cleansed and firm.' She forestalled Lucilla's objection. 'You cannot expect to live in a place like Leeds without accumulating deep grime.'

The horrifying observation gave her something to work on industriously in front of her mirrors. She was encouraged to study her skin minutely, and perform exercises for the face muscles and eyes, as well as her limbs. She revelled in the routines, watching eagerly for signs of instant change.

She was told that the buttermilk locks she'd always been so proud of were in a disgraceful state. She was delivered to a hairdresser, a man, who sucked his teeth and worked so fiercely with the scissors that she was afraid he was hacking ruinously. What he actually did amazed her and gave her fresh delight before the looking-glasses. Little Miriam had to come in every evening and morning and comb and brush the hair for five minutes after massaging cocoa-butter into her scalp. At bedtime, Lucilla had to plait her hair into two. 'So that it can rest while you do,' Mrs Goldman explained. 'Very loosely, though. Tight braiding is only for show.'

Every day Mrs Goldman took a small class of the firm's most promising girls. Only two others besides Lucilla had been signed on as models. The rest were chosen from possibles among the general staff. She felt superior to them all, but found that even she had much to learn. They had to drill in walking, turning, gesturing, drawing long gloves on and off with the fingertips only, stooping to retrieve a handkerchief without looking down or crossing or splaying the legs, curtseying with a heavy book on the head to keep the neck straight and still, smiling in varying degrees, using a fan to convey a wordless language. They did all these in day clothes, then in evening ones with full accessories, which altered the balance enormously. She had to conquer the complications of the train, raised heels, long dangling earrings, swinging necklets and multiple ropes of pearls.

'Quite wonderful, Miss Poole,' Mrs Goldman congratulated her out of the others' hearing. 'A natural gift.'

Mr Ted came to look on once. He said nothing. Lucilla was tempted to look to him for a sign of special approval. Mrs Goldman, who could be sharp as well as encouraging, was down on her at once.

'Miss Poole! The eyes. Looking only ahead. Chin up more. The gaze into the distance. Keep it so.'

When a turn enabled Lucilla to look Mr Ted's way she was disappointed to find him gone. It worried her that he'd seen her offend, but when she chanced to encounter him later he restored her with a smile and a passing 'Good girl.'

Another class surprised and delighted her. The girls, in evening wear, including their new, severe corsets, were led into a room where a long table was fully laid for a meal. Its starched white cloth hung to the floor. Epergnes and vases of flowers were ranged along its centre. Before each chair lay an elaborate setting for many courses and wines.

'I reely couldn't,' murmured another girl to Lucilla, touching her drawn-in stomach. 'If they'd warned us I'd have skipped breakfast.'

But there was neither food nor drink to trouble her. The lesson was in etiquette and the handling of each piece of cutlery and glass. A professional waiter in full fig offered imaginary servings from empty dishes and tureens. An older man, in evening dress, with white hair and a trace of foreign accent, supervised from the table's head, instructing, correcting, criticizing the protégées through an entire invisible meal.

'Couldn't I eat it now!' the other girl declared to Lucilla as they waited for the non-existent pudding. 'If this damn' girdle would let it past.'

'Miss Horrocks,' Mrs Goldman's voice close behind made them jump. 'Never let me hear an expletive again. All of you note that, please. It is not permissible under any circumstances. As to references to undergarments and the digestion, they are in the worst taste. Always remember that Maurice et Cie demands the very highest standards of its young ladies.'

Lucilla had expected her experience at Langenbach's would put her streets ahead of the others in the dining lesson. She soon found how simple those four-course settings had been. Sixteen, with four wines, was very different. She didn't altogether see what it had to do with modelling clothes. Then she remembered Mr Ted's mention of going out into society. She was impressed again by the pains they were taking over her. They seemed to have thought of everything that would enable a girl to hold her own.

A second dining-table class presented a double surprise. The food and drink were real – though in tiny quantities – and so were the men in formal evening wear who joined them at the *table d'instruction*. They varied between young and smug-looking and elderly and courtly. They took their seats condescendingly between each pair of girls. Lucilla's theatrical experience told her they were not wholehearted ladies' men. She judged it by their mannerisms, not conversation, for no talking was allowed. Hard-up gentlemen or out of work actors, she thought.

'Young ladies,' Mrs Goldman said at the end. 'This has been a lesson in table manners and etiquette. Conversation is a study on its own. You'll be practising it tomorrow with these same gentlemen in turn.' She nodded to the white haired instructor. 'Before they leave, I shall ask Signor Martini to introduce everyone.'

Lucilla marvelled again at the company's thoroughness. She saw why they chose so carefully, and why they covered themselves financially against girls wantonly leaving. All this training and ex-perience must be priceless. She determined to absorb every particle of it. Another fair rule, she thought, was that they mustn't go about town without escorts provided by the firm. They were meant to stay in their lodgings, beautifying themselves and practising the speaking exer-cises Mrs Goldman taught them. She was only too happy to obey.

Joe Pearson took her out, though. He didn't call for her but sent a message and then a cab. She thought it most considerately managed. Only Belle and Floss knew of the outing.

'You're great company,' he complimented her, after a giggling exchange of saucy stories across a Soho restaurant table. 'It's something for a man to hit it off with a girl first go. Spend hours breaking the ice, then find nothing underneath – pardon my French.'

'I don't believe it. Not you.'

'I'm shyer than you'd reckon. Here, you don't think I do this with all the girls?'

'Isn't it all in the training?'

'The advanced class? No, love. Like I say, I like being with you. I'll help you along, you'll see.'

He was the best company Lucilla had ever had. Attentive, generous, free and easy. Endlessly talkative, jokey, yet polite. He didn't treat her at all like a boss. It made her confident that she would soon be ready to look in anyone's eye as an equal. She would say 'madam' and 'sir' if the job required, but they would see that it meant nothing. She was more than half-way to learning that she had something that those without it couldn't buy or make or borrow. Looks, and knowing how to use them, were the greatest gift a girl could have.

She was aware that if Joe demanded anything of her it would be hard to refuse him. But he didn't. He kept his hands strictly to himself throughout the cab ride he took her afterwards through the West End, pointing out the sights.

'A wicked city,' he reiterated, as they passed through the Haymarket and Piccadilly. The pavements were thronged with sauntering men and loitering girls in flaring colours. 'What I told you about a girl on her own. Too easy getting caught up in that. Ignorant. Never a thought where she'll finish up.'

He got out of the cab in Mortimer Street and sent her home in it. Riding alone, after the heady evening out, added to her rapidly growing confidence. She compared her situation with that of the mindless, degraded creatures on the street corners, and felt properly superior.

Early the next evening she got another message that he'd be sending for her. Floss offered to help her dress.

'Where's he taking me to?'

'Covent Garden. The masked ball.'

'Masked ball?'

'First of the season. Supper before. You'll love it.'

'What am I to wear?'

'He's sent everything. I'll fetch them up now.'

The gown proved stunning. It was in what Floss told her was Bacchante style. It was vivid rose chiffon, accordion-pleated, a compromise between fancy dress and a dancing frock, off the ground to expose her ankles and pink bowed shoes. The skirt and bodice were trimmed with representations of vine leaves and grapes. A wreath of the leaves and purple grapes coiled about her hair, a tendril snaking down on to her generously exposed shoulder. She was to wear no jewellery. Seeing herself in the full-length glass, she was startled how young the outfit made her look. Floss's meticulous work on her eyes and lips corrected that. When her shoulders and arms were finally powdered and glowing Lucilla had never seen herself so radiant. When the cab had come she merely touched Floss's hand and hurried down, totally absorbed in herself.

Joe joined the cab in Soho Square. He was dapper in a suit of tails, white double-breasted waistcoat, and white tie. She noticed what looked like diamonds in his shirt front. He had a large buttonhole. She thought what a handsome man-about-town look he had.

'Knock their eyes out, we will,' he said. ' "She walks in beauty like the something." Not up to my stuff, but it fits. By the way, slip these in your purse.'

He had brought out a dozen or so trade cards. 'Plenty more,' he indicated his tails' pocket. 'Be ready to pay a visit to the Ladies' whenever I give you the nudge. Anyone comes up there to ask about your outfit, give 'em one of these. No sales talk. Can't have our young ladies involved in sordid commerce.'

'Do you suppose anyone will?'

'If they don't, it won't be your fault or the gown's. It's what walking-out's about.'

She was a little disappointed. She'd hoped the evening out was for herself, and that he'd arranged the special gown as a surprise for her. When no fewer than three ladies spoke to her on her first cloakroom visit, complimenting her and asking her dressmaker's name, she saw that it made sense to mix business with pleasure. Very agreeable, in fact. They dined at the Continental, among distinctly classy company. She saw Joe hand cards to several men whom she'd seen eyeing her. He pointed out some other walking-out couples. She recognized a girl from Maurice et Cie's. The others were from rival houses. She identified two of Signor Martini's gentlemen. It was obviously quite the accepted thing. Lucilla's confidence grew.

They arrived at the Covent Garden Opera House with a great crowd. Joe had said the first masked ball was always packed out, which was why they'd come early. Normally, around midnight was the time to arrive, and things started 'hotting-up' at three or four.

'How do they hot-up?'

'You'll see, though don't think I'm keeping you out that late. Mrs Goldman would have the hide off me. Matter of fact, this might be the last season for the balls. They used to hold them all over town, but they've had to shut up, one by one. Too rackety by half.'

She had expected a dignified assemblage in dress to match theirs. But for every evening dress there was a fancy one. She saw a man in full cavalier costume, with a huge feathered hat; one in a monk's cowl and his nose painted red; another in a pirate's striped vest, eye patch and cocked hat. A woman was got up as an Eastern dancer; another in a soldier's tunic and hat and striped pantaloons. Some of the fancy dresses, she noticed, revealed a great deal of the women in them. Joe saw her looking.

'Ever seen high-kicking?' he said. 'You'd be surprised what some wenches forget to put on.'

Many women and men had obviously come unaccompanied. That was soon remedied among them, at little tables for two where the girls sat beside a vacant chair. Waiters, and pretty waitresses in coloured dresses and sashes of gay ribbons, hurried about with bottles in ice buckets.

There were masks and dominoes for hire at a counter beside the entrance. Joe took two black masks. He put Lucilla's on for her. Her mirrored reflection gave her a fresh thrill. She thought he looked quite sinister in his mask, but he lacked the necessary scowl.

She caught her breath when they entered the ballroom. All the fine theatre's seating had been taken out and the floor polished to a high gloss. Festoons of coloured lights were reflected in it. Dazzling floodlighting heightened the glow of plush and ornate gilding. It made the women's skin seem luminous and dazzled off the men's shirtfronts. An excellent orchestra was playing briskly in a decorated bandstand on the stage. Long rows of dancers advanced, retreated, passed and twirled, clapped and stamped.

'It's wonderful! Can anybody join in?'

'Sure. A lot of those are professionals, that's why they're so good. It gets wilder later.'

She expected him to lead her into the dance, or up to one of the boxes in tiers around the arena. Most were occupied already with merry parties. He took her instead to one of the little tables near the bandstand. It had a 'Reserved' card on it, and a bottle in ice. One of the maids hurried to seat them and pour the wine. It was champagne.

'No point hiding you away,' Joe explained. 'You're here to be admired, while they can still see.'

He directed her discreetly to look at the nearest set of dancers. She saw she was being ogled already by women and men. A woman in evening dress turned her head to take a backward look at her as she was danced away.

'You'll be meeting her in the Ladies',' Joe predicted. He was right. She gave out more cards there. She noticed, though, that not all the women's looks were admiring. She caught some glares, especially when Joe left her alone at the table for a time. Twice, men came up to ask her to dance. And she was aware that not all the men's looks were solely at her clothes. She pointed out to Joe one of the girls who had glared hardest at her. He winked. 'Underwear model.' She was surprised for a moment. At Maurice et Cie's that specialized modelling was done solely on the premises, supervised by older saleswomen. Then she realized what he meant.

'Wait till you see the Paris opera balls,' Joe said. 'This is nothing.'

She looked at him. He was sipping his champagne and watching the dancers. The mask made his eyes impossible to read.

'Do you go to Paris?' she asked.

'A fair bit. Brussels. Amsterdam.'

'On business?'

'Connections all over. We aren't Maurice et Cie for nothing. Not just a fancy name.'

'Is it a French firm, then?'

'In a way. Goes back to Regency days, when Frenchies were coming over here in droves. Bad times after their revolution. Old Jules Maurice set up in a back room and basement in Charlotte Street. No shop window. Himself, his missis and daughter, working all the hours. Once they'd started getting word-of-mouth they never looked back.'

'Are the family still connected?'

'Just me and Ted.'

'You're really called Maurice?'

'No, Pearson's legit. Our dear old mamma, God rest her, was old Jules Maurice's granddaughter. Only child, so the business came down to her and our Dad, who ran it for her. He went, too, a few years back, bless him. It's been old Ted and me ever since. We ought to be dancing, not talking shop. They're going to do The Lancers.'

They went to join the line-up. The band set a cracking tempo, artfully increasing it through a light opera medley. Lucilla, a good dancer, found herself clasping hands and linking arms with men and women in evening dress, fancy dress, and day clothes. Some were masked, some not. Some were less steady on their legs than others. What all had in common was enjoying themselves. Whoops, laughs and rallying cries punctuated the music. There was great applause at the end of a very hectic ten minutes. Lucilla was hot and glad to see freshly filled glasses on their table. A new bottle was in the ice bucket.

They touched glasses and she drank thirstily. She could feel her cheeks, already glowing, start to burn. She thought she'd better go and cool them in the cloakroom, but Joe, himself coloured up, put a hand on her arm.

'Don't worry. You look terrific. Soon as I can breathe I want to talk to you.'

He topped up their glasses. Lucilla was careful to take only a sip this time. Joe had left his other hand on her arm. He moved it down to her hand. She readily grasped it. He was looking at her intently, as if seeing her more than skin-deep. He slowly took off his mask. She moved to follow suit, but he stopped her again.

'No. It suits you. Mysterious.'

'I'm not mysterious.'

He didn't follow it up or start to tell her whatever it was he wanted to say. She didn't like to prompt. After some more moments he shook his head dismissively.

'No. It was just a thought. But, no.'

'What, Joe?'

'Forget it. You'd only be disappointed.'

'I will if you leave me wondering. Who's being mysterious now?'

He gave her hand a squeeze. 'Got carried away with the dancing. Well, all right, you're a sensible girl. No harm in telling you. It was us talking about Paris. Remember I was slow on the uptake about you at Roundhay Park? I guess this time I was being too quick.'

'How? Please, Joe.'

'Well, to be honest, the firm's not quite what it used to be. We aren't a Continental house any more. Our designs have got more and more English over the years. Bound to happen, I expect. They just aren't French modes any more, and it gets harder to sell them on the Continent.'

'I'd have thought a dress like this would sell anywhere.'

'With you in it, yes. Put a Frenchie woman into that and you'd see the difference straight off. Believe me, they're not the same shape. Or the Belgians. Especially the Dutch.'

'But you make them to measure.'

'I know, I know. It comes down to style. There's styles in women, like in what they wear. Frenchie women have got more idea of it than ours. They know what wouldn't suit.'

Lucilla said, 'They can't be all that different. Anyway, plenty of things you buy never look half as good as they did on show. It's like the theatre. If the audience could see close to they'd know it's tricks.'

The champagne had loosened her tongue, and lecturing her boss had embarrassed her. She covered up by taking another swig.

'You amaze me more and more,' Joe said. 'Simply amaze. I never met a girl in all my many days who could hit a nail on the head like you. You've seen it exactly. The whole fashion business. What it's about. Put the most fabulous gown ever created on the wrong woman, and phut! Pour the right girl into it, and pow!'

Praise for her intelligence stirred Lucilla in a way that compliments on her looks didn't. She felt excited. Bold enough to suggest what she sensed he'd been on the verge of saying.

'Use English girls to model over there. Haven't you ever done that?'

He was shaking his head slowly in wonderment at her brilliance.

'Thought of it. Even got old Ted to see it might be worth giving a try, but for the snags.'

'What snags?'

'Jealousy. Prejudice. Think all fashion begins and ends with them, the Frenchies. Hard enough to get them to look at things on French models. Lovely girls, some of them. Naturals. But not in London modes.'

'There you are, then. Use English models.'

Joe laughed. 'Such as *you*, you mean.'

'*Me*?' Her surprise was less than sincere.

'That's the idea I'd had.'

'But . . . but I've only just started.'

'You started the morning you were born, my dear. Well, that afternoon.'

'Then . . . why did you say to forget about it?'

He did his melodramatic trick of looking round, as if expecting to find listeners gathered about their table. He picked up his mask and put it on, before leaning forward to speak lower.

'The *age* thing. Remember?'

'You said forget that, too.'

'This is different. There'd be passports, work certificates. They can get ugly over there. Hate competition. Love to catch us out. It's too risky.'

In her eagerness to get her glass to her mouth Lucilla spilt a little wine down her chin. She freed her other hand to dab at it with a napkin. That lack of three-and-a-bit years had been got over easily enough once. She wasn't going to let it rob her of a chance like this.

'Can't it be fixed?'

He hesitated. 'It's not only the Frogs. There's old Ted.'

'You got him to turn a blind eye before.'

'Like I said, this is too official. False declarations and all that. He'd never have it on. Sorry it slipped out, love. My fault. We might give it a try with one of the older girls. Then, if it goes well . . .'

'Like hell!' Lucilla said.

It was her turn to look round. The noise was so great that no one could have heard. Not that they would have cared. She had shocked herself, though, swearing at him.

He seemed amused. 'Strength of character, too.'

'Please, Joe. I'd give anything for something like this.'

But he still shook his head. 'If it was just my say-so, I'd chance it. You know that. But, Ted . . .'

The wine swept her frustration beyond any point of caring.

'It isn't fair! You just said I'd be ideal. If trade's rotten over there it might all be shut down by the time I'm old enough. Then I won't even have had the chance. Joe – *please*!'

She was pleading like a child again. She knew, but didn't care. He took her hand and she squeezed his so hard that he grimaced. The din of other people enjoying themselves while she despaired maddened her. She could have flung the champagne bottle and everything else off their table into that grinning, capering mob. She wrenched off the silly mask. Joe took his off, too. He took both her hands. She needed no pulling towards him. He kissed her, firmly, tenderly, pledgingly.

'Leave it to me, love.'

'Oh, Joe, yes.'

'Don't let on to anyone. It'll need managing.'

She kissed him. 'You'd still be coming there sometimes, wouldn't you?'

'Try keeping me away.'

'No fear of that. Ever.'

CHAPTER 19

CRIME FOR A CRIME

JENNY went next day. Old Mazurka told Nightbone when he came back to the shop a couple of days later.

'A bird in a cage. What? Never still. I know she goes soon.'

He led Nightbone through to the back and gave him a slip of paper:

DEAR MR M.,

THANKS YOU FOR TAKYNG ME IN I DINT KNOW WERE TO GO. WILL BE ALRIGHT NOW AND TELL N. NOT TO BOTHER, ITS STILL A SHAME BUT I WONT PUT MY ORE IN AND STIR IT UP.

YRS FAITHFULLY,

J. JACKS

PS. LEFT R'S THINGS AS FOUND.

Nightbone handed it back. Her flit didn't surprise him. She was the last sort to hang about doing nothing, especially without a drink. He had expected it might resolve itself like this. Hoped it would.

Mazur was glad, too. He hadn't been sure how to handle her. He had been tempted briefly to give her some money to go to a pub, but thought she would simply run off with it or reappear drunk and bring down disgrace on him. He compromised by getting in a bottle of gin. It proved a complex operation. He didn't use drink, and didn't wish to be known to have bought any. It would have given the locals ideas that he was fallible after all. On the other hand, going out himself to find a dealer in spirits who wasn't too adjacent meant leaving the shop for an unprecedented time. He contemplated asking Jen to serve, but quickly thought again. She was unmistakably what she was. It would stimulate business briefly, as all his customers flocked in to look at her, but his status would be in ruins, along with his family trade.

He gritted his teeth, locked up, and sped to Oxford Street. He was not away more than half an hour. He rushed the bottle into the kitchen cupboard where the coffee was, then hurried out to harangue his mystified and inconvenienced customers. When eventually he went back to the parlour to see if the bottle was gone he found it still unopened with her note under it.

It was early afternoon when he showed Nightbone the note. Raining and windy, and dark already. Customers were a blessed unlikelihood. Nightbone sat down opposite him. The fire in the range between them had been left to burn out.

'So, now she is gone, maybe we talk a while,' Old Mazurka suggested. 'She won't split on you?'

'I doubt it. You didn't tell her where I'm stopping?'

'No. You like Martini's place?'

'Does he owe you?'

'Plenty. I call it in and break him when I choose. I leave him there instead. I know some day I can use him.'

'Have you tried?'

'I use his place, not him. I put you in there. I use you.'

'Does he know the story?'

'Not from me.'

'But you think there's a connection?'

'You see his type?'

'Hard not to.'

'He has plenty friends the same. He escapes trouble in the past, but still he plays with fire. He runs a club near his house for them. He procures men and boys. He is of that type.'

'What about females?'

'He trains them only for models. Like a dancing master. For the rag trade. The best houses. He trains their girls and hires them men. One house is named Maurice et Cie. It is where Becky was. It is enough connection for Old Mazurka. What?'

'The man worked there?'

'In Paris. He has his own business. He comes to London for trade. He meets Becky at Maurice. He offers a better job.'

'Frenchman?'

'Is Robinson French?'

'Did you meet him?'

'She is going to bring him, but I tell her I don't want to know him.'

'Young? Old? Did she say?'

'Smart young fellow, maybe. I don't ask.'

'Was she walking out with him?'

'She's a good girl, Becky. There's nothing like that.'

'Did she want the job in Paris?'

'I wonder since. She brings home papers. I have to sign to give permission.'

'You refused?'

'At eighteen?'

'How did she take it?'

'She doesn't do nothing her papa and mamma don't want.' Mazur glanced round his dingy, untidy room. 'It wasn't so bad then. Her mamma keeps it good. But ... She is young. Maybe she's disappointed. Who can know with a girl today? What? It's not like in the old days. The old country. Maybe her mamma and me don't understand. I don't know.'

'These papers she brought ...'

'I throw them in the stove, to show her what I think.'

'Can you remember any of the particulars?'

'I don't read them. I don't want to hear.'

'What about her employers?'

The yellow eyes blazed back. The grin was a snarl.

'You know what? There comes one of her bosses from there. She isn't turning up for work. He believes she runs off. She owes for clothes and wages. Fifty pound. He demands I pay. Fifty quid, for losing her! You know what the police tell me? What? I must pay. Crazy!'

'Didn't they ask him about Robinson?'

'He never heard of him. Fifty quid! They treat you bad, Nightbone? You see how their crazy laws treat Old Mazurka? Now you see why I pay you everything for him.'

Jenny hadn't gone straight back to Ma Costigan's. She didn't go to the cellar, either. She wanted a drink. Several drinks. It was cash down in both establishments, and she hadn't any. She went instead to a public house on the edge of the beat she and Nell had shared. It was one of those where Nightbone had come searching for her.

'Here, where've you bin?' she was greeted by Hetty, the large young woman who had spoken sorrowfully of Nell to him. 'They're saying you've gone off with that Nightbone.'

'Nightbone? *Me*? Give us a brandy straight, love. Pay you soon as I'm earning.'

She sighed as she tossed it down. 'Another with a splash, ta.'

'But where've you bin?' Hetty persisted, pouring and splashing.

'Wanderin' round. Couldn't get over Nelly. What's that about Nightbone?'

Hetty told her the tale. Jen responded with the proper mixture of contempt for the police, qualified sympathy for Nightbone, vulgar derision of Bailey Watts, and a request for just one more brandy. She took over the initiative.

'What about Bailey, then? Nightbone sorted him out yet?'

'Nobody's seen neither of 'em. Your friend Bodger's gone, too.'

'Bodger? Friend of mine!'

She knew where Bailey lodged. After finishing the third brandy she went there.

'Here! What're you arter?' demanded the unkempt hulk she took to be his landlord. He had found her on the stairs, wondering which might be Bailey's room.

'Just visiting. Fancy a tickle, ducks?'

His dull eyes opened and he licked his lips.

'I ain't payin'.'

'Who said? Mr Watts owes me. He'll pay.'

'Like 'ell 'e will. I flogged his stuff to the barrowman. Didn't fetch what I'm owed.'

'Done a moonlight, has he?'

'Wouldn't you, expectin' that Nightbone coming arter you? Come on, then. In 'ere.'

'Where's he gone, the swine? He owes me, too.'

'Said 'e was orf to his quack's. In a real state, arter that bashin'. I could go thruppence.'

Jen had got between him and the street door. 'Ho, no. Nothing under three guineas at today's prices. Let me know when you've saved up.' She nipped out of the door and round the corner before he could curse her. In at a public-bar door, straight out the back, and she was clear and walking quickly away.

She made for Paddington. She knew where Bailey's doctor hung out. Anything to make a bob, Bailey had arranged for the local girls to go there when they'd got up the spout. Jen had been there herself. There had been one time when she'd feared she was getting the glim. Not wanting it spreading that she'd been seen at a regular pox doctor's, which was beneath her dignity anyway, she'd paid Bailey to get his chum to give her the once-over. The way the man had handled her showed her that he and Bailey were two of a kind when it came to women. She remembered the mews house where he'd examined her. Luckily for her, she hadn't needed any longer acquaintance with it or him.

She went in cautiously. Once again she was listening in a narrow hall, at a couple of doors shut on silent rooms. No one seemed to be about. She went quietly up the stairs, not touching the banisters which looked creaky. She was going on up the further stair to the attics when she heard a moan. It froze her. Then she crept up to the top and listened at the only door there. The moaning was inside. The key was in the lock. She had to turn it.

She found Bailey as he reached the bottom of the pit of his torment.

Some of those who would not yield under *peine forte et dure* were allowed 'humane' release. A sharp wooden block was put under their back. When the weights became too heavy for the spine to bear it snapped across the block. Friends sometimes paid the torturer to let them hasten things by jumping on the victim. Bailey Watts had no such easement. Jenny stood staring at the ghastly pale yet sweating face on the ravaged pillow. The head moved ceaselessly from side to side. The hands twitched outside the sheet. Low rattling moans, like troubled snores, came on each jerky breath. The washed-out eyes were wide open but unseeing. She'd imagined tracking him down smug and full of himself, with feigned injuries and lying low from Nightbone. Seeing him like this, she didn't know what to do. There was a little water in a scaly glass. She tried putting it to Bailey's cracked lips. His head's movement made it spill and dribble uselessly down his stubbled chin. She put the glass down and steeled herself to a grisly task.

It was nothing new to Jenny Jacks to pull up a recumbent man's nightshirt. No woman was more familiar with and indifferent to the sight exposed. What she found this time startled and horrified her.

The swollen belly was one huge blotch of angry colours: red, black, green, grey, blue. It seemed straining to burst at any second and gush with those same vile hues.

'My God!' she said aloud. Averting her look, she quickly covered up the sight. She tried again with the water. Moistening the sheet's edge, she dabbed the restless brow and wiped around the eyes.

'Bailey,' she called into his coma. 'Bailey. Try to speak. You got to. It's . . .'

She had been about to speak her name, but hesitated. Sudden inspiration made her say instead, 'It's Nell. Nelly Jacks.'

It worked dramatically. The head abruptly stopped swivelling. The eyes blinked several times, struggling to focus. Jen moved her face closer to them, guessing it would make it harder for him to see she wasn't her sister.

'Nelly,' she repeated. 'Come to see how you're doing, Bailey.'

His wild gaze was trying to concentrate. She leaned her face even nearer, then suddenly pulled it back, before approaching again, still closer.

'Why'd you do it, Bailey?' she half-whispered. 'What'd I done to you?'

The thin lips twitched but shaped no word. Jen tried all she could think of – water, the damp sheet, Nelly's name and then her own. Nightbone's, even. Twice she thought he might speak, but he only moaned.

She thought she heard a sound downstairs. If Bailey had been left locked up in this state, she knew what she'd get if she were found. From across the room by the door he looked a goner already. His head was still and his eyes open. Faint movement of his fingers on the sheet was a surviving flicker of life. Jen slipped out. She shut the door quietly, remembering to turn the key. She crept down the two flights. There *was* a noise. It came from the basement.

She made a short tiptoed dash for the front door. Once she was out she didn't look right or left. She just walked and walked. Nobody came from behind to drag her back. She was soon in crowds and clear.

Her strength of purpose sagged as she trudged back towards Ma Costigan's. She needed to start earning again. At once, or Ma would sling her out. Then it would be out on the street for as long as she lasted. She hadn't energy or will to try to set herself up afresh.

The thought gave her the shudders. On the higher slopes the fog was creeping back. The air had that smell of chilly wet iron. The street lamps were blurring already. Deep autumn was advancing on all sides. She shivered again. Maybe she'd been better off in Turkey. At least they didn't have peasoupers.

CHAPTER 20

WALKING OUT

'Miss Poole. Lucilla. I'm going to give you a surprise.' Mrs Goldman had surprised her already by drawing her aside, with some indications of secrecy, into the little room where she had first measured her. The door was shut and they sat on the sofa.

'You're coming along splendidly. I'm going to give you the chance to walk out this evening.'

Lucilla just managed to stop herself exclaiming. Her expression gave her away. Mrs Goldman smiled.

'Sooner than you'd expected? Between ourselves, it's well before I'd risk it with most. There'll be a little jealousy if it gets known. See how highly I think of you?'

'You're very kind to me, madam.'

'Your outings with Mr Joe will have given you confidence.' (It surprised Lucilla that she knew of them.) You'll find it very different with a total stranger. I mean, not a professional.'

This was a further surprise. She had understood the term 'walking out' to refer only to going with partners in the same line. Mrs Goldman went on to explain.

'Our clientele is very widespread. Home and abroad. Gentlemen visiting London come to us for gifts to take back to their ladies. A hat, gloves, a gown on approval. If the lady likes it – they always do – it's sent back to us with her measurements and recreated for her alone. Maurice et Cie is known as *the* place to find that service. We have by far the biggest range. Our exclusive designs really are exclusive, and our discretion is known to be cast-iron.'

'How do you mean discretion, madam?'

'Perhaps you haven't learnt yet that men who buy ladies' clothes very seldom do so for their own wives. Wives buy their own. A gentlemen might talk a lot to you about his wife – you'll find they often do – but he's almost certainly admiring the clothes you're modelling with someone different in mind. They don't tell you as much about those. Whatever you hear – about *anything* – must go in one ear and out the other. That's discretion.'

'And we have to go out with these gentlemen?'

'There's no question of *having to*, my dear. It's a privilege reserved to only the top two or three. You're at liberty to decline.'

'Oh, no! I didn't mean that.'

'I'd have been disappointed if you had. You're not shocked?'

'No, madam.'

'You need a broad mind, too, in this trade. Anything where luxury is concerned. But I can see you wondering how far you're expected to go to please these valued customers. There's a very simple answer, Lucilla. You do nothing whatever that isn't decent and in public. You refuse absolutely to go into any places where there aren't other people. If any suggestion of that sort is made to you, you refuse. Politely, but absolutely. It's their privilege to be allowed to spend the evening with you. Not many are. And evening does not mean night. Does that set your mind at rest?'

Lucilla assured her it did. Uncle Ed and Langenbach had been enough in that line. Joe would be different. But no one else till him. She listened interestedly to Mrs Goldman.

'There are bound to be times when you won't find it easy. You'll be treated to rich food and drink, but it's up to you to keep control of yourself. You'll find yourself praised and flattered, as well as the clothes. You accept that as any girl would. But just occasionally you might have suggestions made to you that go beyond what we expect from a privileged customer. You might be offered money, gifts, all sorts of promises. You must refuse everything of that sort. Then you must report it to me. Without fail. This is one of the strictest rules governing your employment. Do you understand it clearly?'

'Quite clear, madam.'

'It's for your own safety as much as our reputation. We can't watch how these men behave with you. We can only rely on what you tell us. But what you do tell me must be completely truthful. No half-truths. No inventions. We can deal with it quietly if we need to, but we must be sure of absolute facts.'

'I understand, madam.'

'Good. Now, Lucilla, in that connection I've a warning to give you that might not sound kind. It is that if you break any of these rules or give any offence to a customer other than by refusing overtures of that kind, you will be dismissed at once. Mr Ted is not one to listen to excuses. You'll be sent packing, and the company will make sure that you or your parents – guardians, in your case – pay back every penny owing for clothes, lodgings, training, and broken contract. That's a great deal of money, you realize?'

'Yes, madam.'

'The last thing we'd want is for you to feel you're some sort of slave. You've got an idea of what modelling involves. You can see there's more to it than beauty, or many more could get in. I don't talk like this to all my girls, because only a few are ever worth it. But you are, Lucilla. So you must realize that if you go through with this evening's engagement satisfactorily, you can go on to all the things we can offer you. If you find it too much to manage, and don't wish to be considered for that sort of work again, you must come and tell me. You could work out your notice in the stockroom so that you could leave without any penalty. It's up to you.'

Mrs Goldman stood up, glancing at the watch at her waist.

'Only remember that a girl's prime isn't very long. It would be no use ever blaming anyone but yourself for what you'd let slip by.'

Lucilla had risen too. 'No!' she said emphatically. 'I want to go on.'

Quit the stage, with the curtain only just up, and all her big scenes still to play? Not likely!

The businessman from Southampton came by hansom cab to Flobell Select Lodgings for Ladies. He was in evening clothes. Tall, though not exceptionally so, and well built. Quite good looking. He would be about thirty.

'More man than some of them,' Floss murmured to Belle. 'Angelo must be casting his net wider.'

'Looks can deceive,' her partner reminded her.

They were standing shoulder to shoulder, peering into the separate lenses of an optical device in their parlour wall. It gave a magnified view of the lobby, where the spyholes were too insignificant and cleverly placed to be spotted. The landladies believed in keeping an eye on their residents' interests, though without being seen to be doing so. One couldn't be too careful nowadays.

'Army, perhaps?' Floss suggested.

'Ex-, no doubt. The usual trouble. Might almost have been police with that build. I didn't think they went in for that.'

'Would Angelo risk a bobby?'

'There must be quite a few glad of the job. They don't owe the force any favours. He might well trawl one or two, even if they're not queer. Pay them well enough and they might have other uses.'

'There she is!' Floss exclaimed. She pressed closer to the lens to see Lucilla come downstairs in a blue velvet dress with an elaborately embroidered waistcoat and lace jabot, and silvery-grey directoire coat. 'Oh, she is lovely, that one.'

Belle gave her a sideways glance.

'Don't you get making a fool of yourself again.'

'Oh no, dear. I wouldn't dream.'

'Dream if you must, but that's all. Remember what I warned you last time.'

'Yes, Belle.' A few months ago Belle had ambushed her fondling a handsome dark Welsh girl lodger. The girl had been sent packing. Belle had given her partner what amounted to a beating-up. She had watched her jealously since.

They returned to the eyepieces. But for glancing away they might have detected a quickly suppressed reaction by the visitor to his approaching escort. He recovered himself instantly.

Nightbone had added only slightly to the change that being out of uniform had made. He hadn't had to use disguise in his work, but he knew that detectives considered the simple effects best. Nothing to attract curiosity. Definitely nothing false that might slip, or run, or fall off. He had got a barber to recut his hair, so that it parted down the middle instead of the left side. That was all. That and being Mr Hilling, from Southampton.

Lucilla didn't recognize him, so briefly and differently seen before. All her thoughts were concentrated on the impression she would produce. Whether she could make the assignment the success that her future hung on. They shook hands.

'How do you do, Mr Hilling?'

'Pleased to meet you, Miss Poole.'

He had known her straight away. King's Cross. Upright carriage. Chin high. Yellow hair. Luggage on the ground. Great Titchfield Street. At first sight then he'd thought her older than she'd proved close to. Now she was older again. Differently, though. He'd taken her first for a lady. Then for a girl playing at being one. Now he realized.

Something to do with professional get-up. Provincial girl with a bit of style, new to London, new to life, on the first step to being a fashion model. It quite amused him that he'd been made part of her training.

Angelo had said that morning, 'Feeling ready to make a start, Robby?'

'What, already?'

'I told you how busy we are. Maurice et Cie have asked for a man this evening. They particularly want one their girl hasn't met. I was able to tell them I had just the chap.'

'What's the idea?'

'Brand new girl. First time out. Normally, one would send an experienced hand, to help her confidence. They don't want that. They believe they've found something special. They mean to try her out. Toss her in, and see how well she swims.'

'Sounds like me, too.'

'In a way. It's a happy chance. It will teach you a lot.'

Nightbone laughed out. 'So long as she doesn't.'

'Now, now! She's being told you're a good customer of theirs from out of town for a nice evening out with Maurice et Cie's compliments. You must play up to that. Don't even hint you're in the business, too. They don't want her thinking she can afford to make a few mistakes. They want her on her mettle.'

'I'm the one could make the mistakes.'

'Nonsense. You've both been to the same school. Equally well taught, since I'm teaching both of you. I assure you, she knew little more when she started a few days ago than you did. She'll be so busy trying to impress you, she wouldn't notice if you used your dessert spoon for the peas. Or think it a rich man's eccentricity.'

'Rich, am I?'

'You'll give that impression. Her firm pays in the end.'

'She's bound to see I'm not a gent.'

'Businessmen seldom are. A customer's a customer, is the theory. Treat him well and he'll come back.'

'Didn't you say these judies are strictly hands-off?'

'Just remember it – if you need reminding. But there are others available for the right customers. Not only females. One thing can lead to all sorts. You'll learn. I told you, Angelo has all the connections.'

In the cab from Flobell's, Mr Hilling told Miss Poole he hardly knew London. Only started making big money recently. Just beginning to find out what it could do. He tapped his pocket. Wherever she wanted to go would suit him. Following Mrs Goldman's advice, she directed the cabby to Earls Court. Joe Pearson had included it in their first evening's round. She knew what to do there. One of Maurice et Cie's membership passes was in her purse.

The vast showplace was thronged, awash with movement and light, music and laughter. Oncoming winter would soon end the season. Life would be duller for those who nourished their spirits on the skating rink and the dance floor, the big wheel and the roller coaster. The nutriment provided at the bandstands and the bars, the theatre, the diorama, the shopping avenue, the lake, and by the strolling crowds themselves would be withheld. The patrons were out in force, greedy to lap up as much as might sustain them through the drear months.

Lucilla's pass gave them admittance to the Welcome Club, which had its own dining room and outside lounge all along a side of one of the squares. To both their secret relief there was a *Table d'Hôte* menu available. Lucilla chose easily and Nightbone said he would keep her company by having the same. He invited her to choose the wine. Following Signor Martini's rules it gave her no problem.

Now that he had been given her background he could hear her faint northern accent. She spoke well, though, without seeming to have to put it on. She certainly showed herself confident at table. He felt easy with her. They chatted about London, from their strangers' point of view. About the dynamiters, and the fighting in the East. About the people around them. With the excellent meal inside them they went to sit outside, to watch the passing parade. With so much happening, and so much light and noise, they felt no coldness, sitting with liqueurs beside them and Nightbone taking the opportunity to luxuriate with a cigar.

'Look at that chap in the straw boater!' he said. 'Girl with the white boa. Passed each other twice. Sizing up. Next time, *click*. What'd I tell you?'

Lucilla laughed. She, too, was wholly at ease now. She had been careful to drink hardly anything. He didn't seem to notice. He didn't drink much, either, but he was obviously enjoying himself. If this was walking out, it suited her. She'd known her place was sitting at a table, not waiting on one. Seeing her like this would make old Frau Langenbach's eyes pop.

Mr Hilling was being considerateness itself. Bob, rather. He'd insisted on exchanging Christian names. She wasn't sure what Mrs Goldman would have ruled about that. He'd admired the dress and coat. She'd been told not to say anything that sounded like sales talk, or ask about his business or private life. He volunteered nothing about either, about his wife or any other ladies. He seemed more interested in her.

'You don't want to know about me,' she objected coyly.

'Please.' He tilted his top hat down over his forehead, resting on his eyebrows. He lounged back, eyes shut, to listen.

She decided to tell him the truth. Apart from the matter of her age there was no point in not doing so. All she pretended was that she'd been with Maurice et Cie for some time. He might not be pleased to learn they'd palmed him off with a novice. She saw a flicker of surprise when she said she'd been a waitress. She'd thought briefly of saying actress, but it might sound too fast and give him ideas. She remembered Mrs Goldman's warning.

'Fairy tale come true,' he suggested, still not looking at her. She agreed.

'I can hardly believe it. It was the end of lunchtime. This young gentleman from London happened to be sitting by himself. Well, you probably know him. Mr Pearson. Mr Joe. Mr Ted's brother, who does the travelling.'

He only grunted. She realized that perhaps she oughtn't to talk about her bosses and how the firm was run. But she had to finish the story she'd begun of the way one thing had led to the others. She thought it couldn't hurt to mention the kind way Maurice et Cie were treating her. If it got back to Mr Ted it might please him. Anyway, she meant it. Sitting in the privileged enclosure at Earls Court, with a glass of *creme de menthe* at her hand, and wearing an outfit that would knock them in a heap in that posh shop back in Bond Street, she felt years away from Aunt Doris's.

'What's amazing,' she gushed, 'is that it's such a small world. I mean, all the folks in London to pick from, and I meet Belle and Floss at the railway station. And even if I hadn't, I'd probably have finished up at their place all the same. Isn't that a fluke?'

'Incredible,' he agreed.

He daren't question her particularly. If he'd been trained as a detective he would have known ways to get more information without seeming to ask for it. The questioning he'd been used to was of the blunter kind that expected admission or flat denial. That kind needed the authority of a uniform over subjects who knew better than to give any fancy stuff. It was not for using on a pretty supper partner who was only earning a crust the same way as himself.

He had to be careful, too. For all he knew she might be questioned about how the evening had gone and how Angelo's new man had managed. Perhaps they'd been set to test one another without either knowing. She might be more experienced than she'd let on, able to tell a story about herself that would tell her things about him. She might indeed be older than she seemed. He didn't think so. Through her professional poise he could still recognize the uncertain girl he'd helped at the railway station. A girl playing at being a woman. Striving to be one, but not there yet.

He could see nothing flukey or incredible in the smooth way things had worked out for her. He couldn't be sure that her kindly landladies were professional pickers-up of forlorn females. They sounded like it. And from what Jenny Jacks and Mazur had told him of the procuring game he thought Lucilla Poole a natural target. But she obviously believed in her good luck and was following it up eagerly. He didn't dare question it.

He was under orders to deliver her back at her lodging no later than ten thirty. The beginnings of another fog were showing. He paid the bill and they left Earls Court in a cab, whistled up for them by a chucker-out.

The fog thickened as they rode eastward. By the time he saw her into Flobell's lobby it was looking like the makings of another pea-souper. The landladies still didn't appear. With his suspicions now thoroughly alert, Nightbone had a strong feeling of being watched as he shook Lucilla's hand and gave a little bow.

'Once again, Lucilla – Miss Poole – I've enjoyed myself very much.'

'My pleasure, I'm sure, Mr Hilling.'

'I hope we meet again.'

'You never know.'

He sauntered out without looking back. He stood for some moments as if making up his mind where to go next. Then he started strolling in a casual manner towards the Tottenham Court Road. He drifted from there to the junction with the Euston Road, where the traffic was heavy in all directions. He joined a crowd crossing the road and then turned his steps determinedly northward. When he had gone a few hundred yards, and was sure he wasn't being followed, his tread fell into the policeman's rhythm, regular as a machine. In unaccustomed evening pumps, his feet took him back into familiar terrain towards Pentonville. As he went, he pulled his dark coat across his chest. Partly so as to cover himself against the wet chill of the gathering fog, but also to mask the gleam of an evening shirtfront. Silvered buttons had been meant to be seen. For a change, Nightbone preferred to pass unnoticed.

The fog filled the street where Jenny had been alternately standing and pacing. She was chilled through. Her nerves were rotten. She wanted to give up and go back to Ma Costigan's kitchen for a warm and a wet, but she was still flat skint. There'd been no trade, and wasn't likely to be now. Her rent would run out tomorrow. She was hanging on, hoping against hope for just one feller.

She heard the footsteps coming. They were light, not like the clump of ordinary boots. She stuck out her hip and rested her hand on it, ready with her 'Hello, darling.' The dark shape, steaming with fog, loomed quicker and closer than she'd expected. It made her gasp. Nobody else was about. She was suddenly scared.

'Jen,' she heard.

'Who . . . ?'

'Keep it down.'

'What d'you want?'

'Shut up and listen . . .'

'There's somebody coming . . .'

There wasn't but he saw she was going to cry out. He grabbed her arm with one hand and clapped the other over her mouth.

She tried to scream, but she couldn't. As he held her helpless she thought about him and Nell.

CHAPTER 21

A SCENT OF HERBS

'WHAT's it to do with me?' she demanded. She reached for the gin bottle. Nightbone got it first. He poured a little for her, then kept the bottle beside him. 'Silly little cow sounds ready made for them.'

Nightbone glanced at Mazur across his parlour table. The grin was fixed, the yellow eyes impassive. He hadn't winced at a reference that could have been applied to his daughter.

Jen stared sullenly into her glass. Nightbone had as good as dragged her into a cab, stifling her cries. The cabby hadn't asked questions. He didn't want trouble in a dark, foggy place. He'd done as he was told and driven them to Mazur's. Nightbone had to hold her fast all the way. Often his hand went back over her mouth. She'd squirmed and heaved. Whenever she could get a hand free she'd tried to claw. She was like a struggling cat, but he was much too strong for her.

She'd been really scared when he'd come on her sudden like that. In her state of near-panic she could believe anything of him and what he meant to do. It had taken her half the journey to realize that if he meant to kill her he'd have done it out there in the fog. He'd hardly have hung around, keeping her from screaming or running away until a cab came along. During the journey he said a couple of times that she needn't be afraid. He was taking her back to Mazur's, where she'd have a room for the night. There was some gin waiting. The last touch made her extra suspicious. Perhaps he was in with white slavers. Thought they might give him something for getting her back. No knowing what a busted cop might try.

He'd bundled her in through the back door. The old fellow was hunched over his table, doing nothing. He looked surprised to see them. Jen could tell there wasn't anything going on between him and Nightbone over her. Nightbone locked the door and took the key out. He went to the cupboard where the bottle was. He put it in front of her, and a glass. She put wariness aside and went at the gin till he took it back out of her reach.

'I want your help, Jen.'

'That's a laugh.'

'Shut up and listen.'

'And who do you think you are?'

He ignored her and told them about his evening at Earls Court.

'That why you're got up like the dog's dinner?' she sneered. 'Nightbone. Taking a tart out to supper. Wouldn't know what to do with a tart on a dish.'

Mazur surprised her by interrupting firmly. 'Listen to him. Please.' She glanced at his grin, and the eyes, and obeyed.

Nightbone told them what Lucilla had revealed about herself and how she'd come to be a model.

'You know the game, Jen. Is she being set up?'

'Sticks out a mile.'

He glanced at Mazur again. He had to risk Jen contradicting her version of Rebecca's death. The living girl mattered more than the dead one.

'Sounds like she'll love it,' she scoffed. 'Can't wait to get on her back. Anyway, what you asking for? Gone soft on her? Don't say you're thinking of buying her out! I'll tell you something for nix. Try and horn in there and they'll make dog's meat of her.'

'Who are they?'

'How should I know?'

Mazur intervened again. 'Jenny, when you come here, the first time, you don't want for Old Mazurka to go on wondering about Becky. What? Why do you do that?'

'He made me.'

'Why does he make you? Because of something you tell him?'

'Ask him. It wasn't my idea. Then or now.'

'You come to tell me Becky is lucky because she is dead. Is this girl also lucky if she is dead?'

'Words! I don't know what you're both on about.' She beat the table. 'For God's sake, give us a drink!'

148

Nightbone held the bottle over her glass but didn't pour. 'Would you have wanted Nell to go through it?'

'She's dead, lucky cow.'

Mazur said gently. 'He is trying to help. Not only this girl. Many more. He only asks if you know these people.'

'Here! Are you paying him?'

'Maybe.'

'So that's it! That's why he's acting so interested. Well, make sure he delivers before you cough up. Doesn't always finish his jobs, doesn't Nightbone.'

Nightbone trickled more gin into the glass. It silenced her enough for him to tell her what Mazur was paying him for.

'That's great,' she said. 'If I'd a load of tin you'd find who did Nelly?'

'I pay him for you, too,' Mazur said.

She got the last drop from the glass. 'Chuck your tin in the river, mister. He won't do it. Will you, Nightbone? Too near home, what happened to Nell. And Bailey. What about Bailey? Got an eyeful, did she? What did she see you doing to him? Afraid she would split, were you? Poor bitch with a soft spot for you? For *you*!'

She made a sudden lunge and got the bottle. Nightbone nearly upset the table to come round to her. Mazur accidentally got in his way. The confusion gave her time to guzzle almost all the remaining gin. She threw the bottle away, cackling triumphantly. Her laughter turned into a coughing fit. Nightbone dragged her back to her chair, sagging already from the huge last draught, her eyes starting to close. He shook her angrily. She slumped against him.

He shrugged at Mazur. Then he picked her off the chair and heaved her lolling over his shoulder. Mazur went first up the stairs, to hold Rebecca's room door open. Nightbone put her gently on the bed. He undid her bodice and Mazur covered her. She was snoring already. They locked her in and went down. Mazur picked the bottle off the floor.

'You move quick, Mr Nightbone.'

'Those Pearson brothers . . .' Nightbone began to ask.

'It was Ted Pearson comes here. After Becky is gone. Wanting their money. Fifty pound for losing her!'

'The other?'

'I never meet him.'

'Where the girl's lodging. Flobell's, Newman Street.'

'I've seen it.'

'Landladies called Floss and Belle. Any connection with Rebecca?'

'I don't hear any.'

'Can you keep her safe till morning? Angelo may be waiting up for me.'

Mazur flourished the bottle in a gesture of braining someone. Nightbone nodded.

'I mean *keep* her this time. We need her. She's our link.'

He picked up his top hat and went into the fog again.

'I didn't expect you'd be so late, Robby.'

'Don't say you've sat up for me, Angelo.'

'Your first engagement.'

'Very inconsiderate of me, then. If I'd have thought, I'd have come back sooner. Mind if I have a drop of your port?'

'Sit down and I'll give you it. Tell me how it went this evening.'

'Nice bit of goods, as you said.'

'Is that all? Where did you go?'

'Earls Court. Good health!'

'We don't say "good health" with port.'

'Learn something all the time from you, Angelo.'

'A fair step, Earls Court. I trust you got her home by her time?'

'On the dot. You aren't narked with me, are you?'

'Disappointed, shall we say. It struck me a teeny bit ungrateful. I thought perhaps you'd got lost in the fog, but I reminded myself that her lodging is only five minutes from here. I wondered what else could be keeping you.'

'Just a stroll.'

'Whenever I looked out it was quite thick.'

'Still is. A man can be by himself in a fog. Those landladies strict about their birds, are they?'

'Like their employers. Quite a responsibility.'

'Bit of a temptation, though. Juicy morsels like that on the premises. Hire out a few latchkeys. Ever thought of it yourself? Nice discreet house like this.'

'Robby, I'm afraid I'm not enjoying this conversation. I should hate to have to ask you to leave, but my business is only as good as my reputation, which I hope I need not emphasize is spotless. If I were to hear the least whisper of gossip attributable to your rather uncouth mind I should have no alternative.'

'Hold on, mate! Uncouth I may be. Have I pretended? But what's this about gossip? Who do you suppose I go shooting my mouth off to?'

'I've really no idea. Your friend Mazur, for instance?'

'The old bloke at the shop? I told you, he isn't a friend of mine.'

'Just a little warning for you then. That crazy old man has one of the most wagging tongues in London. He can make something out of nothing at all, and does. All those customers of his, standing there lapping it up. He didn't manage to lend you anything, by any chance?'

'Manage? No. Come to think of it, he did offer.'

'He would. If you're short, Robby, come to me. And do keep your mouth shut about my business, there's a dear. For all our sake.'

'Trust me, Angelo.'

Nightbone grinned and winked. He finished his port and went off yawning to his room. The smell of herbs met him as he unlocked his door. His attentive landlord's search had been that thorough.

CHAPTER 22

BLOOD AND FLESH

BREAKFAST at Angelo's was a movable feast. Rich supping and hard-working evenings made his gentlemen boarders follow actors' habits, and sleep in late. There were their equivalent of matinees some afternoons, but mornings were mostly free. From about eight o'clock, though, Michael Angelo Martini himself seemed always on view, drifting about his rooms, reading his post, doing his accounts in a vestibule office whose wide-open door commanded a view of all comings and goings. The small staff of female domestics who did the housework and cooking kept to themselves in the basement kitchen and scullery, where, by needlessly unwritten rule, lodger's foot never trod.

Nightbone's habit of going on duty at all hours, for long, irregular stretches, didn't allow for lying in. He was up at seven, to a house that was still, apart from the parlourmaid's mouse-like scurrying. She offered cringingly to tell Cook that Mr Hilling wanted early breakfast. He told her not to bother, and went out.

When he had gone to bed a keen wind had been rattling his sash window and hooting in the chimney. Long before morning it had driven away all the fog. When he went out it was still gusting, whipping leaves off the plane trees. He strolled all round the square, looking casually at the house fronts, noting those with the pink and red shades. He made a point of not heading in the direction of Mazur's, just in case Angelo was watching. He was more interested in clearing his head of the fumes of last night's wine.

The smell of breakfast was in the house when he got back.

He ate heartily. Angelo was the only one who joined him. His air of suspicion seemed to have gone. He turned the meal into a further lesson in etiquette, and when it was over insisted on sacrificing an hour of his precious time to instructing Robby in further facets of the walking-out profession. Then he went to his office, saying that he must get his work done before going out to see a client about arrangements for an autumn trade showing. It was mid-morning before Nightbone could get away unseen to Mazur's shop. Old Mazurka was busy serving. There was no sign of Jen, though. Nightbone went up to the bedroom and looked in. When Mazur was able to come through to him his grin was not at its most marked. His manner was despairingly apologetic.

'She goes again. Like a cat. I listen at the door, and there's nothing. I take her some coffee and listen some more. Nothing. When I'm opening the door she flies out. Like a cat. With coffee in my hand what can I do?'

Nightbone swore one of his rare oaths. 'Did she say anything?'

Mazur shook his head. 'She must have planned it ready.' He passed a hand across his eyes. 'You stay and drink a cup?' He went out into his shop. Nightbone sat down heavily. He had been planning, too, while strolling around the square. He was sure he saw Lucilla's situation exactly. She was being put through a classic process. Hand-picked for it. Looks and ambition. No close family or friends. Fed up with her job, and under the threat of the dreaded mill. Tyrannized by her guardians and pestered by her employer. Suddenly flattered, encouraged, made to feel important. Well paid and accommodated.

He knew where it led from there. The best girls, the ones they could mould with pampering and promises and training, fetched prices that made them worth investing time and money in. Keeping sweet and intact till agents abroad had found a taker. It made no odds who that might be, so long as he was bidding highest and would take her far enough from England. A wealthy old rajah with a taste for nubile white wives. An exclusive South American brothelier. A Hong Kong trader, wanting to put his rivals in the shade. No further questions would be asked. Certainly no concern raised about how she might be treated or eventually end up. The merchandise of this trade was strictly disposable.

He guessed Rebecca hadn't been in the same class as Lucilla. They'd tried the soft approach, but dropped it as soon as her father got in the way. Simply snatched her for the eastern brothel trade, where there was always the biggest demand.

'I wanted to make her look at them all,' he told Mazur when he came through again. 'The landladies. These Pearsons. Martini. She'd been through the trade since she was twelve. She says she played along, so they had no reason to hide themselves from her. She only has to identify one.'

'How you plan to make her do it?'

'Promise her I'll find who killed her sister. It's all she cares about now. It's the only hold I've got over her. Until she knows, she'll keep coming back at me to find out.'

'She says you killed her.'

'That was the gin speaking.'

'You know who did?'

'I think so.'

'You really going to find out?'

'When I've time. Nelly's dead. This other girl's alive.'

'You work for me, remember?'

'For your money. We're on to Lucilla, being put through the system. We've got Jen, the only girl we know who's been through and come back alive. Thanks to you, we've this connection between Angelo and Maurice et Cie. And now me, with my nose in both. We're well placed. But it only wants one slip-up. Only one of them to get suspicious of any of us. They'll ship Lucilla out so quick we'll have lost her for good. They'll make sure Jen never opens her mouth again. I wouldn't doubt they'd make some arrangements for you and me. No, Mazur, I'm not working for you only. You aren't the only loser in this game. I made a deal with you because it's given me a chance I'd never have got without.'

The bell summoned Mazur once more. Nightbone poured himself coffee from the can, and considered.

He hadn't allowed for losing Jen again. He should have worked on her harder last night. Persuaded her to help. Made her, somehow. He couldn't go looking for her again. He didn't want to be seen on that patch, and for her to be spotted with him might be fatal for her. Anyway, he'd never get near her. She would be watching out. He couldn't get to Lucilla, either. As if she'd even listen to his warning. She'd tell someone and blow it all open.

Angelo's prying in his room was his least worry. He guessed he did the same with all his lodgers. There was nothing among his things to give away who he really was or what he'd been. His confidence on that score got a jolt, though, when Mazur came through from his counter.

'Your friend Martini. Just been in. Asking questions.'

'About me?'

'How long I know you. How you come here. What you tell me of yourself. Can he trust you in his house.'

'Did he ask if I've been back here?'

'Nothing direct. I told him I never seen you before or since.'

'Has he gone?'

'I watch him across the square. He doesn't look back.'

Nightbone told him of his room being searched. Mazur nodded. 'He suspects everybody. Me especially. He can't figure out what I do to him.'

'What way?'

'Like I say, he owes me plenty. He's afraid I lend him more.'

'I don't get that.'

'When a man fears too much is known about him, he pays for silence. What?'

'Blackmail.'

'And all the time he is scheming to get free.'

'Or goes to the police.'

'No police for Martini. And crazy English laws can't call Old Mazurka blackmailer, because I don't ask for nothing. Only lend.'

'You *make* him borrow?'

'Sure. Or I split. *Then* it's police for Martini.'

'I never heard of a blackmailer paying. What's the idea?'

'I keep him sweet. I keep him uneasy. He does what I want him, like taking you in his house. So he thinks you spy for me. He knows if he complains, I split.'

'I suppose you've got something on him?'

'Plenty. Him and his friends and their nancy house across the square.'

'The police aren't always interested.'

'What Old Mazurka knows interests them. Things even crazy laws don't allow.'

'White-slaving?'

'Not that. No women. Only men. Boys. Children.'

'If you've that kind of proof you have to inform.'

'Now you talk like a copper again.'

'Withholding evidence is a crime.'

The grotesque grin vanished abruptly. Nightbone was startled by a savagery in the warped features and yellow eyes more acute than he'd

seen in the most desperate criminal. The man's tone of voice became
correspondingly changed.

'You think I care? I care for nothing. Nobody. *I* am nothing. I am
only gelt, and what I know, and revenge. In this hand, tin. In this,
proof. Inside here' – he thumped his breast hard – 'revenge. Only this
in here matters. I spend all the tin. I use all the proof. I help you
through Martini to find this monster. Then I buy him, but I don't sell.
I keep him in stock.' He pointed to the floor. 'In the cellar. I keep him
while he pays me back, with compounded interest. For every day
since Becky goes he suffers an agony. I ration it to him. I save him for
it, day to day. All day and night he waits his next agony. And again.
And again. He knows he can never escape, and I will not let him die.
Not until I see I can hurt him no more. Then I leave him to rot. The
shop door says CLOSED. Everyone is wondering what has become of
Old Mazurka. At last they break in, and then they know they are safe.
Old Mazurka never calls in his loans.'

'No,' Nightbone said.

'You wait. You see.'

'I'd not let you.'

'You aren't a copper. We make a deal.'

'Not knowing this.'

'Now you know it, you're in it.'

'Don't try that, Mazur. Not with me. I understand your feelings.
I've bent the law sometimes. Maybe broken it, rather than let villains
walk over it. There's some laws no decent bobby ever would press.
But what you're planning doesn't belong anywhere. So, there's a man
somewhere who took your daughter. As good as murdered her,
maybe. You do a deal with me to find him. I think there could be a
chance. If we nail him, we hand him over with all the evidence you
can offer and I can get. Him and maybe some others, too. I'm with
you that far. But what you mean to do goes beyond human reckoning.
I won't have any hand in it, and I'll stop you.'

Mazur leaned forward. 'Where comes human reckoning? When a
monster can take away a maiden from her home? When he can keep
her a prisoner, weeping always for what she is become? Wishing she
may die? But not permitted, until God releases her, in a way so
terrible? Where comes human reckoning there, Nightbone? You take
the law in your hands. You take your own revenge. You will deny me
mine?'

'Don't forget me, while you're about it.'

It was a woman's voice. Mazur, who had his back to the door, spun round, shading his eyes. Nightbone saw her in silhouetted outline. For the briefest moment he thought he was seeing Rebecca. Or her ghost. It was Jenny.

She was wearing an uncharacteristic outfit of green and black checks and a small dark hat. The style was ridiculously young for her blowsy figure. The bodice bulged tightly across her chest, the sleeve cuffs were high up her forearms. But it made her look younger and more respectable than Nightbone had ever seen her.

She sat down to the table with them. Mazur fetched her a mug of coffee. She cocked her nose at Nightbone.

'Change of uniform,' she said.

'I'm glad to see you, Jen. Relieved.'

She looked surprised. 'I told him I'd be back soon as I could.'

Mazur's grin was almost sheepish.

'Didn't he let on?' Jen said.

'What have you been doing?' Nightbone asked.

'Better bobby than you, he'd make. Said certain parties needed looking over. If I put some of his girl's things on I could hang about without the likes of you moving me on. Clever, that. Bloody tight, though.' She released buttons at the front. They flew open, revealing a chemise-filled gap.

'Did you see anybody?'

'What do you think? If they were what you reckoned, they'd be hopping off to King's Cross to once-over the morning trains. Came out of their door like clockwork. Into a cab and off.'

Nightbone's normally steady heart thudded fast. 'Did you know them?'

'Old Belle Roche? Anywhere. Mister Minchin, we called her. Looks as if she found herself another missus since. I didn't know her.'

'What is this mister and missus?' Old Mazurka said.

'Ask Nightbone. I'm parched. And my head!'

She drank her coffee with an air of some triumph. Nightbone reminded Mazur how Mrs Minchin had bought Jenny from her mother and later shipped her abroad. Jen recovered to explain, not too politely, how Belle Roche had been Ma Minchin's partner in more ways than one. They'd split up when Mrs Minchin got off the baby-farming charge and retired to Brighton and respectability.

'I never heard of Belle starting up on her own,' she admitted. 'The lodging place could be legit. Just a front.'

'It's enough,' Nightbone said. 'Thanks, Jen.'

'Wasn't for you. For him.' She jerked a thumb at the shop door, where Mazur had gone through to serve. 'Felt sorry for him. Waking up in his girl's room. Listening to him scratching round down here on his own. That story you made up never washed.'

'You've told him?'

'What makes you think that?'

'Something he said about how she died. He knows.'

'Dead cunning, he is. Brought me coffee and sat on the bed jawing. Like I was her in her own room. Asked me bits straight out. Said he hadn't never believed in her getting drownded. I only told him bits. Honest. He could turn savage, that one. You can tell from their eyes.'

'So his bit about how you got away was eye-wash?'

Jen laughed. 'Fell for it, did you? I told him to say it. Run rings round you, telling fibs. Anyway, I helped you, didn't I? You going to help me now?'

'Soon as I can. This business has to be finished first.'

'Oh yeh. Your silly tart comes before me.'

'There's more to it than her. You've got time, and she hasn't. You have to trust me better, Jen. Stop here a few days. He'll pay for anything you want. No boozing or running off, though. I want you in one piece.'

'What's that mean?'

'Anyone thought you were on to them you could be in trouble.'

'You and me both. You ready to listen about Bailey?'

'Forget him. He'll keep.'

'That's what you think, Mr Clever!'

She told him, exulting in the surprise he showed.

'Who's in trouble if he's a goner?' she asked. 'Murder, isn't it?'

Nightbone walked the street several times before he went in. The hospital-house had no number but Jen had described it well. She had offered to come with him, though nothing was going to get her inside again. He'd preferred to come alone. Even in Rebecca's clothes she might just be recognized.

He could see no sign of life. The windows had the implacably sightless stare of an empty house. He went up and rang the bell. At the same time he surreptitiously tried the door. Jen's account of how she'd found it open and simply walked in had given him the shivers.

An unlocked door meant there was either someone inside or they'd just stepped out for a few moments. She'd been lucky to come out.

Its being locked now didn't guarantee anything. Dr Charles – it was the only name Jen knew him by – could be in there performing one of his operations and not able to answer the door. Rather than risk working the lock, Nightbone went round to the back. The mews was busy with men and lads grooming horses and polishing vehicles. No one seemed to have a glance for him. He walked briskly to the premises he wanted. Its coachhouse door was shut, with a look of disuse. There was no activity going on outside it, and the cobbles hadn't been wetted that day. He went unhesitatingly to the iron area steps and quietly down to the back door.

Again, he rang the bell. Twice. Between times he craned across to the barred window. A blind was drawn across, but no chink of light showed. Easily picking the lock with his penknife he slipped inside.

The smell in there made his scalp crawl. Blood.

The source was very close at hand. He was in a disused kitchen. The dim light allowed a faint gleam of equipment on a dresser. Going nearer he could make out knives, a cleaver, a small saw, enamel bowls, and various containers. A heavy table stood in the middle of the floor. No chairs surrounded it. There was nothing on it, but he could make out large dark stains. He forbore to test them with a finger.

His foot rang dully against a metal pail under the table, obviously full. The reek of blood and meat was as strong as from any open-fronted backstreet butcher's.

A deep sink contained further instruments of butchery, soaking in water smelling of disinfectant. A large can of Jeyes' Fluid stood on the draining board. Scrubbing brushes and cloths were near. Something draped over the sink's rim proved to be rubber gloves.

Nightbone had had his experiences of backstreet abortionists. The smell of human blood and sight of unhygienic squalor wasn't new. Never on this scale, though. The operation performed here had been a major one indeed.

He stood listening. Perhaps the doctor was upstairs, getting his patient to bed before coming back to clean up. Nightbone doubted it. He doubted there was enough of the patient left. With eyesight adjusted to the gloom he saw a mound of crumpled bedsheets. Near it was a roll of canvas. He found heavy string and a huge pair of tailor's shears. Going round the rest of the surfaces he was almost relieved not to find the kind of thing that would have clinched beyond doubt what had been going on. Having to handle it and wrap it into a bundle would have been beyond him.

The door at the top of the short staircase was shut. A voluminous rubber apron was draped over the banister. He avoided touching it as he went up the stairs and tried the door. It opened. He was through into a hall. It was dark and musty, but the smell of blood was left behind when he closed the door. He listened again, as Jenny had done in that same hall. Faint noises from the street in front and the mews behind were all he heard. Ignoring the ground floor rooms and the ones he passed on the way up he made straight for the top attic where she had found Bailey.

One look into the fetid room told him all he needed. The bedclothes she had lifted were gone. Only the pillow remained on the iron bed frame. The indentation of the head was still there. The clouded drinking glass Jen had put to Bailey's lips was empty on the small table. There was nothing else to show he had ever been there.

In fact, Eddy Watts's departure from this world had been as medieval as his last suffering. After *peine forte et dure* he had been drawn and quartered. The same once-dear friend whose hand had done it had made him into parcels, bundled them into a couple of sacks, and delivered them by cab to addresses in the Paddington area. Charles never found difficulty in disposing of the remains from his illicit operations. His male acquaintances included a number of medical students who welcomed subjects for dissection in their rooms. It was so much more satisfactory than having to share in class with a dozen others.

Nightbone didn't speculate on the way the remains had been dispersed. What it signified for himself, that Bailey Watts was gone as completely as if he had never existed, didn't occur to him then. All he thought about was the distant sound of the front door opening and closing.

He didn't stay to listen. He gave no consideration to creeping downstairs. He had no uniform, no handcuffs, no truncheon, no whistle. All in all, there was not much to be said for tackling, on his own blood-drenched ground, a maniacal butcher with a cleaver and scalpels to hand.

Nightbone climbed out of the window, heaved himself up to the roof, and emulated Tommy Cox's example.

CHAPTER 23

DOWN TO BODGER

'Lost your appetite, Robby dear? And all that walking!'

He wasn't pretending he couldn't eat. The reek of that blood-bathed room wouldn't go away. He imagined it clinging to his clothes, though no one had wrinkled his nose when he'd joined them at Angelo's ten-foot table for the communal lunch. It was still his only day suit, so he couldn't change. He'd hurried straight from that place, except for a brief call at Mazur's to make sure Jen was still there. He begged her to wait there till he could get back that afternoon. He didn't explain, but his way of asking and the look of his face convinced them there was something serious doing.

He returned a wry smile to Angelo, at the table's head.

'Your breakfast on top of all that rich stuff last night. Laying on my guts like lead.'

Angelo looked pained. The others laughed. There were half a dozen of them as well as him and Robby Hilling: the Wellingtonian Frank, the plump, suave Arthur, and four prettier young men, who seemed specially eager to please their landlord and mentor, smirking secretly at anything in the least witty Angelo uttered.

'My dear Robby, your Irish stew and boiled potatoes, and the rest of that curious fare they give to soldiers, will be soon but a ghastly memory. Champagne, oysters and *bombe glacé* shall be your rations.'

'Partial to exercise, are you, Robby?' asked Arthur.

'Habit. Marching miles a day. Take a while to settle down, I expect.'

'How dreary,' one of the young men commented.

'Only one sort of exercise you like,' his young neighbour jibed. 'Well, one or *two*.'

Angelo rapped the heel of his fork on the table top. He scowled at the speaker. 'Whatever you meant by that, Hamish, I fancy it was something crude and ugly. You know very well I don't permit such talk at my table.'

'No, Angelo. I'm sorry.'

'Coarseness doesn't become you. Someone like Robby, straight from those years in the service, may be forgiven an occasional solecism. With your background there is no excuse.'

'I apologize, Angelo. Please forgive me.'

No one stirred while he suffered in silence. At last Angelo said sternly, 'Very well. Your apology is accepted.' He turned to smile at Nightbone. 'There, Robby. You see how we do things. No sulks here. No rivalries. No jealousy.'

'Quite right, Angelo. Sight different from the barrack room, I can tell you.'

'Pray don't!' Angelo shook with an exaggerated shudder. Everyone laughed and the meal went on. When they had reached the pudding he addressed them all.

'Arthur, Hamish, Jimmy. You're all booked for this evening. The rest I'll expect to see across the way. Cuthbert, dear, I had a message this morning from that particular friend of yours. He'll be coming in at about nine thirty and should feel devastated if you weren't there. I had an inquiry for you from Maurice et Cie, but in the circumstances I told them you weren't available.'

'Awfully kind, Angelo, darling,' said Cuthbert. 'Is it a party night?'

Nightbone saw one or two glances flicker his way.

'Not this evening,' Angelo said. 'I'm sending invitations for the next. Sunday, so that you can all be there.'

'Oh, goody!' burst out a fairheaded youth whose complexion might almost have been a girl's. 'I'll be able to wear my new ...'

'Yes, Douglas, dear,' Angelo interrupted firmly. 'We all look forward to admiring that.' He stood up, and they followed suit. 'Thank you, gentlemen. I have a lot of things to do.'

Nightbone hung back behind the others. He waited at a discreet distance while Angelo inaudibly but vehemently admonished the girlish young fellow before sending him on his way.

'Nothing for me tonight, Angelo?'

'Alas, no, Robby. I could have proposed you for the booking I turned down on Cuthbert's behalf, but it needed someone more experienced. Early days, my dear. Besides, it means you're free for me to take to our little place over the way. Introduce you to some more friends.'

'What place is that, Angelo?'

'A little club I have an interest in. High class. Society and the learned professions only. I make all my gentlemen members.'

'Nothing society or learned about me, is there?'

'That's your charm. My patrons have enough of their own sort of company. They like to relax among friends whom they find congenial but *different*.'

'Oh, I get it. What do I wear?'

'Your nice new evening suit. You'll find it's been pressed for you.'

'What's this party on Sunday? Do I get to it?'

'Certainly. Everyone's expected.'

'Not in my party frock, I hope.'

Angelo gave him a sharp look. 'I don't envisage you in that role, Robby. Now, I suggest you go and have a nice lie down. Settle that tummy. There'll be champagne and smoked salmon this evening. We can't have you not enjoying yourself, can we?'

They left the room together. Nightbone locked his door and lay on the bed. He spent half an hour thinking. Then he delayed a few more minutes before putting on his coat and going downstairs. Angelo looked up enquiringly from his desk beyond his open office door.

'No use,' Nightbone told him, pulling a face. 'I'll have to walk it off. Only way.'

'Another of your little strolls!'

Nightbone shook his head. 'Light infantry pace. Gives the guts something to think about.'

He clapped his hat on, gave an army salute, and strode out. Angelo left his desk to watch through the window. He considered following, but when he saw the pace Robby went off at he knew he couldn't hope to keep up. Anyway, his direction was towards Marylebone Road, presumably heading for Regent's Park. It wouldn't take him anywhere near Mazur's. Angelo sat down to his work again.

Instead of crossing to the park, Nightbone turned left along Marylebone Road, then left again into Portland Place. Once out of Angelo's sight he had slowed down to his habitual pace. A few hundred yards southward was enough to outflank Angelo's. Then he turned along Mortimer Street and into smaller ways, his policeman's instinct guiding him through the heartland of the West End rag trade.

He had to cross Great Titchfield Street. He went along it a short way, to look at Maurice et Cie's corner building. Men and women were passing in and out by the front entrance. From a side door two attractive girls were wheeling a rack of dresses to a van. He might have been tempted to hang around in the chance of seeing Lucilla. There was no point, though. Even if she believed her last night's escort just happened to be passing there was still nothing he could do. He carried on to Mazur's.

Jen was still there. She'd changed back into her own flamboyant outfit. It suited her more than Rebecca's, and certainly fitted better. He told them his morning's experience. It horrified them both.

'Diabolical!' Jen said. 'Why'd they want to do it to him?'

'So he'll never be found. Disappeared for good. Some do every day. If he'd been chucked in the river or put on the railway there was a chance he'd be identified.'

'If his quack signed that paper about him they'll be on to him.'

'He's only to say he never saw Bailey again. They've no call to suspect he'd have kept him like that.'

Old Mazurka had been listening keenly. 'Why does he keep him, but not help? His own doctor. What?'

'That's right,' Jen said. 'They were old chums.'

'Bailey had plenty of them,' Nightbone said. 'Not as chummy after he came out of quod, though. He wasn't the Eddy Watts they'd known. Not the sort they'd want to know any more.'

'That turned him against them? Against everyone, Bailey was.'

'Right, Jen. And he decided he'd make them pay for their neglect.'

'Blackmail again?' Mazur said.

'Threats, at least. He can't have come down strong on them, or he wouldn't have got so down and out. I guess they kept him happy. Just enough to keep afloat. Finance some of his con tricks. When he couldn't go on pulling those, after he really got on the bottle, he saw he was nearly on the last slope. One more go for the big payout from them.'

'What, and then let them get hold of him?' Jen said. 'Too fly for that.'

'He hadn't done it yet. He was getting his nerve up to do it when he had the bright idea of screwing me as well. I was well up on his list.

He'd been trained up for the Law. Saw how the new Commissioner was bearing down on the force. Perfect chance for Bailey to show his old mates how sharp he still was. Not done for yet, and they'd better notice and toe *his* line, or he'd fix them, too.'

'He fixed you.'

'But it went wrong. I didn't hurt him.'

'Didn't matter. His quack said you did.'

'That way there was a reason for Bailey disappearing. All down to me. He hadn't reckoned they'd pull a stroke like that on him. They knew sooner or later he'd do something crazy. Split on them. Or just shoot his mouth off. Anything to get his own back once they'd told him no more cash.'

'But he *was* hurt,' Jen insisted. 'Real bad. I *saw* him. You did it, Nightbone. Didn't you? Own up. Went back in the fog.'

Nightbone shook his head. Before he could answer, Mazur put in, 'If they will finish him off, why do they keep him in bed?' His eyes were on Nightbone's. 'Unless they do it slow.'

Nightbone answered, 'They didn't kill Bailey. They let him die. He was hurt, Jen, but it wasn't me. He knew he was bad enough for a quack. There was only one he could go to without getting asked questions. He had to trust his old mate. It turned out he couldn't, any more than they could trust Bailey.'

'Very smart, Nightbone,' Old Mazurka said. 'So, you prove that and they make you Sergeant again. Maybe Captain yet.'

'Here!' Jen had been thinking. 'This is where Nelly fits in.'

'That's right,' said Nightbone. 'And Bodger.'

They started at Covent Garden. Jenny, in her tart's gear, looked less out of place there than she would in Rebecca's things. She went with Nightbone on foot. He trailed a few paces behind and kept apart from her in the bustling market. It was her idea to go there. Bodger hadn't any lodging. He slept where he could, in the cellar mostly. He wouldn't have gone back there, though. Not with Nightbone expected to come for him.

He kept his few belongings in a bundle, knotted in a filthy old horse blanket. Sober or drunk, when Bodger made a move to go anywhere his hand went instinctively to his bundle. It was so unsavoury, and Bodger so terrible, that no sneak-thief would have tried lifting it.

The market had been his patch in his good times. There was spilt fruit to eat and plenty of places to hide. Some of his mates there would stand him a drink. Jen didn't know that he'd been warned off. The porters and stallkeepers did, and there were considerations of loyalty when a strange tart came asking questions. While a boy nipped off to fetch some of the regular girls the men ran her a verbal gamut. Nightbone kept his distance, leaving her to do it the hard way.

'Blimey! Look what crep' aht o' this 'ere barrel.'

'Cor! Eat the spiders alive, she would.'

'Thought I saw her before – on a bloke's shovel.'

The girls came hurrying, furious.

'Wot you want 'ere? Git off to yer own patch.'

'Bodger Blandy. Anybody see him?'

'Owe yer fer last time, does 'e?'

'Crikey, she must 'a bin hard up!'

'So must 'e!'

'All right, you cows,' Jen yelled back. 'Only asked a civil question.'

''Ere's a answer,' screeched a big girl in a fur tippet. She let fly something that squelched against Jen's breast and oozed down her dress.

''Ere, nark that!' cautioned the trader from whose stock the missile had been lifted. He wasn't in time to stop another handful being seized and flung. It sailed over Jen's shoulder and splurged on a hotel buyer's bowler hat. The reason it had missed her was that she'd stooped to gather a handful of something to retaliate with. The girls scattered, hooting and cackling. Jen was left red faced and red handed, clutching an incriminating fistful of burst tomato. The buyer had his hat in his hand. He was staring outraged at the mess.

'Oh, give it here,' she snapped impatiently. She grabbed it and rubbed it hard with her skirt, making it worse.

'Wouldn't wear that again, guv',' a porter cautioned. 'Catch something 'orrible.'

Jenny swung round to abuse him. Nightbone thought of extricating her quickly, but saw a uniformed bobby moving in. He hung back. The bobby sent everyone about their business, then lectured Jen from a great height.

'You know better than trying it off your own patch.'

'I wasn't. I was asking after Bodger Blandy.'

'You won't find him here any more. Warned off for a nuisance.'

'Why didn't they just say?' Jenny adjusted her hat and rubbed at the mess on her clothes. 'If it wouldn't be troubling you, hofficer, you wouldn't happen to know 'is whereabouts?'

'Is this some trouble?'

'Ho, no. A gentleman friend of mine wants a good man to carry a board for his business. Thought I could do poor old Bodge a turn.'

'All right. When he's working there's three or four billstickers' depots he goes. They give their lads a doss down.'

'That's Bodger's way.'

'They're rough parts.'

'I've bin in rough parts. Same as you, I'm sure.'

'Not doing favours, I haven't.'

They found him at the second of the warehouses. It was in the oozing strip between The Strand and the river, near Charing Cross Station. Or rather, Jen found where he'd been until a few moments before. His one good eye had been enough to spot her. He was away and running before she could catch sight of him.

'Was here,' a billboard-paster told her. 'Horrible.'

'Jest stepped aht fer a word wiv 'is bank manager,' quipped a bright old colleague. 'If yer want to wait, we'll make yer comfy.'

Jen told them where to go and what to do there. The boss had seen them jawing. He came to add his own instructions. She stood her ground.

'Where's he doss down?'

She surprised him into pointing to their sleeping corner. The briefest look was enough. Bodger's bundle wasn't there.

'He's hopped it.'

'If you see him, say how we'll miss him.'

She went off to where she'd left Nightbone watching the yard entrance. He wasn't there. The bundle was, though. It lay where Bodger had dropped it in order to have both hands free to fight. She picked it up and followed the sounds of combat to a littered space outside the wall. No houses overlooked and there were no loungers to see Bodger and Nightbone in punishing embrace. Jen could only watch helplessly.

Bodger hadn't recognized the bloke who'd grabbed him as he ran out of the yard. True to instinct, he'd just ducked his head down and started boring into the other's ribs. Nightbone was far stronger and fitter. Bodger's way of life had sapped him. But the instincts he'd lived off once had survived. His forearms couldn't jab as hard and fast, and his fists weren't the iron clubheads they'd been. But the pummelling caught Nightbone unready. The piston-like one-two shook him badly. He clung on, to prevent Bodger getting away, but having to take that close-quarter punishment.

It hadn't been Nightbone's way to fight much. A swift armlock and snapping the ruffles on quick was his method. He'd used his fists sometimes, though. Knees, boots, and head, too. Bodger was too close and energetic to be got into a lock, and there were no handcuffs. Nightbone had to fight him.

Left–right, left–right. It had been Bodger's way to come out fast and put in the bodiers. Make his man gasp and cover up instead of boxing him off. It had always worked, until the other pros got used to his ways. He was slower by then, and they were ready for him. That was how the Islington Monkey had done his eye. A rigid straight right, that Bodger had rushed blindly into. Nightbone was lucky not to get winded.

'Bodger!' Jen shrieked as close as she dared come. 'Give up. It's all right.'

He didn't hear, or didn't care. Just fought on. Nightbone was surprised by his strength. Bodger had been living relatively cleanly. Since he'd left the cellar there'd been no one keeping him topped up with booze. The warehouse boss knew better than to pay out before Saturday night, so he'd no money to buy any and his mates were skint as he was. He'd had grub and a good sleep in the straw. For him, he was clearheaded and firm on his pins. Not clear enough to recognize Nightbone without his uniform. Only a big bloke who'd stepped into his way and grabbed him saying 'All right, Bodger. No trouble.'

With a supreme effort Bodger tore himself free at last. He lowered his head further and lunged with it. The impact was almost enough to jerk the eye out of its socket again. Nightbone, caught on the point of his chin, was lucky not to bite his tongue through as Bodger once had done. He staggered, half-dazed.

'No, Bodger!' Jen yelled as he reeled away. 'Hang on!' She went a few steps after him, holding his bundle up to show he was safe to come back for it. He didn't look round. He hurried on as fast as legs wobbling from the grinding fight would take him.

She turned back to Nightbone. He was shaking his head hard, impatiently trying to clear it. He dragged an arm across eyes half-blind with tears of sweat and pain. His mouth hung open and he was gasping heavily.

'Which . . . which way?' he wheezed.

'The bloody railway! He can hardly stand up. He'll get himself killed.'

There was a stone embankment, foundation for the tracks out of the station and on to Hungerford Bridge. The trains moved slowly at this point. Bodger would only have to cling on to one somehow for the few hundred yards across the river, then drop off before London Bridge Station. He'd be lost then among the warehouses and slums of The Borough.

Jen pushed Nightbone that way. He reeled like a drunkard, and she supported him. He recovered, but didn't risk running. He could see Bodger having trouble trying to climb the steep embankment.

'Bodger,' Nightbone shouted, staggering forward. 'Come down. I want to help you.'

Bodger went on clawing at the stone face. His leading hand could almost grasp the top, where the girder framework began. Nightbone started to climb.

The stone was in great blocks, giving holds for hands and feet. Nightbone dragged himself upward by bruised hands and wobbly legs. Looking up, he saw Bodger already gripping a girder, trying to heave himself through to the track. The rumble of train wheels vibrated even through the stone.

'No, Bodge, no!' Nightbone heard Jenny cry. He saw that Bodger had got his head and shoulders inside. He was getting his legs through. Then his face appeared, looking down at Nightbone. A fist followed it, and opened. Nightbone ducked his head as a shower of track ballast fell. He got some of it on his shoulders and the back of his neck. If Bodger found a big chunk, and could aim it, it could smash his skull.

A locomotive whistle blasted near, urgent with warning. Nightbone saw that Bodger had disappeared. He wasn't going to waste time. He meant to take his chance with the train.

Risking missing a hold with a hand or foot, Nightbone plunged upward. He grasped the lowest girder. He hauled himself up by it. The noise was great. The train was almost there, coming from the right, whistle shrilling. From track level it seemed to be racing towards them.

Bodger was crouching, waiting to jump on it. He wasn't watching for Nightbone.

Nightbone called out to distract him. 'Bodger! It's Nightbone. And Jenny. Don't be afraid.'

Bodger turned. He picked up a big stone that he'd been going to drop on him but had put down again. He lifted it menacingly. His crouching attitude wasn't one for throwing from. The action unbalanced him. He swayed and fell forward on to his knees. His arms were across the rail, his hands in the ballast. He tried to get up, but failed. He fell forward again. His head and shoulders sank on to the rail.

Nightbone got him just before the locomotive could. He hauled him off and flung him down at the trackside. Hot steam deluged them as the engine clanked by. Nightbone thought he heard shouts from the footplate, but didn't bother looking up. His attention was all on getting Bodger's arm in a lock, with a knee into the small of his back.

He stayed like that for long moments as the carriages rumbled by, so close that their passengers didn't see down to the pair of prone men. When the train had passed he still couldn't move, except to get his head through the girders and look down for Jen. She was lying back against the sloping stonework. Her arms dangled limply, but one hand was still clutching Bodger's bundle.

It took Nightbone another five minutes to convince Bodger that he wasn't a cop any more. He wasn't nibbing him.

'I've never done you harm, Bodger,' he said. 'No more has Jen. You're a hard man to fight, though.'

Under assurances and some flattery, Bodger was won round. When he learned that Jen had his bundle safe for him down there he was convinced. Nightbone released him and they stood side by side, wringing their limbs back into use for the climb down. They got him into a closed fourwheeler. To the cabby, it looked like the familiar tart and her bully, taking a half-drunk bloke off to their lair. From the blood on them, the blokes had been having a duff-up. Every man to his trade.

On the way to Mazur's Jen did all the talking. Nightbone and Bodger rested wearily. If Bodger had had strength to do another runner, Nightbone would have found it hard to chase him. It didn't arise. But when Jen gave up reassurances to start trying to explain to Bodger what was going on, Nightbone shook his head at her. Even now, a wrong word could explode Bodger's anger or fear. There would be mayhem in that confined space.

Inside Old Mazurka's parlour Nightbone kept close to Bodger while Jen went through to interrupt the flow of commerce. Mazur came hurrying back with her. He peered doubtfully at Bodger's battered features.

'Is it him?'

'No. He'll help us. He wants a safe place meanwhile. What about your cellar?'

The old man took down a big key from a fireplace hook. He gave it to Nightbone and pointed out the cellar door under the stairs. He returned to his shop with a distinctly deflated air. The padlock was heavy and well oiled, in a strong hasp. As Nightbone unlocked it he reassured Bodger that he wasn't being imprisoned.

'Here, you can take it down with you,' he said, and gave him both the padlock and key. Jen lit the way with a candle. It smelt fusty and mouldering. There was no light down there.

On the stairs Bodger mumbled in alarm. He had seen, in the candle's glow, the plank bed in a corner, with chains hanging from the wall at its head and feet. Nightbone knew Mazur hadn't been talking emptily about what he intended this place for.

'It's all right, Bodger. They aren't for you. Jen'll bring you some blankets and a pillow for that bed. And some beer and a tightener later. Doss down and feel safe. There's people after you. Out to get you. Understand? You'll be safe stopping here.'

Bodger looked from one to the other of them like a suspicious child. In spite of what he'd said, Nightbone could chain him up and beat hell out of him down here. And maybe worse. Nightbone saw his fear.

'Fetch him some coffee,' he told Jen. 'Any grub there is lying around. Biscuits. Anything.'

She hesitated suspiciously. 'What you going to do?'

'Talk.'

'I want to hear.'

'Get a move on, then.'

She left the candle and went back upstairs. Nightbone drew Bodger towards the bunk. The rest of the room was piled with boxes and barrels. This was the place where Mazur meant to put his unknown victim to slow and agonizing death. The thought gave Nightbone the creeps, but he sat on the bunk and Bodger joined him.

'It was Bailey. Wasn't it?' he said.

He had placed himself on the side of Bodger's functioning eye. What little confirmation it gave was visible.

'Bulley. Yuh. Yuh. Bulley.'

'Who did Nelly?'

'Bulley.'

'What for?'

Bodger didn't answer. Nightbone asked again, but still got no reply. He supplied it.

'Saw you and him. In the fog. He was waiting for you to duff him up. Saw her watching. Told you to do her quick.'

Bodger squirmed violently. His feet threshed.

'Din't! Nell a' ri'.'

'*He* did her? Bailey?'

Bodger turned full face to Nightbone, in awful display. The mangled features, freshly torn and bloodied from their fight. The misshapen mouth, contorting to frame words from a maimed tongue. He made an abrupt movement that took Nightbone unawares. Bodger was on his feet. But not to run to the stairs, where Jen paused, with a mug in her hand. Bodger stood in the floor space, the way he'd always done in the ring. Front knee flexed, the other rigid behind. His hands were up, but not as fists. They mimed a strangler's grasp on someone facing him. They came together and shook with the act of throttling. His face tightened.

Then, still miming, he cast his insensible victim from him. His hands came up again, but in the fists Nightbone had felt recently. Bodger's head lowered, and the fists with it. They worked in the vicious one-two one-two of his favourite body-blows. But there was an uglier curving blow from each of them that went lower and ended the exhibition. As Bodger turned to Nightbone again his expression showed the satisfaction he had had in avenging what he'd seen Bailey Watts do.

Jen did just the right thing then. She came the rest of the way down the stairs, making enough noise for Bodger to hear and not be alarmed. As he turned to her she held out the mug of coffee. She gave him a smile with it.

'Ta, Bodge, love,' she said.

Bodger took the mug and a fistful of biscuits from the tin she held. He sat on the wooden bunk again. Nightbone joined him.

'He only wanted marking,' Nightbone explained to Jenny. 'Enough to use against me. He saw Nell watching. Knew she'd split. Told Bodger to do her. He wouldn't, so Bailey did it himself.'

Bodger nodded repeatedly, swallowing and crunching. He lifted a fist and shook it in front of his ferocious eyes.

'You did him over proper?' Nell said.

Bodger nodded again. Nightbone told her, 'Took it all out on him. Everything. The ring. Cops. Me. What he'd come down to. But Bailey mostly, for his scoffing and sneering. And for hunting Nelly.'

A convulsion from Bodger conveyed that he was right.

'Then what?' Jen asked Nightbone.

'Thought he heard somebody coming. Nell was on the ground. He'd get blamed for her. Bailey would shop him. Panicked. Ran off in the fog. Yes, Bodger?'

'Yuh. Yuh.'

'Bailey was hurt more than he'd asked for. He heard Mary and the two blokes calling out for Nell. He had to get clear. But he was bad. Hurting. He went off in the fog and found a cab. Went to his place and then to his quack friend's. Nobody else to help him.'

Jen subsided on to the stairs. 'That it, Bodge?' she said flatly.

'Yuh. Bully?'

'Gone. All over town. Turned up his toes. Good riddance to rotten rubbish.'

Nightbone saw Bodger's fresh alarm. 'It's all right,' he said. 'Not down to you. Leave it to me. I want you to stop here. Jen'll be near. She'll look after you. Won't you, Jen?'

'Bloody boarding house. Fetching your tart here next. Don't expect her looking after.'

She took his place on the bunk next to Bodger. Nightbone went upstairs, to clean himself up as best he could before hurrying back to Angelo's.

THE HOUSE WITH
GREEN SHADES

ANGELO missed very little concerning his gentlemen. In return
for the work he got them he withheld a percentage of their
fees. Since these were paid directly to him by the fashion
houses he had no difficulty in collecting his full due.

When they had been introduced into his green-shaded house across
the square, and had found favour with its paying patrons, they were
on their honour to give him a share of whatever money or gifts they
received. He took no fees from his patrons. It would have made him a
brothel-keeper. Worse still, a target for blackmail. He did nicely
enough from profits on champagne, brandy, cigars, music, cards,
suppers fetched in, and so forth. But he dared not charge for men, still
less for boys. Angelo's commission was left to his gentlemen's honour.
Mostly, they played fair, but he searched their rooms periodically,
and followed them sometimes, to see where their own concerns took
them. And always he watched them.

Bodger's technique of attacking the body meant that Nightbone's
many bruises were mostly hidden. His chin was swollen and marked,
though, and his hands were torn from fighting and scrambling. His
suit had suffered most. He thought of finding an old clothes shop on
the way back to Angelo's and getting another. But that would look
even more suspicious to a man who knew the extent of his wardrobe.
He was luckier than he'd anticipated when he entered the house, late
in the afternoon. The office door was shut. Angelo had stepped across
the square for a few minutes.

Safe in his room, Nightbone changed quickly into his dressing-
gown and took down the herb jar. The delicious aroma was soon at
large in the passages as he steamed in the fragrant water. His ribs and

forearms were a sight. He was thankful none of Bodger's blows had landed where Bailey had been fatally hit.

He felt soothed and refreshed as he climbed into evening rig. He quite fancied himself in it. He heard voices in the passage and found Cuthbert and Douglas just passing his room, dressed like himself.

'Nice timing, Robby. Coming over with us?'

'Don't mind if I do, ta.'

'I say, that bath stuff of yours makes a treat.' Douglas leaned forward to sniff delicately at Nightbone's neck. 'Mm! Clings, too. Nicked yourself, have you?'

'Walked into a lamp-post.'

'Naughty!'

Darkness had fallen some time ago. It was a fine evening with only the light haze of autumn dampness. The gaslamps around the square and at the street ends were yellowing walls, pavements, railings, and the almost bare trees. Many of the houses were in darkness or dotted with lamplight. In three places shades glowed red. The house Cuthbert and Douglas steered Robby towards with linked arms had pale green blinds. They were lit so discreetly that it might have been an ordinary house or club. It was the latter, but not ordinary.

Outside, it looked to him much the same size as the lodging house. In the vestibule he felt more space, rooms beyond rooms. The ground floor ones had been combined by opening walls into arches. Soft drapes hung about. There were couches, and bright cushions, and little brass-topped tables. A smell of cigar smoke. A piano was being played softly somewhere out of sight. An elderly man and a young one from Angelo's were chatting close together on one of the couches. Another he knew as Peter was listening with a smirk to something being whispered by a thin, bearded man, whose flowing tie made Nightbone think he must be an artist. A chubby young waiter was serving wine.

'How do you find our little place, Robby, dear?' Angelo asked at his shoulder. He was dressed like everyone else in tails, though with a maroon coat and silvered cap. With his long hair and puffy pink skin he looked benevolent and distinguished. He frowned at Nightbone's chin. 'What *have* you done to your face?'

Nightbone had his tale ready. He scowled. 'Had a bit of a dust-up in the park. Chap who knew me from the army. Sapper up from Chatham. Heard why I was kicked out and wanted to make something of it.'

Angelo looked perturbed. 'No police trouble?'

'No witnesses. Didn't take long.' He held up one of the scraped fists.

'I don't approve of brawling, Robby.'

'I don't brawl. Just give 'em the hint.'

'In future, I'd prefer you to walk away.'

Nightbone looked suitably disgusted.

'I insist, Robby.'

'Have it your way, then. Yes, nice place. Is it all free?'

Angelo brightened. 'For you, dear boy, of course. Drink and eat whatever you wish. Be moderate, though. And no slipping away upstairs without telling me.'

'I don't know what you mean.'

'Oh yes, you do! But you must always ask my approval.'

'What if you're not about?'

'I'm *always* about. I am here to see that our patrons get what they desire. You are not to push yourself forward, so to speak. Merely mingle and chat. See what transpires.'

Nightbone lowered his tone. 'On the straight, Angelo? No cop trouble?'

'Not so long as everyone behaves himself. In the most unlikely event of a visit you simply go on being a young member of an exclusive gentlemen's club. Leave any talking to me. There's the doorbell. I make a point of greeting all my guests in person.'

He tripped away. Nightbone wandered about looking at possible exits in case one of those unlikely police raids did happen. He found the pianist behind a screen of drapes, and had to listen to the ageing man's tale of frustrated ambition to be a classical composer.

When he got back into the main body of the room he found it much fuller. The patrons were of all sorts and ages, some elderly and handsome, some young and gross. During the evening he saw a good deal of hand-holding and arms around shoulders and waists. Once he interrupted a kiss behind a pillar. The men broke apart smiling coyly. He recognized the drill. Chatting and supping downstairs. Other things in the rooms above.

He saw Angelo usher occasional couples to the stairs. To his great relief no one paid him the dubious compliment of inviting him, though he chatted easily enough to everyone he was introduced to. Much of the talk was beyond him, about theatres, parties, and people he didn't know. He got some appraising looks, with obvious hints in them of future interest. There was likely to be more free-for-all on 'party' night, when he guessed the gowns and wigs and high heels would be out to attract him. He was asked several times about his bruised chin. He got the impression that his story of how he'd got it stimulated interest in him.

One couple who had arrived together were in their thirties, elegant, immaculate, and obviously devoted friends of Angelo. He introduced them to Robby as Charles and Simon. They were correctly polite, but their aloof manner showed him there was no place in their relationship for a third man.

A little later, needing to get away from a group gossiping meaningless scandal, he brought the melancholy pianist in the alcove a glass of champagne. He leaned on the piano with his own glass, half-listening to the monologue that the languid music accompanied. He became aware of other voices approaching the draped grotto and pausing outside it. One was Angelo's.

'So, Simon dear, what will interest me very much?'

'Carlotta will tell you. It was her idea.'

Nightbone heard the third voice. 'It's about poor little Blanche.'

'Eddy? What about her?'

'Won't be troubling us any more.'

'Not taken up again?'

'Ssh! Some bother with a policeman. Got herself hurt.'

'Badly?'

'Fatally.'

'Will there be questions?'

'No. We may breathe again, Angelina dear.'

'Goodness! One ought to feel sorry, but ... This calls for a little celebration. Across at my place afterwards?'

'Not tonight. We must be flying.'

'Party night, then? Come over afterwards and I'll have a special bottle up for us. Poor Blanche. So sweet, once.'

'But things were getting rather *ominous*, weren't they?'

'... and Brahms himself told me, "Any time you're passing through Ischl, my boy, you've only to send in your card." But, of course, I never was ... '

Nightbone's other ear was reclaimed. He was in time to look out and see Angelo escorting Charles and Simon to the door. Dr Charles Darbry, of Paddington. He found himself regarding his right hand. It had shaken the one that had chopped and sawn Bailey Watts into joints.

'All alone still, Robby dear?' Angelo came beaming back to him, clearly showing his relief. 'I'm afraid it's a case of Little Boy All Alone this time. There won't be any more in now. Never mind. I hope you've enjoyed yourself?'

'Nice company.'

'Did you meet anyone who seemed to fancy you?'

Nightbone looked him in the eyes. 'I'm choosy who I play with.'

'I'm sure you are.' Angelo moistened his lower lip. 'I hope Angelo qualifies?'

Nightbone held his look. He smiled. 'How much longer does all this go on?'

'Do you want to leave?'

'Might do. What time do you get away?'

Angelo's eyes sparkled. 'I must see to a few things. They can close up after me. Why don't you go back now? Pour yourself a drink in my room. Anything you like. Only, don't go strolling off again!'

Angelo was relieved to find Robby waiting in his parlour. He had taken longer than he expected to get away from the club. He hurriedly exchanged his evening things for a purple ecclesiastical-style gown and matching cap. He put on some eye shadow and dabbed himself with a little perfume.

Nightbone was lounging in one of the fireside chairs, still in his evening things. He saw Angelo's automatic glance towards the closed writing bureau. He grinned. 'Could've been away with your spoons.'

Angelo was in high, nervous humour. 'So droll, Robby. I'm sorry to have taken so long. Never mind, my dear. The night's young. You haven't given yourself anything to drink.'

'Just sitting thinking.'

'Something delightful, I'm sure.' Angelo went to the decanters. 'Port? Brandy? Let's have it over there on the sofa table. So much more comfy.'

'A little port, thanks. You have a brandy. You might need it.'

Angelo turned. 'What's that?'

Nightbone indicated the armchair opposite him. 'Why don't you sit there? I'll stop here. There's a bit of talking to do.'

Angelo hesitated. Perhaps Robby was starting up some exciting charade they would play. He handed over the port glass and sat down obediently.

'Good health!' Nightbone said.

'Oh, Robby, we really don't . . . Never mind, you incorrigible dear. Angelina forgives. What is it you wish to talk about? Mm?'

'What I'm here for. Mr Mazur sent me.'

Angelo's benign expression changed to sudden anger. The pink cheeks flushed. The mild, moist eyes froze over. His voice turned to ice, too.

'So that *is* it! I've always thought there was something between you. You and that old villain. Come on, then. What trick is it to be?'

'No trick. I'm to tell you he's decided to foreclose.'

Angelo laughed sharply. 'Oh, is that all? There's no need to be devious about that, you ignorant boy. He could have saved your impertinence by telling me in his shop. No doubt you know about the money he insisted on "lending" me. I never wanted it. I told him so. It's all intact, against the day when his insane whim should make him ask for it back. So it's come, has it? Well, you may tell him he shall have every penny. Not a halfpenny interest, though. And he will have to come for it himself. I don't intend trusting it into your sort of hands.'

Nightbone nodded. 'I'll tell him all that. Except the last bit. He trusts me, Mr Mazur.'

'More fool him.'

'Going to pay me well, too. All you give him back. I'm getting that, and more.'

'I see. So it's really you behind this. Found out something to hold over him. Making him pay up. I can't pretend I'm sorry. You deserve one another. Now, get out of my house.'

Angelo had started to get to his feet. Nightbone stayed where he was.

'I'll tell him that, too,' he said mildly. 'Only, it wasn't money he sent me for.'

Angelo sank down again. 'Don't say you've the effrontery between you to want my property instead!'

'Not even that.'

'Then what?'

'Some names.'

'Whose?'

'The man who took his girl. His daughter, Rebecca. Who went missing and finished up killed.'

'Killed?' Nightbone thought Angelo's surprised look and tone were real. He nodded.

179

'Murdered, some would say. Maybe you didn't know. I don't suppose they report such things back. Mazur didn't know for sure till today. I found him a witness. Eye-witness. Ready to testify if it goes to the cops.'

'Not against me, I can assure you. I have had nothing to do with Mazur's daughter at any time.'

'No? She worked for that Maurice firm you're so thick with. Young fellow made up to her there. Wanted her to go to Paris with him. She couldn't, so they snatched her. Don't tell me you don't know all that.'

'I heard of it. Mazur told me. More than once. You know the way he chatters. But I had no connection with it.'

'Doesn't stop you knowing who had. Mazur's been waiting a long time to ask you, but he knew you'd not tell. Hadn't got the knowledge to put pressure on you with. I have, though. Against you and others. Paid me to get it for him. Bit of a turn-up for a chap who's skint.'

'And you thought of me as the easy victim. Thought I was a little bit vulnerable through other activities. Convince that lunatic I'm involved, take his money, and run for it. Isn't that your plan?'

'Very smart, Angelo. I hadn't thought of that. Now that you mention it, it's a good wheeze. If you don't give me what I've come for I'll take you along to him. Give him something for his tin. He'll believe me if I tell him you're the one he's after. You do know how crazy he is, don't you? That grin. Those eyes? They're nothing to what's behind them. Any guesses what he means to do?'

Nightbone saw stark fear come into Angelo's eyes. He heard it in the tremor in his voice, though he was trying to hide it.

'I'll pay you, Robby. I owe you a bit, of course, and I'll add to it. Be sensible and take it and go away. You don't know what trouble you could find yourself in. Please, Robby, stop this for your own sake and mine. I haven't done you any harm. I took you in in good faith. I was pleased to help. How was I to know Mazur was using you?'

'Sorry, Angelo. He's hired me to find who took his girl, and I've promised. Tell me, and you're off the hook.'

'I swear I'd nothing to do with it. Not my sort of thing at all. All I do is teach those girls modelling. Provide male escorts. Anything that's beyond that is no concern of mine.'

'You don't care?'

'I don't *know*. Most of them go on being models. Quite a few get married.'

'What about the rest?'

'They . . . just go. There one day, gone the next. Ted Pearson's very strict. The least breach of his rules and it's instant dismissal. Girl or man.'

'Off the premises and never seen again. Just like that?'

'In effect.'

'Straight down to the docks? Neatly done. And you didn't know?'

'I don't. I don't wish to. I don't want to say any more about it.'

'Mr Mazur will make you.'

'I'll go to the police. I don't care what it means.'

Nightbone got to his feet, He advanced on Angelo, who half started to rise again then cringed back into his chair. Nightbone stood over him, one big, cut and scratched fist raised.

'You won't go to the police, Angelo. I'm here to stop you. If you try any tricks, such as squawking out, I'll do it by force. Tell me who it was got round Rebecca Mazur, or I give you to him for it.'

Angelo asked with a dry mouth and lips that scarcely moved from numbness: 'Make me a promise, Robby. Please?'

'What?'

'You won't say I informed. They'd kill me.'

'I only work for Mazur. It's up to him.'

'Ask him for me. He can have the money as well. And more.'

'I'll ask. It rather depends what you say. Who you name.'

Angelo shook his head desperately. 'Robby, you've got to make him believe me. He'll think I'm trying to trick him. You will, but I swear I'm not. I'm too frightened. Of you and Mazur. Of them. I swear by anything you like that what I tell you is nothing but the truth.'

Nightbone lowered his fist. He moved a half-step closer to Angelo, who cringed back as far as he could. He stood so near the chair that his shins touched its front. He stared down at the face that had turned as white as the hair fringing it. Nightbone's stare. The stare that penetrated, and burned, and laid bare.

'Who?' he asked.

Angelo told him. Nightbone stayed motionless for a full half-minute, still staring him down, but with eyes whose penetrability was diffused with thought. Then he seemed to rouse himself. With a movement that made Angelo wince fearfully again he stooped and picked up the neglected brandy balloon. He took it to where the decanters were. He poured a measure into it, then brought it back to Angelo.

Nightbone returned to his own chair. He picked up his glass and raised it.

'Good health, old fruit!' he said. And drank the rest.

CHAPTER 25

COLONEL-SAHIB

'ood-looking young fellow. About your height. Nothing like so bulky, thank heaven, or he'd never have passed. Naturally black hair, which was an advantage. Rather swarthy skin. He had to black up a little, but not extravagantly enough for it to show. Carried only a tent and what he could get into a small tin box. Made himself out to be a traveller from the plains, seeking spiritual enlightenment among the hills. When he got back, two years later, General Fairbrother told him the information he'd gathered was worth a year's scouting in force. And you've got this result inside a week. Extraordinary!'

'Bit of luck thrown in, sir,' Nightbone acknowledged.

'Essential,' the Commissioner boomed. 'All the planning and hard work can go for nothing if the luck isn't there.'

Nightbone was seated in a somewhat rigid and uncomfortable armchair. Colonel Saltby was leaning against the mantelpiece, one foot raised on the brass fender rail. There was a roaring fire in the grate, and a full coalscuttle standing by. The Colonel felt the cold after India.

They were in his study at the top of the Kensington house, the sanctum into which his wife would no more venture than would any housemaid. When he left it, for even a few minutes, he locked its door and kept his key on him. There was only one other. That was used and guarded just as conscientiously by Mangi Lal, the orderly the Saltbys had brought home with them. The Commissioner's papers were safe with him. He spoke only Urdu, and couldn't read or write. Had he been able to, he wouldn't have presumed. Mangi would be willing to give his life to defend the Colonel-Sahib's study's contents, even down to the latest issue of *Punch* and the evening newspaper.

That morning, the day after the interview with Angelo, Nightbone had sent a personal telegram to the Commissioner at Scotland Yard. Its brief message would have been incomprehensible to anyone but Col. Saltby, who had thought it up originally for Nightbone to memorize. It meant that he would come to the Kensington house that evening at ten o'clock. He had no need to ascertain if the Commissioner would be free and willing to receive him. He had been assured that, whatever else was engaging him, he would make himself available when the message came.

Nightbone made a most circuitous journey there. He walked much of it and used three cabs, backtracking twice. He made certain he wasn't being followed or watched as he approached the house. He spent five minutes in cautious reconnaissance before ringing the side-door bell. This was not the entrance leading to servants' territory. It led from a conservatory and was only used for that purpose, bolted finally at dusk. The bell wasn't in the customary place of bells, to one side of the door, at waist height. It was close to the ground, so hidden by ivy that no unsuspecting eye would see it.

It rang quietly in only two rooms, inaudible outside them. Col. Saltby's study was one. The other was a small pantry next to it. Mangi Lal sat patiently there, hour by hour, content to do nothing but be on hand for the Colonel-Sahib's call, or to pad quietly down to admit whoever had given the prearranged ring at that clandestine bell.

Mangi Lal had never seen Nightbone before. He was just another barra-sahib, who identified himself with the one word that Mangi required before letting any visitor across the side door's threshold. This sahib was quite young compared with some who came, though twenty-eight was definitely middle aged by Mangi Lal's standards. He was big, but, there again, most sahibs were bigger and heavier than the millions of Mangi Lal's race.

Left alone with the Commissioner, who had greeted him with a firm handshake and a searching, serious gaze, Nightbone took the proffered chair and began his narrative. There had been no preliminary chat. No inquiry about his well-being. No refreshment offered to put him at ease. He felt far from easy, in that chair, in that company.

The Colonel maintained his mantelpiece attitude throughout. He didn't interrupt once as Nightbone gave him every detail of what had happened to him between quitting Scotland Yard and prising that name out of Angelo last night. When it was over the Commissioner made no comment. Instead, he told this story of his own. It was of a young regimental lieutenant, whom he didn't name. He had volunteered to wander as a native among the hill people of Afghanistan and Nepal, to find out what intention there was to help Russia's long-threatened invasion of India.

'Of course, we had native informants galore already,' Col. Saltby said. 'Some are still out there at this very moment. They go off for two and three years at a time. It's appallingly risky. Even to be suspected means torture and slavery, with some particularly nasty form of execution if the suspicions seem justified. Hence the long missions. The distances and terrain are against easy movement. They have to live as poor men, so as to assimilate with the greatest masses. Much of the time they're working to keep themselves alive, and moving on. Their coups are few and far between, and all of it for pay no better than a coolie's. Shocking way to live. Two or three such expeditions wear out even the hardiest of them. Yet they're dedicated to the job. Proud to be accepted for it and to prove themselves faithful servants of the Queen.

'Naturally, most of the information they send back – and you'd be astounded how they contrive to do it – merely confirms or negates intelligence we already have. Few of them have the skills to evaluate, draw conclusions, hypothesize. It struck young . . . the subaltern who is the point of this tale, that someone capable of those things ought to go out and see for himself. He brought his plan to me confidentially. I was immediately against it. I knew such enterprises had been tried in the past, in India and elsewhere. The results weighed poorly against the loss in gallant young lives. I need not picture for you the treatment of a soldier caught masquerading like that.

'He stuck to his guns, though. I knew he was fluent enough in tongues to be able to pass himself off as a sort of peripatetic traveller of no orthodox religion. His build and looks were in his favour. The cheeky young devil proved that. He turned up one afternoon, rigged out as a rug-seller. Got the usual kicking from one end of the lines to the other, and offended the Adjutant so much that he dragged him in front of me. He even let me have the sharp edge of his tongue for a few minutes, before peeling off his layers and showing who he was. He'd waited till we were quite alone before doing so. He knew, and I knew, that he'd made his point, but to ensure absolute security over what he was planning to do it had to be known to only the two of us.

'A great deal of arranging, it took. I had to post him away from the regiment on some excuse. He had to make sure he subsequently disappeared from all sight of family, fellow officers, friends, anyone who knew him. When he eventually came back, he had a story of having been abducted in the bazaar to serve in the household of a ranee, until he could give her a couple of fair-skinned offspring. It was so bizarre, and gave rise to so many jokes in the mess, that everyone believed it. Only he and I knew what real hardships he'd lived under. And the information he brought back may have averted invasion.

'So, Nightbone,' Col. Saltby finished, 'you will understand the tradition under which I sent you forth to operate. I took a calculated chance. I've made no secret of my intention to run the Metropolitan Police, if not as an army, as embodying some of the strategic and tactical aspects that experience has shown. The criminal is our enemy in the field. He exists in strength and is up to every nasty game. It should not be incumbent upon us always to let him have the initiative.

'This white-slaving disgrace has existed far too long. The Law's deficiencies have been made the excuse for inaction. I'm assured in high places that there are to be changes. From all I have read among the documents, my predecessor was given such promises. I decided to do something positive. I determined to send out my own equivalent of one of those brave fellows we use in India. Someone with a penchant and natural talent for working alone. Who could blend in unnoticed and discover things that no amount of bobbies in uniform or rulebook detectives could. I was well aware of the risks. Had things gone wrong, your lot and mine, though different, would have been dire. You were not the only officer I considered for the task, Nightbone, but, so to speak, fate delivered you into my hands. I'm grateful to you, not only for having achieved a notable police result, but for justifying the risk I saw fit to take with both our futures.'

Col. Saltby descended from the fender as from a podium. Nightbone moved to get up but was waved back into the lumpy chair. To his surprise, he heard himself being asked if he would care for a whisky and soda. His host must have pressed a bell, for the door opened quietly and the turbaned Mangi Lal slid in.

'*Do to barri whisky-soda,*' Saltby ordered.

'*Achha, Colonel-Sahib.*'

Without having given Nightbone a glance the little man glided away, to return almost instantly with the drinks and a syphon.

'*Shabash*,' his master commended him, and he and Nightbone were alone again. Col. Saltby served equal measures without consulting Nightbone's preference. 'Your very good health, Nightbone. Well done.'

'Yours, too, sir, thank you.'

The Commissioner followed his sip with a long, expressive sigh. At last he allowed himself to take the armchair adjoining Nightbone's. He went so far as to lean back and let his neck rest against its scroll top. He turned his eyes to Nightbone.

'Well, now. Tell me how you recommend proceeding from here on.'

'Well, sir, thinking it over since yesterday, it seems to me that perhaps ... '

'Nightbone. Be a good chap and just say what needs doing. Eh?'

'Yes, sir. If you're up to another risk I'd leave most of it as it stands. Don't show them we're on to them. Let them go ahead and run the girl, Lucilla. Nab them on the ship or over the other side. As if by chance. Under age. Falsification of documents. Procuring for the purposes of prostitution. Everything in the book. It's a hundred to one it'll be Joe Pearson escorting her. He's worked her this far, and she'll trust him till the minute he leaves her in the lurch.'

'How long before they move?'

'Inside a week. They were quicker off the mark with Rebecca Mazur, because they had to be. But it won't take them long to get a good offer for this one. Then they won't delay.'

'How does she stand meanwhile?'

'Safe enough. They won't want to spoil the goods, if you'll pardon the term, sir. It could lose them their top price.'

'Filthy business! Flogging would be too good. You're quite sure this Angelo won't warn them?'

'Scared of his own shadow, sir. I've made him realize what his fairy friends are capable of. He knows the white-slavers are, too. And there's Mazur. He's hemmed in, and knows it. He's agreed to tip me off when they make their move with Lucilla.'

'You don't think he's one of them?'

'Just a ponce. A fixer who doesn't want to know what he's fixing.'

'Are the doctor and the lawyer in it?'

'I don't think so, sir. Strictly male sex with them. We can take them any time we want. And Angelo. Best leave them be for now.'

187

'This business of Watts, though. We can't let that go by.'

'No proof, sir. Only what Jenny Jacks saw and I, er, smelt. Prosecute with insufficient evidence and all hell could break loose. Their kind are in a lot of high places.'

'As I'm discovering,' the Commissioner said grimly. 'One has to tread warily indeed. What of those women and their lodging house?'

'Again, sir, their business is as much above board as below. They're in with Joe Pearson, for sure, but there's no evidence of keeping girls against their will. Shutting them down might give away more than it's worth.'

'Set up somewhere else? Like sweeping muck from one place to another.'

'As Mazur would say, sir, "crazy laws".'

'Well, Nightbone, our job as policemen – if I may use the term of myself – is to make the best of the laws we have. But if crooks won't observe the proprieties, I believe we're entitled to an occasional lapse.'

'The way I've always felt, sir.'

'But not overstretching it. That would make us provocateurs, inciters, tyrants. You realize, do you, what this success of yours means to yourself?'

'I don't think I've taken it in yet, sir.'

It was true. He had given his own position no real thought. Events had swept him along so rapidly that he hadn't had time. The Commissioner proceeded to explain.

'No going back, I'm afraid. No rejoining the regiment. I sent you out there to sniff after organized crime in general, and you happen to have started with white-slavery. There's plenty more. Besides, there are no circumstances in which I could retract your dismissal. Without, that is, admitting that I had made a mistake. Watts and his injuries have ceased to exist. The Home Secretary is not going to order an inquiry into the Commissioner of Metropolitan Police discharging an officer, simply because a prostitute and an ex-pugilist say it wasn't justified. As I see it, Nightbone, you stay where you are and carry on, with your cover intact. Incidentally, where *do* you propose to be?'

'I suppose Angelo's would be best for now. He daren't throw me out, and he's got useful connections.'

'Mm! Far be it from me to expose you to hazards beyond the call of duty.'

'I can always smack his wrist, sir.'

'Very well. What about Mazur? Do you think he suspects you?'

'I've wondered that. The way he watches. Little hints he drops. I don't think he'll come out with it. As for Jenny, she'll just go back on the game. Take Bodger Blandy back to Pentonville with her. They won't change.'

'The other girl, when we get her back? Broken home, you said.'

'She'll be all right. Bit sadder and wiser, which will be all to the good. Change of lodging and she can go on at Maurice et Cie's. Mrs Goldman is a hundred per cent kosher. Like Ted Pearson. They'll look after her.'

'Assuming Martini told you the truth, that Ted Pearson wasn't in the racket.'

'Too scared to lie, sir. He says Belle Roche started it all up after she left Mrs Minchin. Her fancy piece, Floss, hadn't any form, so she fronted when they set up their lodgings. They needed a man for picking up top talent round the country. They got a pal of theirs, Joe – real name Cook, by the way. One of your bright-eyed villains, charmers on top, ruthless underneath. They also found Ted Pearson, who'd compromised himself on the homo scene. Honest and strait laced otherwise, and dead scared of losing his name and business. They made him take Joe in, posing as his brother. The fashion house was a perfect cover for their trade. Mostly straight. When they had a girl earmarked for the trade they could just lift her when they were ready and give out that she'd been sacked and sent home. The girls never knew what they were really being trained up for till they woke up somewhere foreign and found it happening to them.'

The Commissioner exhaled disgustedly. He stood up. Nightbone made to follow suit, but the conformation of the chair didn't help. Col. Saltby gestured him to stay put again. He returned to his fireplace stance, holding his whisky glass.

'Lastly, for tonight,' he said, 'Watts. What of Watts?'

Nightbone cudgelled his wits. He wasn't a spirits drinker. The soda bubbles were distributing whisky pleasantly about his system. He was tired from the period of hectic mental and physical activity. He put down his glass unfinished.

'When Bailey came out of jug, he was done for,' he explained. 'I mean, so far as his career went. Prospects, family, all that. He knew the only way he could get back in was to buy his way. His fairy friends weren't out to help him much. He pulled a few con tricks, but nothing big enough. He tried to spot where the real money was to be made. He saw white-slaving. He never did have any opinion of females. Smart, well-spoken gent, able to talk them into anything, he reckoned. No capital outlay. Just some obliging contacts. His father had been in shipping, so the transport was easy to fix. Cash on delivery guaranteed. But he came a cropper first time out. He'd lighted on Mazur's girl. Easy. Poor old foreign couple, scratching their way with a shop. Be glad to let their girl have her chance. Bring credit on them.'

Col. Saltby nodded. 'The Hindus have a word for it. It isn't a monopoly of Jews. Carry on.'

'He was sure it was all in the bag. But the old man defeated him. He wouldn't let her go. So Bailey had her grabbed and shipped off within twenty-four hours.'

'Why didn't Martini tell Mazur this himself?' the Commissioner asked. 'Let him have his revenge on Watts?'

'He thought of doing. But he talked it over first with Bailey's other chums from the days when they were all girls together. They agreed that Bailey had been a fool, trying to get into the trade. It's run by professionals. They wouldn't stand for any outsider ruffling the waters. He promised his chums he wouldn't try it again, and they agreed to chip in together from time to time to keep him afloat. He was owed that much from having saved them and himself from an airing in court in full drag. It would have ruined them all.'

'Ah, the Fitzroy Square business. It was the talk of the mess when it came out in the papers. A certain officer asked me if he ought to resign. His younger brother was one of 'em. I told him if he wrecked his life in connection with money or a married woman I'd let him go tomorrow. But I'd be damned if I was allowing a tarted-up poofter to deprive us of the second-best tent-pegger in Rajputana. I'm sorry, Nightbone. You infer they kept quiet about Watts and the Mazur girl for old times' sake?'

'Yes, sir. But, as I've explained, lately their patience with him had started running out. Him deciding to have a go at me, and playing into their hands in consequence, was a godsend to them. I can't prove it, and nor can Angelo, but we reckon my version of what they did is right.'

'Remarkably neat,' the Commissioner mused. 'They get rid of Watts. You yourself escape the possible charge of manslaughter in the event he'd been found dead of his injuries. The prostitute, Jenny, has at least the satisfaction of knowing that the man who killed her sister has met his own death thoroughly unpleasantly. And presumably your friend Mazur can enjoy peace of mind at last, from similar sentiments.'

'Presumably, sir.'

The Commissioner glanced at Nightbone keenly.

'You're not sure? You don't suggest that being deprived of his blood-lust will make him go seeking someone else to vent it on?'

'I don't know what he'll think, sir. It's why I came to report to ask your orders before telling him.'

'Do so,' the Commissioner said emphatically. 'Don't delay. If word were to get out that there's a fellow in the West End of London with his cellar set up like a medieval torture chamber, and the police haven't acted, the press and the Home Office would be howling after us.'

'I can see that, sir. The problem is, will he believe it was Bailey?'

'Why shouldn't he?'

'Because I told him I was out to stop him taking his own revenge. He never believed the first story I made up to ease his mind about her. What's he going to think when I try to convince him the man he's been waiting to get his chains on has been knocked off by somebody else?'

The Commissioner actually beamed.

'If that's all the problem you have left on your hands, Nightbone,' he said, 'the sooner you busy your talents with some other form of villainy, the better!'